"You don't

Sara eased back a fraction, her nerves tensing.

"Oh, I think I do. You have this need to give, to share, to do for others. I know you've loved someone once and were disappointed, even deeply hurt, as I was."

Nick held her steady. "You have a buried passion you want to deny. Like you want to deny that you're attracted to me. How am I doing?"

Close. Way too close. "Conjecture. All of that's conjecture." She put a hand to his chest to push him away, to give herself some breathing room. She felt his heartbeat pick up its rhythm, thrumming beneath her touch. Slowly she raised her eyes and found his—deep, blue and aware.

"Still think I'm conjecturing?" And then he was wrapping his arms around her and crushing his mouth to hers.

Pat Warren

is the mother of four and lives in Arizona with her travel-agent husband and a lazy white cat. She's a former newspaper columnist whose lifetime dream was to become a novelist. A strong romantic streak, a sense of humor and a keen interest in developing relationships led her to try writing romance novels, with which she feels very much at home.

This book is dedicated to Dee Simpson and a friendship from girlhood to grandmotherhood, and still going strong.

Pat Warren
OUTLAW LOVERS

Silhouette Books

Published by Silhouette Books
America's Publisher of Contemporary Romance

Special thanks and acknowledgment to
Pat Warren for her contribution to the
Montana Mavericks series.

Text and artwork on page 8 is reprinted with permission from
NEVER ASK A MAN THE SIZE OF HIS SPREAD:
A Cowgirl's Guide to Life, by Gladiola Montana.
Copyright © 1993 Gibbs Smith Publisher. All rights reserved.

 SILHOUETTE BOOKS

ISBN 0-373-50170-6

OUTLAW LOVERS

MONTANA Mavericks

*Welcome to Whitehorn, Montana—
the home of bold men and daring women.
A place where rich tales of passion and
adventure are unfolding under the Big Sky.
Seems that this charming little town has some mighty
big secrets. And everybody's talking about...*

Melissa Avery: Looking for answers behind the death of her father, Charlie, she'll have to turn to someone outside of town for help. And always willing to lend a hand is Whitehorn's finest...

Judd Hensley: The sheriff thought he'd heard the last about the remains found on the Laughing Horse Reservation. But this mystery won't go away, along with a name he's heard before...

Lexine Baxter: Rumored to have had an affair with Charlie Avery, she may be responsible for his death. But she left town years ago. And someone else is on the mind of...

Homer Gilmore: An eccentric hermit, maybe, but he does know what he saw in the woods. And the person he's particularly suspicious of is...

Mary Jo Kincaid: She claimed she hurt her ankle bird-watching in the woods. But what was she really doing hanging around where Charlie's remains were found? Luckily for her, the spotlight has suddenly fallen on...

Ethan Walker: This reclusive brawler had been known to tangle with Charlie, even threatening his life once or twice. And his alibi wasn't exactly airtight....

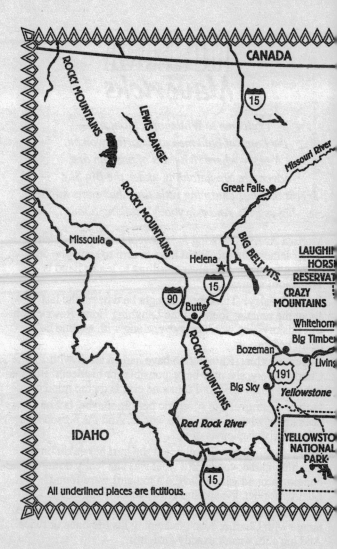

CANADA

ROCKY MOUNTAINS

LEWIS RANGE

15

Missouri River

ROCKY MOUNTAINS

Great Falls

Missoula

Helena

BIG BELT MTS.

LAUGHI...
HORS...
RESERVAT...

90

15

CRAZY
MOUNTAINS

Butte

Whitehorn

Bozeman

Big Timber

191

Living...

ROCKY MOUNTAINS

Big Sky

Yellowstone

Red Rock River

IDAHO

YELLOWSTO...
NATIONAL
PARK

15

All underlined places are fictitious.

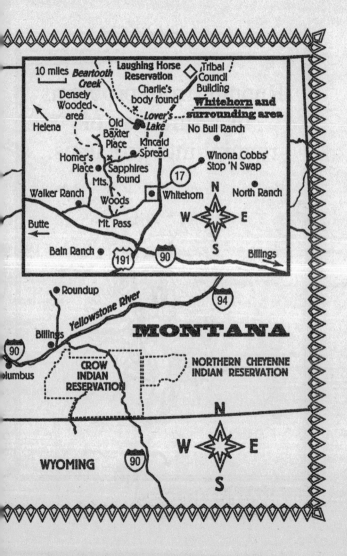

Runnin' from problems is a sure way of runnin' into problems.

One

All small towns have their secrets, Nick Dean thought as he drove north on Montana's Route 191. Some more than others. The town of Whitehorn, northwest of Billings, seemed to have more than its fair share, or so he'd discovered these past few days.

He swung his blue Blazer into the passing lane to go around a slow-moving station wagon, its windows steamed up by a carload of kids of varying ages and a harassed-looking woman driver. It was dusk, that nebulous time of evening just before the streetlights come on. A cold October wind whipped occasional clumps of tumbleweed across the highway, adding to the feeling of desolation. With a shiver, Nick rolled up his window.

Of course, having been born in Red Lodge, near the southern border close to Wyoming, and having spent most of his adult life in Montana, he was used to often-frigid weather. He even enjoyed it much of the time. The day's high of thirty-eight, dropping at least ten degrees since midafternoon, was warm compared to what it would be at the height of winter, when the wind-chill factor could take it down to thirty below in an hour. Glancing at a darkening sky thick with churning gray clouds, he decided it was entirely possible that the first snowstorm of the season was building.

That was all he needed right now.

Nick rolled his shoulders to get the kinks out. He'd been on the move from early morning, starting off with breakfast at the Hip Hop Café, hanging around over coffee refills, trying to overhear conversations or bits of gossip. Some people had been chatty and friendly, others outright suspicious. He'd learned several interesting things since he'd arrived in town, especially from the older generation, but nothing concrete.

Next, he'd spent several hours at the Whitehorn library checking out old newspapers in their morgue. After a late lunch he'd driven to the Whitehorn County Hospital, where he'd persuaded a young redhead in medical records to allow him to paw through some old files.

After all that he still had more questions than answers as to what had happened to Charlie Avery, whose remains had been discovered recently on the Laughing Horse Reservation north of town. He had a few suspects—men who hadn't exactly seen eye-to-eye with Charlie—but not a shred of proof that pointed to any one person actually doing him in.

Nick ran a hand through his flyaway blond hair, feeling the frustration. For the most part, he enjoyed his work. Being a private investigator meant he was his own boss, worked his own hours and got to call most of the shots. It sure beat the years he'd put in with the Butte Police Department working vice. That job, too, had called for patience, something his father had taught him as a teenager working in the family construction business. The problem was that most of the people who hired private investigators wanted action *now*.

He watched the streetlights come on and noticed that now his was the only vehicle on this stretch of highway, both ahead and behind. Most of the residents of Whitehorn were home having dinner in their warm kitchens. He wasn't really hungry, so he decided to drive on to the Whitehorn Motel, where he'd rented a room, and pick up something from their coffee shop later.

Luck was with him on this case, Nick acknowledged, at least as far as his client was concerned. Melissa Avery, the woman who ran the Hip Hop Café, was anxious to find out what had happened to her father after he'd disappeared some twenty years ago. But because of the elapsed time, she realized that the trail might be cold and that Nick wouldn't have results quickly. The first thing he'd done when he'd arrived in Whitehorn after driving the hundred thirty-six miles from Butte had been to check with the coroner, where he'd verified Melissa's right to be concerned.

Charlie Avery had definitely been murdered.

But by whom and for what reason—that was what Nick was intent on discovering. And he would, he felt certain. He'd never taken a case yet that he hadn't solved, though admittedly, some took months, while a few had been resolved in a matter of weeks.

That's where patience came in. An investigator had to carefully gather facts; keep extensive notes; interview anyone and everyone remotely connected to the victim, his family and friends; ascertain motives, opportunity and means. Eventually, the pieces of the puzzle would fall into place. That's where the satisfaction came in, unlike police work where, often as not, catching the culprit didn't necessarily mean a conviction. Smart, high-paid lawyers, legal technicalities, uncertain witnesses—any one of those and a number of other factors, and the criminal walked.

Nick had found that frustration much harder to deal with than the patience required to unravel a mystery.

His eyes flickered over the hilly terrain to the left, the dormant scrub grass, the scraggly bushes. Winter was sneaking up on them. He flipped on the lights and had barely gone ten feet when something just ahead had him leaning toward the windshield and squinting. He hadn't been mistaken, Nick decided as he made out a form at the side of the road. A woman stood motioning for him to stop, yet he could spot no disabled vehicle. Surely she hadn't been out walking along this deserted strip of highway. Quickly, he pulled the Blazer to a halt.

Leaning over, Nick rolled down the window and studied her in his headlights. She looked to be in her mid-twenties, with long, windblown hair and a thin face. She seemed lost in the folds of an oversize tan raincoat as she approached, carrying what looked like a heavy canvas bag. "Car trouble?" he asked.

She answered his question with one of her own. "Can you give me a lift?"

"Sure." He shoved open the passenger door and watched her climb slowly inside. "Where you headed?"

She had trouble closing the door, but finally managed it. "I—I'm not sure. Where are you going?" She struggled to fasten her seat belt.

Up close in the light from the dash, Nick saw that she was quite pale and, despite the cold, her face looked flushed. "I'm heading for the Whitehorn Motel." Her blue eyes were huge and seemed a little vague. "But I could take you somewhere else. It's getting colder and looks like it may snow." At that, he turned the heater on.

"I don't want to trouble you. The motel's fine." Her voice was so low he had to lean closer to hear her.

Shifting into gear, Nick glanced over again. "Are you from around here?"

"No, no. I just came back to make sure she was all right."

"She?" But the woman was staring out the windshield, apparently unaware of his question. "You came back to make sure *who* was all right?"

Suddenly, she came to attention. "No one. Never mind."

Nick saw perspiration gathering on her face, unhealthy perspiration not caused by the heater, he was certain. "Are you all right? Maybe I should turn around and take you to the hospital."

"No, I'm fine. Really." She huddled in her coat, pulling up the collar.

"My name's Nick Dean," he said, giving it one more try as he downshifted around a steep curve. Another glance told him she had her eyes closed and wasn't planning on giving him her name, whether because she was ill or from a need for privacy, he couldn't tell. He wanted to ask her what she was doing on this lonely stretch of highway hitchhiking, if she knew someone in town and who the mysterious "she" she'd been checking on was. Still, it was none of his business. Perhaps the best thing he could do was to get her to the motel, where she could either check in or call someone.

As he straightened the vehicle after the curve, Nick suddenly felt the jolt of a tremendous explosion. Fire burst forth, flames shooting out from under the hood as the Blazer came to an abrupt stop. The driver's door shot open and Nick was thrown out, hitting the cold ground, then rolling down the embankment. His left shoulder and then his head took the worst of it. He had no time to prepare himself, no time to brace against the tumble and roll into the fall. As he plunged down the hill, he heard another roaring eruption.

He didn't see the black smoke billowing up from the wreckage, nor hear the lone, frightened scream of a woman. Before his body rammed into a cluster of prickly bushes that stopped his plunge down the incline, Nick Dean mercifully passed out.

Sara Lewis checked her watch and saw that it was nearly seven. The wind was really picking up, and it had begun to snow just as she'd left the Whitehorn County Hospital and climbed into her six-year-old white Volkswagen. Fortunately, the little car ran like a top, and the reliable heater had the interior warm in moments. She would have to dig out her fur-lined parka soon, Sara thought as she turned onto the two-lane road that paralleled Route 191. The highway would have gotten her back to the reservation more quickly, but she much preferred the slower pace of Pale Bluff Lane, especially when she was tired.

And she was tired, Sara admitted to herself as she shook back her long black hair. They'd had a shipment of valuable tapestries come in this morning at the Native American Museum where she was artifacts curator. She'd been in charge of the paperwork, cataloging each arrival, checking the authenticity and overseeing the hanging. She'd been anxious to get the job done before the five o'clock closing time, so she'd worked through her lunch hour.

But she'd gotten every piece finished and hung to her satisfaction. So she was comfortably tired, not drained. Afterward, it had been her choice to drive in the opposite direction from her home to the hospital. She had an arrangement with her friend, Dr. Kane Hunter, another Native American who worked in town. They'd grown up together and had remained good friends. One of the children in the reservation's day-care center where she volunteered on weekends—Chad Laughing Face, a chubby four-year-old—had diabetes and a family that had trouble affording insulin. Kane was good enough to tend the boy free of charge and to keep him supplied with insulin if Sara picked it up when needed. She'd been happy to oblige tonight, just one of the things she did on the reservation to make life easier for her people. Things she did quietly, as was her way.

Sara's stomach growled, reminding her that her body wasn't a machine and needed sustenance, and soon. Some hot, homemade soup would hit the spot, she thought, and the wheat bread she'd made yesterday. Then a cup of tea and a long soak in her claw-footed tub.

She smiled as she leaned into the curve she was rounding. By most people's standards, this was probably not an exciting evening for a twenty-nine-year-old woman in the prime of life. But it suited Sara just fine. She didn't crave excitement, never had. She liked her life; her small house on Laughing Horse Reservation, where she'd grown up; her job, which she'd trained for both at Montana State University and at the museum in Bozeman, where she'd worked part-time to pay the expenses her partial scholarship hadn't covered. A woman proud of both her heritage and her independence, Sara knew she was strong and stable.

She also knew that those were the very things that apparently frightened off most of the eligible male population. Sighing, she acknowledged not for the first time that she was caught between a rock and a hard place. While attending college, she'd dated some white men, but hadn't felt totally comfortable with any one of them. Certainly not Jack Kelly, the all-American football star who'd surprised her with his avid interest, then taught her the hardest lesson she'd ever learned. Though there were few Indian males living on Laughing Horse in her age group, she'd dated a couple. And there was the rub.

She'd come to believe that no white man would accept and respect her cultural background. And she hadn't run across a Native American man who was strong, dedicated and as dependable as Sara believed she needed a man to be. She was beginning to think she never would for with the exception of her good friend Jackson Hawk, who'd married Maggie Schaeffer recently, and Kane, who'd been in love with someone else for a long while, few young Indians were comfortable with themselves, had come to grips with their heritage and were therefore able to remain happily on the reservation.

And Sara couldn't picture herself living anywhere else.

Definitely a dilemma, she thought as she crossed over the intersection of Route 191 and turned onto the road leading to Laughing Horse. A dilemma but not a tragedy, she told herself. She had lots of friends, the warm love of her mother and grandmother, who both lived near her own small house, and work she enjoyed. Many people had far less.

Life was a trade-off, after all, and—

Sara instinctively stepped hard on the brakes as a tall figure loomed just ahead of her, caught in the twin circles from her headlights. He was apparently having trouble staying upright, and she might have missed him altogether if he hadn't been wearing a bright red jacket. Pulling off the road, she stopped by a thick copse of pine trees.

Shifting into Park, she left her lights on and jumped out of the car. For a moment she didn't see him, then realized he'd fallen onto the shoulder of the road. She rushed over, noticing that he was trying to sit up.

Dried grass clung to his thick blond hair and there were scrapes and bruises on his angular face. A large gash on his head near his left temple was bleeding, and his jeans were dirty and ripped. "What happened?" she asked quickly.

With his head pounding and his left shoulder hurting like hell, Nick was having trouble remaining in a sitting position. But he didn't think about his discomfort, only of getting help. "Blazer," he finally managed to answer. "Caught fire. Have to get the woman out."

Straightening, Sara looked in each direction and could see no Blazer, no fire, no woman. "Where did this happen?"

He waved a hand vaguely. "Up on the highway. Gotta get help. I started walking. Fell." He tried to push himself upright, but the effort was just too much.

"Here, let me help you." Sara moved to his side and slipped one arm around him.

"Oh!" he cried out. "My shoulder."

She jumped back. "I'm sorry. Look, you're hurt. Let me drive you to the hospital and—"

"No! Explosion. Can't risk it. No hospital." Nick reached a shaky hand up to where the pain centered in his head and saw that his fingers came away bloody. "Never mind me. Go help the woman."

Again, feeling foolish, Sara glanced around and saw nothing. "There's no Blazer in sight and no woman." In the headlights, she studied his eyes. Pupils dilated, his complexion pale. She touched his cheek with the backs of her fingers and found his skin cold and moist. And he was disoriented. Her training under several volunteer doctors during her teens when she'd helped out at the reservation clinic told her the man was in shock. "How long have you been walking?"

"Don't know." Damn, if only he could think clearly.

Gently, Sara peered under his red jacket and saw that the shoulder he'd favored was at an odd angle. Probably dislocated, needing to be yanked back into the socket, an unpleasant experience at best. "Where would you like me to take you, if not to the hospital?" The snow was coming down steadily now and beginning to stick. The wind gusted and had her long hair tossing every which way. Sara brushed a handful out of the way and waited for him to respond. When he didn't, she thought of another suggestion. "You say there was an explosion. Perhaps you'd like me to take you to the police station."

He looked up, his blue eyes suddenly kind of wild as his hand reached to grip hers. "No, please. I don't know what happened or who did it. My head..." He lowered his head into his other hand. "Hurts so much."

"What's your name?" Except for her years away at college, she'd lived in the area all her life and knew nearly everyone in town, by sight if not by name. Whitehorn was only twenty-five square miles. "You're not from around here. Where are you staying?"

"Motel," he muttered.

An organized thinker, Sara took a moment to assess the situation. It was hard to tell if he'd been unconscious after the apparent accident, and if so, how long. If his mumblings were to be believed and he'd actually fallen from his burning Blazer, the thick red jacket had probably cushioned his fall somewhat, but that shoulder needed attention. Evidently, he'd been dazed and had started out walking, wandering onto the reservation. She couldn't take the time to drive back to the highway now to see if there was a charred Blazer anywhere to be found. Taking him to his room at the motel seemed heartless. She couldn't just leave him here by the side of the road, bleeding and nearly incoherent, with snow coming down fast and furious and the temperature below freezing already.

Sara came to a decision. She'd take him home, feeling rather safe since her house was located right behind the tribal police station. The self-defense course she'd taken some years ago gave her a measure of confidence as well, though he seemed in no shape to harm her physically. She'd call and see if she could get a report on a Blazer on fire and the possibility of a woman inside it. And she'd get him some medical attention, taking care of it herself if necessary, guided by Kane Hunter if she could still reach him at the hospital. It wouldn't be the first time she'd followed his phone instructions during a medical emergency.

"Come on," she said, leaning down to him. "Let me help you into my car. We've got to get you out of this cold." She braced herself to accommodate his weight, slipping her arms around him, trying to avoid the area of his injured shoulder.

Nick groaned but made it upright on the second try, leaning heavily on the woman. He wasn't sure he could fold his six-foot-plus frame into her small Bug, but he managed that, too. Closing his eyes, he leaned back his head, scarcely aware when she got behind the wheel. Despite his best effort, shivers shook him. If only he could warm up.

"I'll have you inside out of this cold in just a few minutes," Sara told him, praying he wouldn't pass out. She didn't know how on earth she could get him into her house if he was entirely deadweight. Flipping the heater on high, she passed the last of the pine trees and turned left in front of the tribal center building, circling the complex.

With cold and trembling fingers, Nick clutched his arms, then winced as pain shot through his shoulder. He wondered vaguely if he had the strength to yank it back into place.

He'd feel a lot better if he could figure out what the hell had happened. He'd had the Blazer serviced just before leaving Butte and hadn't had any indication of a problem until the explosion. Had someone messed with his vehicle sometime today? He'd left it for hours in parking lots at the café, the library, the hospital.

But who would try to harm him and why? He was new in town, had met but a few people. Or could it have had something to do with his investigation into Charlie Avery's murder? Who was the mysterious woman he'd picked up? Had she been tossed clear as well? Where was she and where was his Blazer?

With a groan he couldn't prevent as pain sliced through his head, Nick opened his eyes and tried to focus. The lighted sign on the building just up ahead read Laughing Horse Tribal Police. Though it cost him, he swiveled toward the woman driving. "Where are you taking me?" he demanded in a voice that sounded rusty to his own ears.

"To my house," Sara answered calmly. But she hadn't missed the fear in his question. Was it the sight of the police station that had him worried? "Are you in trouble with the law?"

He frowned. "Not that I know of."

As she passed the building and drove on, finally turning into the driveway directly behind, she wondered if she'd made a colossal mistake by taking this stranger to her home. Parking as close to the front door as she could, Sara shut off the engine and lights, then turned to look at him.

He seemed moments away from passing out again, trembling like a small boy sick with the flu. She'd lived most of her life going on instinct. Deep down inside, she simply felt the man posed no threat to her, rather that he might be in danger himself. From childhood, her mother had taught her that to help one another was one of the reasons people were put on earth and that it was the thing that separated humans from animals.

Sara believed that with all her heart.

"I'll come around and help you out." Quickly, she did just that, taking some of his weight as his heavy arm draped over her slender shoulders. Managing the two steps up onto the small porch wasn't easy due to the difference of six inches or so in their heights and the gathered snow that made the painted boards slippery. Finally, she had him standing at the door. She fished her keys from her shoulder bag, maneuvered the lock open and moved inside with her burden. She turned on a lamp, then led him over to the couch facing the small corner fireplace.

He all but fell onto it, shaking so hard his teeth were chattering, pain from his shoulder and head causing him to grimace. Eyes closed, Nick struggled to keep from going under.

Sara shrugged off her coat and was grateful she'd laid a fire yesterday. Hurriedly, she lighted the paper and kindling, watched the logs catch, then moved to the kitchen to turn up the furnace as well. She felt warm enough in a pale yellow sweater her mother had made for her and a navy wool skirt, but she could see that he was still shivering, undoubtedly a result of shock.

First things first. From the bathroom medicine chest she gathered cotton, peroxide, bandages, antibiotic ointment and a basin with warm, soapy water. Before she called Kane, she'd have to see how extensive his main injuries were. Returning to the living room, she saw that he hadn't moved.

Dragging over a kitchen chair, she sat down facing him. Gently, she touched his face and felt that it was still cold and clammy. "Let me help you out of this jacket." His eyes popped open and Sara couldn't help but notice that they were a startling blue despite the dilation.

"No. Cold." The effort to talk had his face beading with sweat.

"I know, and I'll get you a blanket as soon as we clean you up. But first we need to put your shoulder back in place."

Reluctantly, because it hurt even more now to move, he struggled to a sitting position and allowed her to ease off his jacket. Underneath, he had on a plaid flannel shirt in red and blue. He turned to study his shoulder. "You know how to do that?"

"Yes. We don't have a hospital on the reservation, just a clinic. I've worked there as a volunteer for over ten years, on and off. Dr. Hunter stops by several times a week. I've learned a lot from him."

From his visit to the county hospital earlier, he remembered the name as being that of a staff doctor. Had that been today? Nick blinked, feeling wobbly, but at least he was following the conversation, which he felt was progress. He knew she was right, that the shoulder had to be popped back in. He also knew it would hurt like hell, and in his present condition, wasn't sure if he'd pass out from the pain. "Then you've done this before?"

"Once, on a boy about twelve who'd taken a tumble playing football." And she'd felt young Lucas White Water's pain more deeply that day than he had.

"Yeah, me, too. High school football." He swallowed around a dry throat. "Okay, go ahead."

Sara swallowed, too, only around a lump of fear. Lord, please don't let me do more harm than good, she prayed. "It'd be easier if you could stand up."

Nick narrowed his eyes, studying her. He must really be out of it not to have noticed before this how beautiful she was. She was tall, five-seven or -eight, and slender, but with plenty of womanly curves beneath her sweater. Her eyes were large and so deep a brown they were almost black. He saw intelligence there and an enviable serenity, with just a hint of nerves. Her skin was the color of rich coffee with cream and absolutely flawless. And then there was her hair, thick, shiny and black, and so long it fell to her waist.

Maybe he'd died and gone to heaven. "Who are you?" he asked, weaving a bit.

She smiled and her face softened. "Sara Lewis." She wondered how much he remembered, of the accident, of how he'd gotten here. One of the symptoms of shock was this drifting in and out of awareness, of random memory snatches. "I found you by the side of the road, remember?"

Her voice was low and husky, sending shivers down his spine. Sexy. He liked it. "Yeah, I remember." He looked around the room, as if seeing it for the first time, then back at her. "You brought me to your house."

"Yes. Now, let's—"

"How do you know I'm not an ax murderer or a serial killer?"

If he were, would he joke about it? Sara asked herself. "Are you?"

Slowly, he shook his head, his expression serious. "You shouldn't trust strangers, you know. Dangerous, especially for a—a woman as beautiful as you are."

She let the compliment go, considering his present condition. "Would you like me to take you back to the side of the road?"

A log shifted in the grate and he jerked in response to the noise, then stifled a moan as the resulting pain registered. "Not just yet, I think." He glanced down at his arm, dangling at an odd angle. "I'll try to stand."

Refusing her assistance, Nick got to his feet and stood unsteadily. "Okay, just do it."

Sara rose. "I need to see the joint. Could I help you remove your shirt?"

He nodded, then just stood there.

Taking that as her cue, she unbuttoned his shirt with fingers that weren't all that steady suddenly. He was so large, his shoulders so muscular. He was dressed like a rancher and looked as if he worked outdoors. She tugged his shirt from the waistband of his jeans and saw that his stomach was flat, his waist narrow. Curly blond hair darker than that on his head was generously sprinkled on his wide chest. As she pulled his good arm free of the shirt, then carefully disengaged his injured one, she found herself very close to him. Close enough to smell the decidedly masculine scent that emanated from his smooth skin.

Sara cleared her throat, feeling uncharacteristically nervous. She was the calm one, always in control, level-headed. But he was so very male and so near, and it had been a very long time since she'd been alone with a very attractive, half-undressed man.

Keeping her expression bland, she stepped back and to the side of him, shifting her attention to his injured shoulder. The skin was marred by dark, ugly bruises. It was obvious that it had popped forward, probably from the impact of his body hitting the ground.

"Since you've had this before, you know this is going to hurt, right?"

Nick closed his eyes. "Yeah. Just do it."

Gripping his arm with both hands, Sara kept her eyes on the socket. Quickly, she gave a hard yank, pulling the arm forward, then around. She heard the muted sound of bone sliding against bone, and felt him shudder as he let out a deep-throated yell. She watched him fall back onto the couch, his face even paler than before.

"It worked," she told him unnecessarily, needing to speak to cover her anxiety. Sitting down alongside him, she reached into the basin for the warm washcloth. "Next, let's take care of this gash."

The cut near his hairline had stopped bleeding, but it began again as she gently cleaned the area. It was so close to his temple that it worried her. She saw that he kept his eyes closed and didn't move, which she appreciated. She made quick work of cleaning the more-minor cuts, then reached for the antibiotic ointment and dabbed a bit on the worst ones. The deep cut she bandaged carefully, then she picked up his hands.

"You've got some bad scratches here." When he didn't respond, she went to work, wondering if he'd fallen asleep. But his breathing was too uneven, so she guessed he was trying to get through this by gritting his teeth. At least they'd stopped chattering as the heat from both the furnace and the fireplace raised the room to almost too hot a temperature. She'd have to change out of her heavy sweater soon, Sara thought.

Finishing, she rose, setting aside the medical paraphernalia. She picked up his shirt and saw that it wasn't torn, though his jeans had several jagged rips. Since she didn't have anything else for him to change into, his own clothes would have to do. "Let's put this back on."

Nick leaned forward and marginally assisted her in redressing him. He licked his parched lips. "Thirsty. Please, could I have something to drink?"

Another sign of shock. "Sure. I have orange juice, milk, water."

He frowned as the pain in his shoulder began to throb steadily. "Got any whiskey to put in the water?"

He couldn't have known that she'd never served whiskey in her home, Sara thought. Not after her alcoholic father had left her mother and his two children when Sara had been just eight. They'd heard two months later that he'd died in a head-on collision after falling asleep behind the wheel, dead drunk as usual. Far too many other men on the reservation—men under-educated and jobless—had turned to liquor when they'd run out of hope. The sorry situation had left such a bad taste in Sara's mouth that she'd avoided alcohol all her life.

"Afraid not."

His frown deepened. "Not even wine?"

"No. It's water straight or one of the others. What'll it be?" She knew her voice was several notches cooler.

Nick looked up at her, trying in his hazy mind to determine why she was suddenly so distant. "I'm not a drinker, if that's what you're thinking." He touched his shoulder gingerly. "It's just that this hurts like all the fires of hell."

"I'll get you some aspirin." She left the room.

Swell. Aspirin. Nick gazed into the fire, then around the small living room again to keep his mind off the pain. It was in shades of ivory, green and peach. Cozy, his mother would have called it. Two easy chairs set at angles on both sides of a table. The couch, which was not only quite long, but comfortable. A bookcase along the far wall crammed with paperbacks and hardcovers. A stereo on a shelf, some records and photos. A serene watercolor hanging on the side wall. Lots of plants and toss pillows. No television, and he wondered why. Didn't everyone have a TV?

Sara returned and handed him two aspirins and a tall glass of cold orange juice. He drank them both down, then shivered again. "I should be going. You've been very helpful, but..." The very thought of going out into the cold night had him closing his eyes wearily.

"I don't think you're in any shape to go anywhere tonight." Sara walked to the front window and peered out.

"It's really snowing now. And you have no car, remember?" She pulled the drapes shut to help keep out the wind. None of the houses on the reservation were terribly well built.

Walking back to him, she stood looking down into his face. Even with the pain lines, he reminded her of someone. Someone she'd spent many years trying to forget. Sara tilted her head, studying him. A lock of his thick blond hair fell boyishly onto his forehead and she could see a tan beneath his pallor. His eyes were the color of a Montana sky in summertime. This man had more character and maturity than Jack probably had even today. Actually, he resembled Robert Redford when he'd appeared in *Butch Cassidy and the Sundance Kid.* "If you're going to be my overnight guest, do you think you could tell me your name?"

He roused himself, realizing he owed her that at the very least. "Nick Dean. I'm a private investigator from Butte. I'm working on a case in Whitehorn. Charlie Avery. His remains were found on Laughing Horse Reservation recently."

"Yes, I heard about that. About twenty miles from here."

His eyes opened slowly. "From here?"

"Uh-huh. You're on that very same reservation." She watched the knowledge register.

"And you're an..."

"An Indian, yes. Or a Native American, as some prefer." She tossed her long hair back over her shoulder challengingly. "Are you sure you don't want me to take you somewhere now that you know that? I might have a tomahawk tucked in my purse."

He frowned again. "Why would you say that? Don't put yourself down, or your people. And don't resort to clichés. You're Indian, I'm not. So what?" He rubbed his aching head. "I rarely take aspirin. How long before it starts to work?"

Sara was nonplussed, something she rarely was. She'd never heard any white person, man or woman, dismiss cultural differences so casually. Perhaps it was his concussion. She'd have to see how he reacted in the morning. "Not long," she said, preferring to answer his medical question rather than discuss his other comments. "You probably haven't eaten. I'm going to heat some chicken soup for myself. Would you like a bowl?"

"I don't think so. My stomach's a little queasy."

From the shock he'd suffered, she decided. "Maybe a nice cup of tea with honey and lemon."

He almost smiled. "That's exactly what my mother used to fix for me when I had a cold."

"Mine, too. Perhaps we're not so very different after all." Sara started for the kitchen, but his next comment stopped her in her tracks.

"Oh, yes, we are," Nick said to her retreating back.

She swung about to face him, raising a questioning brow.

"I'm a man and you're definitely a woman." This time he did smile. "I may be in shock, but my eyes are working just fine."

Taken aback once more, Sara took her time fixing his tea. When she returned with it, she found he'd managed to remove his boots and was lying on the couch on his good side, sound asleep. She set down the teacup and sighed.

What had she gotten herself into? she wondered.

Two

Seated at her kitchen table, Sara took a sip of her tea, then picked up the wall phone and dialed the sheriff's office. It was time for a few answers.

She'd known Sheriff Judd Hensley, a big, muscular man eminently suited for his position, for years. She'd been saddened when Judd and his wife, Tracy, had lost their only son eight years ago and had subsequently divorced. Tracy had concentrated on her work with the FBI and was one of their finest forensic anthropologists. Judd had also buried himself in his work. Sara had been extremely pleased to hear that Judd and Tracy had worked out their problems and recently remarried.

The phone was picked up on the fifth ring and Sara recognized Tracy's voice. "Hi. It's Sara Lewis. Are you working with Judd on the night shift?"

Tracy laughed. "Not exactly. I came to pick him up, since we had plans to go to dinner and then do some shopping. But he's out on a call and so are both deputies. I only answered the phone because I thought it might be Judd."

Sara gazed out her kitchen window. Since she'd arrived home, it seemed as if at least two inches had accumulated on the ground outside. She'd rather have talked with one of the deputies, but it appeared that she was stuck with Tracy, who probably wouldn't know much. "A lot going on tonight?"

"Sort of. This unexpected early snow's caused a couple of accidents already. Judd left a note for me. Something about rushing to check on a call about a truck catching fire on Route 191. I really thought he'd be back by now. Do you need something, Sara?"

Tracy had already told her exactly what she'd wanted to know. "Nothing that can't wait. I'll catch him later. Was anyone hurt in that fire, do you know?"

"I won't know till Judd returns. Why, is someone missing from the reservation?"

She really didn't want to say more to Tracy, mostly because the sheriff's wife was all too friendly with Lily Mae Wheeler, a woman who lived in town and was the worst gossip Sara had ever run across. "Not that I know of. Listen, I'll let you go. Take care, Tracy."

"You, too."

Sara replaced the receiver thoughtfully. So Nick Dean, private investigator from Butte, had been telling the truth. At least as far as it went. Who, she couldn't help wondering, was the woman he'd wanted her to go help, and where was she now? Was she real or had he imagined her? Sara hadn't dared bring up the subject to Tracy for fear of arousing her suspicions.

Sipping more tea, Sara wondered when she'd aligned herself with the stranger sleeping on her couch. It was just that he'd seemed genuinely worried that perhaps he was in some sort of danger. An explosion, he'd said, then the fire. Luckily, he'd been thrown free, but what of the woman he'd seemed so worried about? Yet he hadn't mentioned her since she'd brought him inside.

Investigators by their very profession, especially when they were looking into what the newspapers had labeled a twenty-year-old murder, were likely to rile folks up. Perhaps the person who'd done in poor Charlie Avery, a man

Sara had never met, was now after Nick. Maybe Nick's asking questions around town, which she'd heard mentioned at work, was upsetting people. People who apparently wouldn't stop with one murder. That seemed to put a different slant on her taking him in.

Sara drained her cup and carried it to the sink, where her soup bowl was soaking. Was her imagination working overtime here? Was she jumping to conclusions because the man was a detective? But still, Tracy had said there really had been a truck on fire up on the highway. Nick could easily have rolled down the embankment, passed out and awakened facing Pale Bluff Lane. Disoriented, he'd likely staggered along, finally reaching the reservation. Perhaps tomorrow he'd remember more.

Again, Sara picked up the phone, this time calling Kane Hunter at the hospital. The receptionist said she'd page him, so Sara waited, watching the heavy snow fall. If this kept up all night, they'd definitely be snowed in by morning. And tomorrow was Friday, the day Jason Eagle, their head curator, usually took off. She knew that her Volkswagen had trouble making it into town in really deep snow, since the reservation had no snow-removal service. Of course, if it got really bad, the museum would likely be closed. That sort of thing happened frequently during Montana winters, although mid-October was quite early for a really severe storm.

"Dr. Hunter here." Kane's voice came on, sounding rushed as always.

"Hi, Kane. This is Sara. I'm terribly sorry to bother you again tonight, but I need a bit of advice." She pictured him at one of the paging phones near the O.R., probably in his green scrubs, his dark eyes impatient.

"No problem. What do you need?"

Kane rarely had time to waste. Quickly, she told him she'd picked up an injured man after an accident, described Nick's wounds and what she'd done so far, then waited.

"Who is he?"

She hesitated, uncertain how much to reveal, even to a trusted friend. She didn't want to put Nick in more jeopardy, or herself for that matter, since he was in her home. "If I tell you, it must be between the two of us only."

Kane thought that over. "I don't like secrets. Is he a stranger?"

"He's new in town." More than that, she'd rather not say. "I'm not sure if he's got a concussion, which is my main worry."

"You want to bring him in?"

"No. Tell me what signs to look for. Right now, he's asleep."

Kane let out an aggravated rush of air. He'd grown up with Sara and knew how stubborn she could be. "You need to wake him periodically, ask him ordinary questions he should know the answers to. If he can't answer them, he probably has more than a minor concussion. Does he have a bump on his head anywhere? Any vomiting or amnesia?"

"I haven't checked for a bump. He's a little nauseated but not sick. He doesn't appear to have amnesia, though he's quite vague about some things." She recalled Nick's last comment—that she was definitely a woman—and the accompanying grin. "Yet very aware of other things. I treated him for shock, as I mentioned, and his pupils aren't quite so dilated anymore. The chills have also stopped." The last time she'd checked, when she'd covered him with the blanket, the clamminess was gone from his skin and his color was improving.

"Is he going to stay the night? Surely, not alone with you?"

Not only because of his profession but because of their friendship and the fact that he was four years older than she, Kane had always been overly protective of her. "Will you stop worrying? I'm fine."

Kane fumed quietly. "I'd stop by later, but I doubt I'll get out of here until very late. I've got a woman in labor, a man who's had a heart attack and an accident case that came in a few minutes ago."

Sara's ears perked up. "An accident? What kind?"

"You don't want to know. A burn victim. Sheriff's office had to all but pry her out of the truck."

Sara swallowed around a wave of nausea. "She's gone?"

"Of course. No one could have lived through that. Judd's looking into it." He glanced at the clock on the wall. "Listen, if that's all, I've got to go. Why don't you at least call Summer to stay with you? I'd feel a lot better knowing you weren't there alone with a stranger." One day Sara's tender heart was going to get her in trouble.

She couldn't ask her mother to come over and stay the night, Sara thought. Summer Lewis worked long hours at the reservation's trading post, took care of her own elderly mother, who lived with her, and most evenings took dinner to several older widows, food she cooked in the early hours of the morning. "I'll think about it," she hedged.

Kane let out a resigned sigh. She didn't fool him for a minute. "Keep an eye on him during the night and give him lots of liquids. If the weather doesn't worsen, I'll stop by tomorrow sometime."

"Thanks, Kane." Again, she hung up. At least it appeared as if she hadn't done anything to harm her unexpected guest.

She stared at the phone, wondering if she should call Clyde White Feather, the tribal police chief. The office was right behind her home, but Clyde was probably in his own house half a mile from hers. What would she tell him—that she'd picked up an injured man, tended to him and he was sleeping peacefully on her couch? What purpose would that serve? Clyde would offer to come over if she indicated she was frightened. Which she wasn't.

No, she'd go it alone and trust her instincts. Turning out the light, she went into the living room.

He was asleep much as she'd left him, his breathing deep and only a little labored. She touched his face and found it warm, but not sweaty. In sleep, his features relaxed, he looked even more appealing she noticed. In his early thirties, she'd guess. Was the woman who'd been in his truck someone significant to him? As attractive as he was, he surely had someone special in his life. Then again, he'd scarcely mentioned her after getting into Sara's car. She'd tell him what she'd learned in the morning, provided he was better. Now, he needed worry-free rest.

Turning, she stirred up the fire, put on another log, then walked to her bedroom. She didn't want to sit around in a bath with a man in her living room, but she'd take a quick shower. Then she'd wake Nick and ask him questions as Kane had instructed.

It was going to be a long night.

The howling wind woke him. Nick came awake instantly, as was his habit. He opened his eyes and, for a moment, wasn't quite certain where he was. Then he saw the fire still glowing, the cozy room and his rescuer asleep on a chair across from him, one long leg stretched out onto the ottoman, the other curled under her. She'd changed into a pink sweatshirt and well-washed jeans. A green-and-white afghan was bunched across her middle. Her cheeks were rosy from the heat of the fire, which was probably why she'd shoved aside the cover.

He lay studying her, wondering what Good Samaritan urge had compelled her to take a stranger into her home. These were dangerous times, as his business all too often made him aware. Sara Lewis didn't look like a careless or foolish woman. It had to be that her caring instincts were deeply ingrained. Fortunately, she'd happened upon someone who would do her no harm. This time. But he hoped she didn't make a habit of picking up strangers.

Memory slammed into Nick. He, too, had picked up a stranger tonight. The woman hitchhiker. His foggy mind had let him forget her for a while, but now he grimaced, wondering at her fate. The wind that had awakened him was testimony that the night weather had only worsened. The woman hadn't seemed well *before* the accident. Had she been tossed free of the burning truck on the passenger side? He hoped so.

That thought brought about another, as snatches of memory came drifting back. An explosion. His mind felt much clearer now and he distinctly remembered hearing an explosion just before seeing flames, and then shooting out of the truck as if shoved by a huge, ruthless hand. Nick knew he wasn't a deeply religious man, yet he silently thanked the gods that he hadn't fastened his seat belt. He knew using seat belts was the safe, prudent thing to do, but he hated the restriction, especially when he was wearing a heavy jacket. In this instance, his stubborn resistance just may have saved his life. He might be nothing but charred remains if he hadn't been able to free himself immediately.

He maintained his Blazer with the careful attention of a man who regularly had to depend on his vehicle in a state where harsh weather was the norm for months on end. That had to mean that someone had tampered with it. He'd been in Whitehorn less than a week, but he'd apparently ruffled some feathers with the questions he'd been asking around town. He was investigating a twenty-year-old murder. Evidently he'd gotten close enough to scare someone enough to want to put him out of commission.

The thought was more chilling than the freezing wind outside.

He returned his attention to the woman sleeping two feet from him. There wasn't a speck of makeup on her face, yet she was even more beautiful than he'd realized earlier. If he leaned just a little, he could touch her, and suddenly, he badly wanted to. There was something about escaping death that made a man want close contact with another human being, to reaffirm that he was indeed still alive.

But he knew she'd probably toss him out on his ear if he awakened her that way. He didn't want to be a problem, since he had a lot to thank her for. In the morning she'd drive him back to his motel and he'd likely never see her again. She lived on the reservation and probably seldom strayed from it. From what he'd heard from the people in town, the Northern Cheyenne who lived on Laughing Horse pretty much kept to themselves, except for a very few. The Indians had been appalled when Charlie Avery's remains had been found on their land, as if his very presence brought with it a taint of guilt.

Nick didn't think so. From what Melissa had told him about her father, twenty years ago Charlie had been young and restless, a man who'd made several enemies in his short life. But among the white people in town, not the Indians. From everything Nick had learned, the Northern Cheyenne were peaceful and wouldn't harm a man who'd wandered onto their reservation. His own inadvertent arrival last night proved that. One of their own had taken him in.

He shifted his gaze back to his reluctant hostess. She had thick black lashes that rested on her cheeks now. Her mouth was full and beautifully shaped. She'd apparently bathed, for he could pick up a light floral scent, like bath powder, over the pungent wood aroma from the fireplace. She'd fixed her hair into a long braid that draped along one shoulder, and he wished she'd left it loose and free. She'd gotten somewhat bristly and decidedly defensive over the Indian thing, and he wondered why.

There'd been Indians in and around the area where Nick had grown up, but his parents had taught him early that the color of a man's skin told you absolutely nothing about him. It was what was in his heart and head that counted. Apparently Sara Lewis had her own prejudices, perhaps fashioned from some bad experiences. During his college days in Bozeman, Nick remembered that some of his classmates had deeply resented the few Indians who'd attended, most on scholarships. Nick had never understood why.

Still, he thought as he watched her chest rise and fall with her deep breathing, Sara couldn't be too prejudiced or she'd never have taken a white man into her home, especially since she lived alone.

Feeling stiff from lying in one position so long, and suddenly realizing he was very thirsty, Nick shifted, moving into a sitting position. A quick stab of pain shot through his shoulder and had him releasing an involuntary groan.

Sara heard him and came awake quickly. "Are you all right?"

"Yeah. I just hurt like hell." Easing his legs from the couch, Nick became aware of other bruises along his back and rib cage. One hip also ached, probably from when he'd hit the ground after dropping from the Blazer. He touched the cut near his temple and felt a bandage. At least his headache was gone.

"What's your name?" Sara asked.

He looked at her, frowning. "I told you, Nick Dean."

"And where are you from?"

He glanced at the clock on the mantel. "Isn't two in the morning an odd time to be playing twenty questions?"

Shoving free of the afghan, Sara got to her feet. "I think you may have a concussion. When that's a possibility, it's best to question the patient every couple of hours to make sure they're coherent and aware. Otherwise, you might need hospital attention." His color appeared normal, she was pleased to see, and his pupils, too.

He rubbed the back of his neck, stretching a bit. "I seem to recall being awakened earlier and someone demanding that I talk to them."

"Yes, that was me. You weren't very nice."

He glanced up sheepishly. "What'd I say?"

"You told me to leave you the hell alone. That was the first time. The second session you told me to go away or you'd punch my lights out."

He saw the hint of amusement in her eyes and relaxed. "Sorry about that. I guess I was a little out of it. I'm not usually so rude, especially not to someone who rescues me."

"Would you allow me to check your head, to see if there's a bump that might indicate a concussion?"

"Sure, if you don't mind if I whimper a little. I hurt in places I didn't even know I had."

Sara stepped close to where he was sitting and slowly pushed her hands into his thick hair. She felt him shiver and wondered if his chills were back. With sensitive fingers, she probed his scalp carefully, looking for a possible cut or a raised bump. It was silly, considering his condition, but she felt a jolt of awareness at touching him so intimately. She forgot for a moment that he was hurt and trusting her to help him. She thought of him only as a man, an extremely attractive man.

Nick took a deep breath and knew instantly that it was a mistake. She smelled so good, like wildflowers on a summer day, like everything female. He felt his body's instant hardening response and shifted uncomfortably, hoping she wouldn't notice. "Find anything?" he asked, his voice husky. He knew he couldn't take too much more of her warm, womanly nearness.

Sara sensed the change in his breathing and stepped back. His lips were parted, drawing her attention. They were full and inviting, causing her to wonder how they'd feel pressed to hers. Appalled at her mental meanderings, she put a chill in her voice. "No, but I wanted to be sure. Dr. Hunter advised me to check."

He sat up straighter, wincing at the effort. "You told someone I was here?"

Sara backed up farther and sat down on the ottoman facing him, feeling on safer ground. "Not exactly. Kane's a friend and I called to make sure I was doing the right thing regarding your injuries. But I didn't tell him your name."

He looked skeptical. "You told him you happened on a stranger who might have a concussion, took him home and needed advice?"

She shrugged. "More or less. Kane knows me, knows I'm apt to do just that, but that I'm careful." She tilted her head, nodding toward the rear of the house. "Besides, the tribal police are right behind me." He wouldn't know it was seldom that anyone was on duty all night. "And the chief lives nearby."

He remembered passing the building last night. He'd fleetingly thought she'd intended to drop him there. He'd underestimated her. "You've done this before then—taken in a stranger?"

She debated with herself about what to tell him, then decided the truth was best. "No, I haven't."

"Then why me?"

Sara thought he looked honestly perplexed. "You were in need and I came along. Is that so unusual? I'd have stopped for my neighbor's dog."

That certainly put <u>him</u> in his place, Nick thought.

Sara stood again. "Are you thirsty? Hungry? Do you need more aspirin?"

"I am thirsty, but not especially hungry. At least my head doesn't hurt anymore."

"I'll get you more juice, or would you prefer milk or water?"

"Juice is fine." Holding on to the arm of the couch, he got to his feet somewhat unsteadily. And felt the room sway, causing him to sit back down rather quickly.

Concerned, Sara moved to him. "If you'd let me, I'd help you to my guest room. I think you'd find the bed far more comfortable than this couch. I tried to get you to move earlier, but I couldn't wake you enough."

"Give me a minute." Eyes closed, Nick felt even the darkness swirling. Apparently he wasn't as free of the aftereffects as he'd thought. He hated having to lean on her, but there seemed no other way. And the couch was about a foot short of accommodating his height. "All right."

As he stood, she slipped an arm around his waist and waited until his good arm slid along her shoulders. "It's the first door on the left off the hallway." They walked, Sara very aware he was trying not to let her bear too much of his weight. She'd turned down the double bed earlier and now helped him ease into it. Looking exhausted, he fell back onto the pillows. She pulled the comforter up to cover him. "I'll get that juice."

When she returned with it, she saw that he'd removed his jeans, tossed them aside and bunched both pillows under his head. She tried not to picture those strong, hard thighs under her grandmother's quilt and handed him the glass. As he drank, she heard his stomach rumble. "Are you sure you wouldn't like something to eat?"

Suddenly he did, but he hated being such a bother, especially in the middle of the night. "I don't want to trouble you."

"It's no trouble. I think you'll sleep better."

Sara heated the soup and cut a generous slice of bread to go with it. She carried the tray in to him and saw that he was sitting up. Watching, she saw him take the first spoonful, then look up at her with those deep blue eyes.

"This is really good."

Sara pulled up a low-back chair. He seemed alert enough, with no signs of a concussion and the shock symptoms nearly gone. He was probably hurting, from his shoulder and possibly the gash in his head, as well as from many smaller bruises. A tumble out of a high Blazer onto frozen ground, then a roll down a wintry hill full of brambles and prickly bushes likely had left him sore all over. Fortunately, he'd been in good shape, which meant he'd heal quickly.

"You look more as if you worked outdoors rather than behind a desk," she began, hoping to learn more about him. She had a feeling Kane would be dropping in tomorrow with questions, and she wanted to have some answers for him.

Nick swallowed another savory mouthful. "My father owns a construction business outside Red Lodge. I used to work with him and still help out occasionally when things are slow in my office. My folks also have a small ranch—some cattle, a couple of horses. Nothing fancy."

So that's where he'd gotten those muscled shoulders. She curled her feet under her and let him eat for several minutes before starting in again. "What made you switch from construction and ranching to detective work?"

He chewed a chunk of warm bread thoughtfully before answering. "I get restless. I enjoy building homes and ranching's okay. But staying in one place too long makes me antsy. That's why I took off after college and did my share of drifting. Worked a lot of odd jobs, lived in a lot of places. Finally, I joined the police force in Butte and worked vice for a while. Nasty business." He scooped up more soup.

A restless man who liked a frequent change of scene and new challenges. So many men she knew were like that, a fact that had always puzzled Sara. Perhaps because she had no desire to pack up periodically and live elsewhere.

"After I quit the force, I went back to work for Dad for a while again. Then a college friend asked me to come back to Butte and look into opening a private-investigation firm with him. I always liked Nate, so I did."

"Apparently you enjoy your work."

He shrugged with his good shoulder. "It has its moments. I've got to admit, there's rarely a dull week. The people who come to us for assistance are endlessly fascinating."

Reading between the lines, Sara decided that once P.I. work stopped being fascinating, he'd move on. Men like Nick Dean grew bored easily.

Nick glanced at her between spoonfuls and saw her studying him in her patient, watchful way. She wasn't one to press, it seemed, just let him say what he would in his own time. He liked that about her. Finished, he leaned back into the pillows.

"I got married right after college, but it didn't work out." He checked out her left hand, then met her eyes. "How about you? Married, divorced, involved?"

She wasn't surprised at his question, but rather at how much about himself he'd revealed on such short acquaintance. Perhaps it was the intimacy of the hour or the aftermath of his accident. "None of the above. Who was the woman in your Blazer, the one you wanted me to go help?"

Nick frowned, remembering. "I don't know. She was hitchhiking and I picked her up—not more than five or ten minutes before the explosion. She was just standing at the side of the highway. I didn't see a car around or anyone else. I don't know how she got there, practically in the middle of nowhere."

"Did she tell you her name?"

"No. I asked, but she seemed to be in her own world. The only thing I got out of her was that she wasn't from around here, but she'd come back to make sure *she* was all right. When I asked who this 'she' was, she closed her eyes, looking kind of sick. Next thing I know, there's fire everywhere and I'm sailing down this hill."

Though Sara looked deceptively calm, her interest had been aroused. Two strangers in Whitehorn on the same day was unique in itself. "Describe her."

He did, but Sara shook her head. "I've never seen her. So you don't know any more about her than that?"

"No. Why, do you?"

She looked away for a moment, then back to him. "I'm afraid so. Kane told me they'd brought in a burn victim from an accident on Route 191."

Thank goodness. Help must have arrived while he'd been wandering about, disoriented. "What's her condition?"

"I'm afraid she didn't make it."

Nick frowned, then shook his head. "Poor thing. She was young, you know. Around twenty-five. And she didn't look well." His lips became a thin line. "She had the misfortune of being in the wrong place at the wrong time. In a Blazer that apparently someone had tampered with. If only I hadn't picked her up."

She saw regret, then anger in his eyes, and felt better. A man who cared about others, even strangers, probably wouldn't do harm. "I understand the sheriff's looking into the accident."

His eyes narrowed. "Did you talk to him, too?"

"No, just his wife."

"Who *else* did you call while I was asleep?"

Sara's gaze cooled. "Listen, you're a stranger, one I took into my home, and you told a rather rambling story. I believe I have the right to check it out."

"So when will the sheriff be here, at first light or any minute now?"

Sara crossed her arms over her chest, not letting him see her quick flash of temper. "You're a real trusting soul, aren't you? Seems to me that *I'm* the one at risk here, yet you don't trust me."

"I'm the one whose Blazer exploded. That's apt to make anyone a little uneasy, wouldn't you say?"

"Well, I didn't blow it up. I'm the one who took you in."

He let out a rush of air, feeling tired. "You're right and I apologize."

She heard him, but she had trouble setting aside her annoyance. "For the record, I didn't tell the sheriff's wife one word about you, nor did I say much more to Kane."

That confused him even more. "Why? Why were you protecting me, when you didn't know many of the details and you don't know me?"

Sara tossed her braid over her shoulder. "Probably because I'm a poor judge of people." Rising, she glanced at the bedside clock. "It's late and I have to go to work in the morning."

"Where do you work?"

"At the Native American Museum in Whitehorn." She walked over and leaned down to pick up his bed tray, but before she could grasp it, his long, lean fingers closed around her wrist. His grip was stronger than she'd have guessed after his ordeal. Her eyes flew to his face.

The coolness was still in them, Nick noted and he hated it after her earlier warmth. "I said I was sorry," he told her, "and I meant it. I—I guess I'm surprised at how much you've put yourself out for me."

"I'm fairly bright, you know. I, too, figured out that perhaps someone might have tried to do you in."

He felt her pulse scramble beneath his fingers and wondered if it was from her temper or his touch. Her hand was so much smaller than his, the bones almost fragile. "Then I have even more to thank you for." His gaze drifted to the heavily draped window. "I'm not comfortable with putting you in possible danger."

"No one came along when I picked you up. And no one knows you're here, not even the people I spoke with."

He gave a slight tug on her arm, bringing her down to sit on the edge of the bed. "Then we're in hiding together, two outlaws—one probably already wanted for questioning in a suspicious explosion in which a woman was killed, and the other for harboring a fugitive."

"You make it sound like a bad television cop show."

He was relieved to see her features had relaxed. He didn't want her angry with him. He decided that he liked Sara Lewis. She also intrigued him. "You don't have a television."

"Sure I do. In my bedroom. But I seldom watch it. Not much on worth watching." But her mind kept returning to the problem at hand. "They'll be able to trace ownership of the Blazer to you through the registration or the license plates, if they weren't destroyed."

Nick turned her hand over in his, tracing her smooth skin with his thumb. "Depends on how much was left after the explosion. That fire had to have been very hot. It'll take them awhile, I'm sure." His eyes sought hers. "Would it be a problem if I stayed here, just until I can sort things out? I'd like to heal a bit and try to figure out just who tried to kill me."

Sara's pulse was jumping erratically and her skin was heating from his touch. A problem if he stayed here? Oh, yes, that it would be. But if she refused him, where would he go?

She pulled her hand free and walked to the window, almost gasping as she pulled the drape aside. "The problem may be taken out of our hands. There's about a foot of snow on the ground already and it's still coming down."

She closed the drapes and turned back to him. "We may be housebound for a day or so."

But she'd already been more than kind. "I'll find a way to leave if you'd prefer that." He could always call Melissa to come get him, take him back to the motel, then rent a car when he felt better. Nick didn't want to do that, but he would if Sara didn't want him here. "I don't want to crowd you or make you feel uncomfortable."

What kind of person would send an injured man out into a near blizzard? Slowly, she moved back to the bed, but not close enough that he could touch her again. "I have no problem with you staying and you're not crowding me. It's not a mansion, but there's certainly room enough for two."

He was certain his relief must have shown on his face, for he saw a softening of her features. "I'll try to stay out of your way and not be too much trouble."

"Please, stop saying that." This time she picked up the tray. "Is there anything else I can get you before I go to my room?"

"Uh, the bathroom. It's..."

"Right next door. I've put out clean towels. Do you want me to help you?"

"No, no. I can make it. But thanks." If he had to crawl, he wasn't about to let her take him to the bathroom.

She turned toward the door so he wouldn't see how badly she wanted to smile. Did he think she planned to go inside with him? "Just call out if you need anything."

"Okay. Sleep well." Nick watched her walk out, leaving the door slightly ajar. He'd wait until he heard her bedroom door close, then he'd manage somehow to make it next door.

With a sigh, he closed his eyes, just for a moment. Damn, if only he didn't feel so incredibly weak.

* * *

She was just drifting off when she heard the crash. Jumping out of bed, Sara grabbed her robe, shrugged into it and tied the sash as she hurried down the hallway. She could see a light coming from beneath the closed bathroom door. "Nick, are you all right?"

She heard a groan and decided she'd have to take a chance. She shoved open the door.

He was standing with one hand braced on the sink. Dangling in his other hand was the towel bar that somehow had gotten ripped off the wall. He wore only dark blue briefs and a miserable expression.

"I'm sorry. I got dizzy and grabbed the towel rack. I guess I put too much strain on it."

She didn't quite smile, though it was pretty funny. Or perhaps it was just relief that he hadn't fallen and injured himself further. "It's all right. Are you feeling better now?"

"I'll fix it, I promise."

"Not tonight, I hope. Why don't we get you back into bed?" She took the towel rack from him and placed it on the floor near the tub, then slipped an arm around him. Her fingers touched warm, taut masculine flesh and she tried not to react. More importantly, she tried to keep her eyes above his waist. "Ready?"

Wordlessly, he allowed her to help him back to bed. He watched her settle the heavy quilt around him, noticing the intricate design for the first time. "Did you make this?"

"My grandmother did, many years ago."

"It's too nice to put on a spare bed. You should be sleeping under it."

She checked his eyes to see if there was a double meaning in his comment, but decided there wasn't. "I have others. Are you warm enough?"

"Yeah, this is great. I'll try not to disturb you again."

Just then there was a rough, sliding sound coming from outside the window, then a heavy thump. His nerves on edge, Nick sat up too quickly, pain slicing through his shoulder.

But Sara was already across the room, peering out. "It's nothing. A clump of snow slid off the overhang and landed on the shed. The roof's tin, which is why it sounded so loud."

Nick relaxed, easing back onto soft pillows. "There's that much snow?"

For a long moment she watched the growing accumulation. "Yes. I remember only one other time when we had this much snow this early in the season. I was ten and my brother, Paul, was twelve. The schools were closed and we were thrilled, naturally. We built this huge fort alongside our house. When it was finished, Paul dared me to climb up and slide down."

Drawing the drapes closed, she walked back to the bed, unaware she was smiling at the memory. "I never could resist a dare, so I did it. Only I didn't slide down. I fell down and broke my arm. My mother was furious with Paul, even though I kept telling her it was my own fault. Paul didn't *make* me climb up."

Nick had missed growing up with siblings and had always wanted a brother. "What did your father do?"

Her face changed, closing in. "My father died before that incident. My mother had to be both parents, and she was."

Something there, Nick thought. She seemed to resent her father for dying and leaving them. "Does your brother live here, too?"

Sara adjusted the belt of her robe, wondering why she'd started this with someone she scarcely knew, even though he'd told her half his life story and she'd seen him stripped down to his underwear. "No. He's married, lives in Billings and works for his wife's family business."

Nick got the feeling she didn't approve of her brother's choices. He was probably married to a white woman if there was a family business. Nick didn't think there were many businesses owned by Indians in Billings. There was that Indian-white thing again. "I guess you don't have any family left here on Laughing Horse."

"My mother's here and I have several aunts and uncles, lots of cousins. And my grandmother, the one who made the quilts, lives with my mother. She just turned eighty."

"I envy you," Nick said honestly. "An only child usually envies big families. It's a lonely way to grow up."

Sara shoved her hands into the robe's pockets and studied him. She'd never met a white man quite like Nick Dean. He didn't ask the usual questions, the ones about life on a reservation that annoyed her no end. People from other parts who'd never been exposed to Indians had the movie version of a reservation in their minds, certain that everyone lived in teepees, used war paint periodically and sat around chewing buffalo hides for recreation. Nick listened and seemed to find similarities rather than differences.

It was unnerving.

"I suppose the grass is always greener, as they say. Paul and I are very different and still seldom see eye-to-eye. We used to fight a lot, but now we just have discussions. The adult version of disagreeing."

Nick didn't smile. "Still, I'd have given a lot to have had a brother. The construction crew was like family, since most of the guys have been with Dad for years. But there was no one my age, you know."

"Is that the real reason you left home and wandered around?"

"I suppose. Looking for something. Damned if I know what." He struggled with a yawn, wondering how this conversation had moved onto a track he wasn't all that comfortable with. Middle-of-the-night chats usually ended up soul searching. He didn't mind talking about himself and his past, but in-depth analyses made him feel awkward. "Guess you'd better get some sleep if you have to go to work in the morning."

Sara shot a glance toward the window. "I doubt that anyone will be leaving Laughing Horse tomorrow. We don't have snow-removal service. Could take all day to shovel out."

"Then I guess your doctor friend won't be able to get through, either."

"Oh, I don't know. Hunter's very tenacious." Hand on the doorknob, she looked at him. "Sleep well."

"You, too." To his great surprise, Nick found his eyes closing the moment he heard the door shut behind her. The comfortable bed, the warm quilt and his beautiful hostess sure beat the hell out of the impersonal Whitehorn Motel.

Three

Sara awakened at seven as usual, stretching beneath her hand-sewn quilt. It wasn't until her feet searched for her slippers that she realized she could see her breath in the bedroom. Moaning inwardly, she hoped her furnace wasn't acting up again.

Quickly, she wrapped herself in her robe and opened the drapes. The wind had blown wildly most of the night. Snowdrifts were piled as high as her fence line. She'd have to check the road out front to see if she could make it in to work. She wasn't crazy about leaving a relative stranger alone in her house, but she couldn't seem to come up with a viable alternative.

So much for that concern, she thought as she gazed out the front window moments later. Her car was completely covered over, the walk wasn't distinguishable from the yard on either side and the road had at least eighteen inches of drifted snow covering it. The museum, a mere twenty-minute drive from her house, was likely half buried, too.

Turning, she saw that the fire had gone out and that Nick's door, which she'd closed last night, was ajar. She tiptoed past and saw he was still in bed, the covers pulled up to his ears. Poor man was probably afraid of catching pneumonia if he got up.

In the laundry room off the kitchen, she eyed the furnace. The little house was over thirty years old and Sara felt lucky to have gotten it. Made of wood and shingles, painted a blue she'd never liked, it had thankfully been insulated long before she moved in and the inside walls paneled. However, there was always something needing repair, draining most of her spare dollars. This summer it'd been the roof needing patching, and more recently, kitchen plumbing that had needed replacing. Now, just as the cold weather was beginning, the furnace had apparently decided to take a rest.

Sara punched in the reset button, adjusted the valve and waited. Nothing. She knew zip about furnaces and couldn't think where to begin to look further. Hands on her hips, she surveyed the thing with disgust. With the weather they were having today, who could she get to come out and take a look? As usual, the repair would be up to her.

"Having a little trouble?" Nick asked from behind her, then smiled when she jumped at the sound of his voice. "Did you forget I was here?"

"No, you just startled me." She looked back at the offending machinery. "You could call it a little trouble. The darn thing won't come on."

In his stocking feet, he finished buttoning his shirt as he walked closer. "Have you got any tools?"

How was it that some men with ruffled hair looked unkempt and others, like Nick Dean, looked sexier than ever, even first thing in the morning? Sara wondered as she went to her utility closet and pulled out her toolbox. "Living alone, I've learned to do most minor repairs. Why don't you pour yourself a glass of juice and I'll see if I can get this thing going?"

He reached for the handle of the toolbox. "Why don't you put on some coffee and let me take a look? It's the least I can do after all you've done for me."

Unconvinced, she looked up at him. "I dislike depending on others. I'm pretty handy, and *I* didn't take a fall down a hill."

Nick had always admired independence. But sometimes some people took it a shade too far. "Look, I don't want to make this a contest of wills. I've got years of experience in construction and I've repaired many a furnace. Would you please just let me help as a small measure of thanks for taking me in?"

Put that way, she could scarcely refuse. And she really didn't know a thing about furnaces. It's just that it was *her* problem and she wasn't comfortable having him take over. Reluctantly, she relinquished the box to him. "All right."

Nick picked out a screwdriver and began removing a metal panel.

"Are you feeling any better?"

"I believe I'll live." The truth was he hurt in a lot of places, especially since it was so damn cold in the house. But he knew that a fall like he'd had would take time to get over completely.

In the adjoining kitchen, she ran water into her coffeepot. "Have you looked out the windows yet?" she asked, gazing at the snow still coming down, though only lightly now.

"Yeah. Mother Nature dumped a bunch on us, didn't she?" The storm worked in his favor. It would take longer with this weather to contend with for the sheriff to learn the identity of the owner of the Blazer. If Sara's phone was working, he'd make a few inquiry calls later and see how much he could find out.

With the coffee perking, Sara left to dress in jeans and an oversize, baggy sweater in pale blue. She didn't feel comfortable being in her robe with a man in the house, even though it was full length and serviceable rather than sexy. Or perhaps she didn't feel comfortable with Nick in the house, period. He was so tall, so big, his broad shoulders filling the doorway. Her house seemed much smaller with him in it.

You're being silly, she chastised herself, as she stepped into fur-lined moccasins. In a day, two at the most, he'd be gone. Despite his middle-of-the-night comment, he knew nothing of Native Americans and certainly wouldn't be interested in one, male-to-female. Except perhaps as a conquest, she thought, remembering the heat of his gaze as he'd held her wrist last night.

Let him try. He'd soon discover a frost colder than the temperature outside. She was no man's one-night stand, no white man's Indian experiment. She'd already been down that road once and found it to be full of potholes. A smart woman had to learn important lessons only once.

She was just leaving her room when she heard the furnace click on. All right, so he was handy. Big deal. She probably could have repaired it just as easily had he not insisted on coming to her rescue. His grin when she returned as he was replacing the metal panel was a bit cocky.

"Do you think I've earned my breakfast?" Nick asked.

"So that was your motive all along, eh?" She smiled back, despite her firm convictions of a moment ago. It was hard not to. He was a man who smiled readily and often, she'd guess. Here he was, stuck in a snowstorm in a stranger's home with only the clothes on his back, his Blazer totaled, unknown someones apparently wanting to do him harm, undoubtedly hurting despite his macho denials, yet in a good mood.

It was an optimism of spirit, or perhaps a self-confidence, that was almost foreign to her culture. It was not that Indians were unhappy—far from it. They laughed and joked regularly and often. But mostly within their own groups, with their own people. With foreigners and most especially with whites, they were guarded, hesitant, wary.

Nick was the outsider here, yet oddly, Sara felt more as if she were. She envied his innate good humor and wished she had more of it. And she had to admit that his smiles were infectious.

The first real smile he'd seen on her had changed her face, Nick decided. Softened it, added a touch of vulnerability that she was so good at hiding. Then she'd drifted off into her own thoughts. "Where did you go?" he asked, stepping closer. He'd replaced the panel, put away the toolbox and still she stood there, as if contemplating the mystery of the ages. "You're so serious when you look at me." He dared to reach out and touch the end of her long braid, where it hung to her waist, and found her hair soft and silken, just as he'd imagined. "What are you thinking?"

Even his fingertips on the ends of her hair had her nerves jumping. Sara stepped back quickly. "I'm thinking I'd better make you that breakfast." She moved to the kitchen before she revealed the effect he had on her. Taking a deep breath, she removed a pan from a low cupboard and arranged her features into her usual composed expression. By the time he joined her, she was calm again, her heart rate normal once more. "Would eggs be all right?"

"Whatever you make is fine." He picked up one of two mugs she'd left by the coffeepot and held it up. "Want some?" At her nod, he poured hers, then filled the other, taking his to the small drop-leaf table across the room. He sat down and sipped as he stared out at a sea of white, but he wasn't thinking about the snowfall.

She was an enigma. Nick had never known anyone like Sara Lewis. She was, from the little he'd been able to put together, fiercely independent and very capable. Many women he'd known—beautiful, educated and self-reliant—were often a bit arrogant as well. Sara lacked that superior air, though she seemed quietly prideful. But there was a wariness to her that seemed such a part of her, and an underlying anger he'd caught glimpses of ever so briefly that had him wondering as to its source.

Inhaling the mouth-watering fragrance of bacon frying, he turned to study her as she worked at the stove, her movements unhurried yet efficient. She was in profile so he couldn't read her expression. Actually, he had trouble defining her emotions even when looking into her eyes. And there was the crux of it. Sara guarded her feelings behind a serene composure he'd seldom seen, except perhaps in his grandmother, who'd lived with his family when he'd been a boy. Yet he felt Sara's was a cover-up.

Nick understood the need to guard feelings. When he'd been married to Beth, he hadn't wanted to expose her to the harsh realities of his work in vice. So he hadn't talked about it, had instead bottled up his feelings of helplessness at not being able to lock up some of the slippery sleazeballs they'd had under surveillance. And he'd never mentioned his rage on behalf of so many innocent victims.

In protecting his wife, he'd harmed himself. The department's psychologist had finally managed to point that out to him. But by then, his marriage was over and the satisfaction he'd once found in police work totally gone. He was a slow study, but he'd finally learned to be more open, to share his feelings with the few he trusted. The change in attitude had improved his disposition, his outlook and the ulcer that had once eaten away at his stomach lining.

As he watched Sara fill two plates, he wondered if the careful way she thought things over before speaking, the reactions that fleetingly crossed her face before she quickly masked them, the disciplined way she held her body were from lifelong training or because she was uncomfortable having a white man in her home.

Or could it be because she was as aware of him as a man as he was of her as a woman?

Sara set his plate in front of him, then sat opposite with her own. She was unused to eating a big breakfast, usually making do with juice and coffee on the run as she hurried to work. But she'd thought it would look unfriendly if she didn't join him. Which was basically how she felt at the thought of having to spend the entire day enclosed with him in her small house.

"This is terrific," Nick said after swallowing a generous mouthful of scrambled eggs. "Did you put cheese in them?"

"Uh-huh."

He ate in silence for a while, then glanced over and noticed Sara picking at her food. "Aren't you hungry?"

"I often skip breakfast. I'd rather sleep an extra half hour." Oddly nervous, she got up to refill their cups. At the counter, she flipped on the radio, hoping to get a weather report.

She was fidgety this morning and addressing her remarks to her plate rather than looking at him. Chewing his toast, Nick wondered if he could put her at ease. "Where'd you go to college?" That seemed a safe-enough topic.

"Montana State," Sara said, sitting back down.

"What year did you graduate?"

When she told him, he nodded. "I made it out three years ahead of you." So she was around thirty, an age when many women seemed to take stock and reassess their lives. He was curious about Sara's, where she'd been and who was important in her life. She'd breezily dismissed his inquiry last night, but he doubted if someone as lovely as she wouldn't have men in her life.

Sara wasn't surprised they'd attended the same college. Nearly everyone in Montana went to State if they went to college at all. She nibbled on her toast, thinking that she'd better try calling Jason Eagle, the head curator, and see how the museum had fared in the storm. Sometimes even ten miles could make a difference in the amount of snowfall.

"Why did you decide to return to the reservation after graduation?"

Here it comes, she thought. He probably couldn't imagine why someone with a degree would choose to live in less-than-perfect surroundings. "I'd always planned to return. I feel I have something to offer here that wouldn't be as appreciated elsewhere." Not wanting to hear his opinion about her choices, she rose. "Please excuse me. I have to call the museum." She cleared her plate, took her mug with her and walked to the wall phone, wishing she had an extension in the bedroom. Turning her back to him, she quickly dialed.

Definitely touchy this morning, Nick thought as he finished his breakfast. He tuned her low murmurings out and tuned in the radio announcer, who was explaining that although the snow had stopped falling, the accumulation had closed Whitehorn and surrounding schools and most businesses, a common occurrence in these parts. The voice on the radio went on to advise everyone to stay home if at all possible because road crews were just getting started on the main highways. It would be hours before secondary roads would be cleared.

And Sara had said the reservation had no snow-removal service. Except perhaps manpower. Nick flexed his shoulder and felt ripples of pain race down his arm and across his back. A doctor might frown on shoveling after a dislocation, but he had to do something to win back Sara's approval and warm up her frosty expression if he were to remain in her home.

The problem was he wasn't sure exactly what he'd done to cause the coolness in her tone.

He drained the last of his coffee and carried his dishes to the counter just as she hung up the phone. Glancing over, he saw that she looked thoughtful. "Is the museum going to open today?"

"No, they're snowed in worse than we are, it seems." The two-story building stood on an open corner where Route 17 intersected Pale Bluff Lane, an obvious target for the wind to whip mounds of snow all around it. She'd had to phone Jason at his home.

"Guess you'll be staying in then." Searching around under the sink, he found liquid soap and a stopper. He plugged the sink, squirted soap in and turned on the hot water.

"I have this medicine I have to get over to little Chad," Sara said, thinking out loud. She looked out the window again, gauging the snow's depth. "I could make it on snowshoes." Absently, she glanced at Nick and became aware that he was washing the dishes. "What are you doing?"

"You cooked, I clean up. That's the rule I grew up with."

She eyed him suspiciously. "You grew up on a ranch and working construction, yet you still did dishes for your mother?" It didn't fit the picture she'd been forming of him.

"Sure did, from the time I could reach the sink. Dad does them when I'm not there."

"Well, I certainly admire your mother."

He sent her a proud smile. "You'd like her, too. She's one very special lady. I'm going to tell her about putting cheese in the eggs. Adds a nice touch."

Sara tried not to be charmed. A man who talked so warmly of his mother usually liked and respected women. Yet, as she stood watching him, the way the morning light coming through the window played across his features reminded her so much of Jack Kelly that it was almost uncanny. Jack had loved his mother, too. And had listened to her every word, especially when it came to what to look for in a suitable wife who would one day deliver the Kelly heir.

The remembered anger and shame brought color to her cheeks. She struggled against recalling the pain, the devastation that had followed. But she'd survived Jack and his blue-blood family, and had painfully rebuilt her shaky self-esteem. And she'd vowed that no man would ever hurt her like that again. Except for the infrequent times when someone came across her path who reminded her so vividly of that bitter episode in her life, she was happy and productive.

However, there were lingering effects. Jack hadn't quite managed to squelch her romantic hope that one day she'd meet someone who'd love her truly and honestly for herself alone. Life before and after Jack had done that. Witnessing her mother and father's marriage, which had been one long quarrel, had had a profound effect. Her brother Paul's marriage was a tribute to his ambition, not a great love affair. Her friend Jackson Hawk had a failed mixed marriage in his past, before he'd found Maggie, one of his own kind. And even Kane had been torn up about a white woman who'd left him high and dry.

What did it matter that Sara was attracted to a man who'd literally stumbled into her life and caused the first stirrings she'd felt in far too long? He was trouble waiting to happen.

But she was no longer an innocent nineteen-year-old in love for the first time. She now knew better than to stretch her hand into the flame.

Grabbing a towel, she began wiping the dishes he'd washed.

"You don't have to help," he told her, noting the color spots on her cheeks that told him he'd managed to anger her again. "I'll finish."

She was about to tell him that it was her house and she'd wipe the dishes if she wanted to when the phone rang. Tossing down the towel, Sara grabbed it. She'd no sooner finished telling Jackson Hawk that she was fine when Kane's call came in, asking about her as well. Though she assured him that her uninvited guest hadn't slit her throat during the night and that he was feeling better, Kane still sounded unconvinced. He reminded her that he'd be stopping by the clinic later when the roads were clear and he'd check with her then.

Listening to Nick drying the silverware and tossing it into her drawer, she kept her back to him and dialed her mother. After several minutes of conversation, she was reassured that both Summer and her grandmother were fine and not going outside today, since the trading post would be closed. Hanging up, she turned and saw that Nick had finished, put on his red jacket and was pulling on his boots. "Where are you going?"

"Do you have a shovel? I thought I'd clean off the porch and clear a path, maybe brush off your car."

He'd managed to throw her off balance again. "With a shoulder that was dislocated not twelve hours ago? Do you enjoy pain?"

He stood. "I heard you mention you had to get medicine to someone."

"Yes, a little boy, Chad Laughing Face. He's a diabetic and I picked up his insulin yesterday. His family lives about half a mile from here. Do you plan to shovel a path all that way?"

He remained unruffled, letting her spout off her unreasonable irritation, trying to figure out why she vacillated between a smile that lit up her face and an unfriendliness that had her all but sniping at him. "Probably not, but I'll see how how I feel after I finish your place."

Sara shook her head, praying for patience. "Is that what you did in Red Lodge when it snowed, shovel all around the barns and outbuildings? Or did you simply put on snowshoes like most sensible people and wait for a truck with a plow to take care of the bulk of it?"

"We had a truck with a plow. Do you have one?"

"No, but Ira at the gas station next to the tribal police has one and he usually gets around to clearing most of the main streets as quickly as he can." Apparently, Nick wasn't aware that many of the roads around the reservation were mere dirt paths, especially in the southwest section, where far too many families lived in rundown housing and tarpaper shacks.

There was beauty to be found on Laughing Horse, with its incredible view of the snow-capped peaks of Crazy Mountain, Beartooth Creek with its pristine water and the acres of green grazing land that stretched as far as the eye could see in the summertime. But there was also abject poverty, sections of barren land with no funds to farm it and desolation in the eyes of some people who'd given up believing life would get better. Maggie Schaeffer Hawk was getting the people and government more motivated to change but progress came slowly to the outlying reservation areas.

How could a man whose family owned a prosperous construction company and small ranch know of such things, much less understand them? Perhaps she was unfair to judge Nick. The old adage about not knowing a person's troubles until you've walked in his mocassins was certainly true. Maybe she should loan him her mocassins.

He concentrated on buttoning his jacket, determined to shovel her damn snow even if he dislocated his shoulder again. "Fine. Let Ira clear the roads. I'll do your porch and walk. Where do you keep your shovel?"

"Look, this is silly. You're going to do irreparable harm to your shoulder. I can't let you do that. *I'm* going out to shovel. I've done it a hundred times before and—"

Growing angry now, Nick yanked up his coat collar. "If you think I'm sitting in here while you're outside shoveling, you don't know me at all."

Matching his anger despite her resolve not to lose her temper, Sara planted both fists on her slim hips. "I know you, all right. You're a chauvinist, believing there's men's work and women's work. And you're fixated on being macho, throwing aside common sense—if you have even a modicum of it—which should tell you that if you dislocate that shoulder now, you could very well face surgery."

Nick gritted his teeth. "Do chauvinists do dishes? Did I not lean on you last night? I don't give a damn about appearing macho in your eyes. I just happen to be stronger than you, a fact of physiology. Now, are you going to tell me where that shovel is or do I go looking?"

He really was exasperating. "Neither. I don't think either of us should go out. I'll call around and find a teenage boy to shovel the walks. I know several who are always looking to earn a few dollars."

Her dark brown eyes were spitting fire and her cheeks were flushed from her adamant arguing. It was the most reaction he'd seen since he'd met her, the first strong emotion he'd witnessed. His temper cooled as his blood heated. "You're very beautiful when you're angry. Did you know that?"

It was all she could do not to groan out loud. "What an original line. Did you say it to distract me? Because if you did, it didn't work."

"Then maybe this will." His good arm reached around and dragged her up against his hard body. He heard a quick, startled sound from her before his mouth took hers.

Fury rose inside Sara, hot and heavy. She knew how to handle this and it worked every time. She made herself stiffen, forcing her body to be rigid from head to foot, clamping her teeth together, keeping her lips closed tight. She hung on despite the overpowering male scent of him seeping into her, the surprising softness of his mouth captivating her as it pressed against hers, the devastating taste of him that had her suddenly wanting, wanting.

She must not give in, she told herself, must not let him drag her under. And Lord, he was trying, his clever hands exploring and caressing her back while she kept her own balled at her sides. She tried to empty her mind, to keep resisting, even as her pulse began to pound.

Her unresponsive rebuff cooled him more quickly than a bucket of ice water might have. Nick let her go and stepped back, breathing hard but brave enough to meet her eyes. He'd never seen eyes so dark, yet so frosted over.

"My grandfather had a saying," Sara said, as calmly as she could manage. "'Anything you take that isn't freely given is never really yours.'"

He got the message, in spades. He couldn't let her see how badly he'd wanted her response, so he opted for levity. "Is that an old Indian saying?"

"More like a universal truth. I'm surprised, since you've lived all over, that you haven't heard it before." Turning on her heel, she left the kitchen, went into her bedroom and closed the door. Quietly. She wasn't about to let him see he'd moved her to temper.

Angry with her, with himself, Nick went to the back door and shoved it open. Physical exertion was the only answer when a man felt this low. Stomping through the thick snow, he made his way to the shed.

He hurt like hell. Not just his shoulder, but all over. He'd been a stubborn fool and now he was paying the price. The physical pain he felt wasn't nearly as bad as having to allow Sara to remove the leather boots that felt permanently frozen to his feet. His own hands wouldn't have been able to do it, since he'd worked outside without the gloves that had gone up in flames in his Blazer, along with his gray Stetson. He tried not to cry out when she finally tugged off the second boot over his lifeless toes, all but landing on her backside with the effort.

Sara set the boots by the back door and handed him the blanket she'd left on the kitchen table. "Take off your wet clothes and wrap yourself in this. I'll throw your things in the washer." Without another word, she left the room.

To her credit, she hadn't said I told you so. And her eyes hadn't mocked, her mouth hadn't sneered. He was furious anyhow. Only at himself this time.

Slowly, feeling as if his fingers might snap off with each movement, he took off his clothes and left them by the washer. Then he wrapped the generous plaid blanket around himself and made his painstaking way into the living room. Thank goodness she'd built a fire. Even easing himself onto the couch had his muscles screaming. Now his hands felt on fire as they thawed. Could he possibly feel worse?

He glanced up and saw Sara watching him with her steady gaze. There wasn't censure there so much as a humorous disbelief that he could have been so dumb. Yes, he could feel worse, knowing that she thought he was as stupid as he felt.

"Go ahead, say it. You were right and I was wrong."

Sara shook her head. "I don't have to say it." She went to put his clothes in to wash.

Nick lay his head back and shut his eyes, trying not to groan out loud. He felt as if he were sixteen showing off for the pretty little cheerleader, working out in front of her until his muscles nearly snapped. Funny thing was, he hadn't done it to impress, but rather because he'd been so damn mad at Sara's rejection of his kiss.

He wasn't used to it. Not that he came on to many women. After his divorce, he hadn't wanted to go out for some time. Casual sex had lost its youthful appeal. But the occasional special woman he chose—always someone, who appealed to his mind and libido—never turned from him.

Until now.

It stung. However, as he'd told himself just this morning, Sara Lewis was definitely different from any woman he'd known. More cautious, less friendly. Yet sensitive and caring. Picking up a stranger and dragging him home with her, getting medicine for a small boy and calling her mother to make sure she wouldn't go out in the storm...she was a dichotomy.

He became aware she was back and raised his head. Quietly, she placed a cup of hot chocolate on the end table alongside him. Just like his mother might have done.

But when his eyes moved to her, he wasn't thinking of his mother.

She was actually smiling. He nearly tipped the mug over in surprise.

"How is that shoulder?" she asked, her voice low and husky once more.

"Not wonderful, but not dislocated."

Sara sat down on the couch, not real close, but not at the far end, either. "My brother used to do foolish things like that. Must be something men have to prove, to themselves or to someone else, I'm never sure."

He sighed, a ragged sound. "I don't know, either. Something in the Y chromosome, maybe."

She smiled at that. She liked the fact that he could laugh at himself, even if she'd had to prod him to do it. "Are you always so stubborn?"

He thought that over. "Yeah, probably." He met her eyes. "You, too?"

"I'm afraid so. One of my worst traits."

"I don't imagine you have too many bad traits."

She relaxed, drawing her legs up and shaking back the long hair she'd brushed out of its confining braid. "You might be surprised."

He took a swallow of the hot chocolate and almost purred at the marvelous taste and the welcome heat. Then he turned back to catch the firelight dancing in the ebony black of her hair. His fingers ached to reach out and touch it. Shifting, he gathered his blanket about himself, thinking it might have been better if a big burly man had found him or some motherly older woman who was comfortably fat and no temptation.

He was getting that heated look again. Sara rose and went to the bookcase and her tape collection. "Shall I put on some music?" Anything to distract him. As soon as Ira came by with his plow, she'd put on her snowshoes and go see Chad. But until then, maybe music would lull him into a nap.

"Sure. Got any Garth Brooks or Reba McIntyre?" His slow grin told her he doubted it.

"Afraid not. I've got mostly classical, some collector albums of jazz favorites, show tunes and a couple of operas."

Apparently she wanted him to nod off. "Anything you choose will be fine." He waited, and in moments, the sound of violins filled the small room. He took another gulp of his drink.

"Maybe you'd like to read."

He'd already checked out her titles earlier. Not a mystery or Zane Grey in the lot. Instead there were biographies, gardening manuals and heavy tomes on ancient statuary, sculpting and the lives of painters long dead, as well as books on Indian history. "I don't think so, thanks."

"All right, I tried." She sat back down, this time in her favorite easy chair across from him, and picked up her needlepoint. Sara didn't have much leisure time, since she spent most of her days either working or volunteering around the reservation, weather permitting. But listening to music and working on a new design was one of her favorite ways to pass her free time.

She stitched away, glancing up occasionally to watch him finish his drink and eventually stretch out on the couch. She'd always marveled at how easily men fell asleep. Most women she knew, including herself, often took quite a while. Their disparate taste in music and books hadn't surprised her. Even though Nick Dean was currently a private investigator, he was really mainly an outdoorsman, a westerner through and through.

Which only pointed out their differences. She was a woman who happened to live in the west, but he was a born-and-bred, countrified westerner. There was a huge difference. And she badly wanted to keep in the forefront of her mind all of their differences. Despite an attraction, opposites really didn't belong together. That made it easier for her to ignore her decidedly potent and very disturbing awareness of this man.

So she sat working away while he napped, a cozy domestic scene to an observer, but one with no basis in fact. She got up to toss his clothes in the dryer and to put a chicken in the oven for dinner. When the fire began to sputter, she put on two more logs. Rising, she heard his low moan as he turned, his shoulder irritation probably making itself known.

She walked over and hitched up the blanket that had slipped, covering him again. She then gasped in surprise as his hand caught hers, tugging her down to sit alongside him. His eyes were so deep a blue it felt as if she were staring into the depths of a fathomless sea. He held her gaze for several long heartbeats, then reached up and slowly stroked her cheek, finally cupping her chin.

Her breathing altered, her reaction out of her control. "Don't do this, please."

"Are you afraid of me?"

"No. I just don't want to get involved."

"With me specifically?"

She didn't want to go into why getting involved with him would be like revisiting a mine field that had nearly destroyed her the first time around. "With anyone."

"Why?"

"It's a long story, and I don't want to tell it." She tugged on her hand, but he didn't let go.

"Is it because I'm white?"

He wasn't going to make it easy. "Certainly that has something to do with it."

"It's not important, not to me. Why is it to you?"

It's not important. The very same words she'd heard before. And though that man, too, had insisted their different cultures weren't important to him, they had been of utmost importance to his family.

With determination, Sara pulled her hand free and stood. "Here's the story. You can stay here until you're healed, until the storm's over, until you find out who's after you or whatever. But the offer does not include *me*. If you can't honor that, you'll have to make other arrangements." Thrusting her hands into her pockets to hide their trembling, she went to the kitchen to check on dinner.

With a puzzled frown, Nick watched her leave. Someone had hurt her, undoubtedly a white man. Lewis was her family name. Apparently her father, the man she'd said had died when she was young, had been white. Her features weren't typically Native American, which would back up his theory. Had her father been the man who'd left her distrusting all white men?

Or had it been someone else, someone she'd been involved with as a grown woman? Whichever, Nick felt sure of one thing: he wasn't about to be lumped in with someone who'd hurt her just because he shared the same skin color.

With that decided, he closed his eyes. After a nap, he'd feel better equipped to change Sara Lewis's pretty little mind.

Four

"You say you're calling about a vehicle that caught fire on Route 191?" Deputy Rawlings asked in a drawl that held more than a little trace of the south in it.

Nick held the phone a short distance from his mouth, hoping the deputy he'd met earlier in the week wouldn't recognize his voice. He'd deliberately waited until after five to call, hoping the sheriff wouldn't be in. He had a feeling that Judd Hensley's deceptively quiet way hid a shrewd mind. "That's right. A Blazer, as I understand it. Late afternoon yesterday."

"Yeah, that's right. Not much left of that vehicle. Been towed to the garage where we're going to check it out."

"Do you know what caused the fire?"

"Sheriff suspects foul play. Say, who is this and what's your interest in this?"

"Uh, I was on the road that day. Seemed like I heard an explosion just before the fire."

"You saw it happen? Sheriff'll want to question you. What's your name?"

Nick's mind raced through several possible answers, then he decided he'd better play it safe. "I don't want to get involved."

"Now, hold on," Deputy Rawlings insisted. "You're the only witness to a possible crime in which a woman died. You have an obligation to come forward."

"What was the woman's name?"

"We don't know who she was yet. She . . ." There was a pause and a shuffling sound.

A deeper voice came on. "This is Sheriff Hensley. Would you by any chance be Nick Dean?"

Nick nearly dropped the phone. How in hell had they found out his identity so quickly? There seemed no point in evading the sheriff's question. "Yes. Your deputy tells me you suspect foul play. On what do you base your suspicions?"

Judd decided he'd ask his own questions while he had Dean on the line. The weather was still bad, which meant the man wouldn't be able to get into his office until tomorrow, probably, and he needed answers now. "We hauled what's left of your Blazer into the service station last evening before the snow got too heavy. Our man took a look at it today. He's found fragments of dynamite. I've got a call in to the forensics lab in Billings to send over one of their experts. Can you tell me what happened?"

Nick rubbed the back of his neck. It was one thing to wonder about the explosion and quite another to hear the cold, hard fact that someone had deliberately planted a bomb in his Blazer. He'd been shot at once in his work as a P.I. and had had a knife slice into him by a guy high on drugs when he'd been working vice. But a bomb?

"I wish I could. I was driving along when suddenly there was this explosion, followed by a huge burst of fire. I was thrown clear and passed out."

In his office, seated at his cluttered desk, Judd took notes. "Do you know why someone might put dynamite in your vehicle?"

"The only reason I can come up with is that I'm investigating that old murder, like I told you when we talked last Monday. I haven't been in Whitehorn long enough to make enemies." Nick heard a sound on the front porch, the stomping of feet, and realized that Sara was back. He'd awakened from a much-longer nap than he'd intended having and found her note saying she'd gone to see Chad Laughing Face.

"You've never been to Whitehorn before this week?" Judd asked.

"No, never."

"Who was the woman with you?"

"I was going to ask you the same question. I picked her up hitchhiking. She didn't look well and never did tell me her name."

"Where were you taking her?"

"I asked if she wanted me to take her to the hospital, because she appeared ill, but she refused. I told her I was headed for the Whitehorn Motel and she said that would be fine. She was sweating even though it was cold, and her hands were shaking."

"Describe her." Judd hated to say out loud that there'd scarcely been enough of the poor woman left to make it easy for even a relative to identify.

"Average height, mid-twenties, thin and pale, wearing a raincoat too big for her, light brown hair."

Judd frowned at his pad of paper. That description didn't fit anyone in town, all of whom he knew. Why would a young woman be hitchhiking along such a busy highway at dusk near an unfamiliar town? They hadn't found an abandoned car she might have left behind, giving her a reason to thumb a ride. Whoever she was, she'd had the rotten luck to be picked up by a man who had dynamite under his hood. "Did she say anything that might give us a clue to her identity?"

Nick crossed his long legs and leaned back in the kitchen chair as Sara came through carrying her snowshoes. He'd gotten his clean clothes out of the dryer and put them on.

He saw that hers were quite damp from her long walk. He mouthed the word *sheriff* to her as she glanced at him so she'd know who he had on the line, then answered Judd. "Only one thing. She said she wasn't from around here and that she'd come back to make sure *she* was all right. But when I asked her who she meant, she said never mind."

Puzzled anew, Judd toyed with his pen. "I need you to come in tomorrow. We should make a list of everyone you've been in contact with since arriving in Whitehorn. I've heard tell around town that you've been asking a lot of questions, talking to folks everywhere. Looks like you stirred up a hornet's nest. Someone doesn't want you nosing into their business."

Nick let out a huff of air. "I've come to that conclusion myself."

"Weather should be clear by tomorrow. See you in the morning, say nine o'clock?"

Nick watched Sara pull out the other kitchen chair, sit down and tug off her boots. "I don't think so, Sheriff. I'm not crazy about exposing myself to further danger."

Judd thought that over a moment. "All right. Tell me where you are and I'll come get your statement."

He'd known that was coming. "Can't do that either, Sheriff. Tell you what. I'll write down that list of names and call you with it tomorrow."

A scowl appeared on the sheriff's face. "I'd think things over, if I were you. If you don't cooperate in a police investigation where an unexplained explosion occurred and an unknown woman died, you'll be an accessory to murder. You're our only witness. You and the person who's harboring you would both be in deep trouble. It's not going to help your line of work any to become a fugitive yourself."

"I intend to cooperate, by phone. I'm just not willing to give whoever did this the chance for another crack at me just yet."

Judd's irritation was palpable. He'd had one hell of a twenty-four hours, what with the Blazer fire, the death of an unknown woman and a whole assortment of other accidents due to the storm, leaving him scarcely four hours to grab a little sleep. He was in no mood to fence with this guy. "We'll protect you, assign a man to you, if that's what you want." He wasn't quite sure how he'd arrange that, since they were shorthanded in this freak storm, but he'd do it somehow.

Protection from a small-town sheriff and a couple of deputies who rarely had more to do than catch a speeder or break up a domestic quarrel, Nick thought. No thanks. On Laughing Horse Reservation, which was out of Whitehorn Police jurisdiction, he was in a safe place. He'd go back, but in his own sweet time. "I appreciate that, but I can't risk it. The person who planted the bomb could be any one of a dozen people I've questioned, or someone I haven't met yet but who's worried I'm getting close to a murder they covered up years ago. He knows who I am and I don't know his identity. I don't like those odds."

Grudgingly, Judd had to admit the man had a point. "I guess I'll go along with you, though I don't approve. Call me with that list tomorrow. And Dean, don't do anything stupid."

What could he say to that? Nick hung up and met Sara's dark gaze. "I took a shower. I hope you don't mind."

"Of course not."

"Well, you heard most of my end of the conversation. You think I'm being stupid?"

"No. If someone was after me and had tried to blow me away once and failed, I'd think long and hard about giving him another chance to finish the job." Despite her uneasiness at sharing her home with Nick, in her heart Sara knew she couldn't encourage him to leave and jeopardize his life.

"Even if it means you're stuck with me awhile longer, and that the sheriff warned me that whoever's harboring me becomes an accessory?"

Sara rose to take her boots to the laundry room before answering. "Judd Hensley doesn't worry me. He has no jurisdiction over me, nor you while you're on Laughing Horse. And even if he did, what could he do to me? I took in an injured man. That's hardly a crime." With that, she turned. "I'm going to get out of these damp clothes and then see about dinner. I hope you're hungry."

"Starving, and it smells wonderful." But he had something he had to say. "Sara?"

At the doorway, she turned to look over her shoulder, her eyes questioning.

"Thanks, for everything."

"You're welcome."

Nick took a moment to also thank the fates that it had been Sara Lewis who'd found him wandering along, dazed and bleeding. Then he dialed his partner in Butte to update him.

As the clock on Sara's mantel chimed eight, Nick sipped his hot tea with lemon and studied Dr. Kane Hunter over the rim of his cup. The man's complexion was darker than Sara's, but his hair was just as black. His intelligent eyes were filled with questions, even though Nick had told him much the same story he'd told Sheriff Hensley, at Sara's insistence.

"So, what are your plans?" Kane set down his empty cup and leaned back in the easy chair opposite Sara's uninvited guest. He'd listened to the man's explanation, and even he agreed with Nick's decision to lay low for a while. What he didn't like was where he'd chosen to hide out.

"I'm not sure," Nick stated honestly. "I talked with Melissa Avery earlier. Since she's the one who hired me, I thought it only fair that she be told that I didn't run out on her. She was shocked to hear about what happened to my Blazer. I didn't tell her where I was, but I did say that I was nearby and still working on the case, only from a distance for a while. And I asked her to keep her ears open in her café in case she learns something, and said I'd check back with her in a day or two."

"Then you plan to stay here until...until when?"

A relentless man, pushing harder than the sheriff, Nick thought. But then, the sheriff wasn't a lifelong close friend of Sara's.

Sara had had about enough of Kane's unfriendly interrogation. He'd been acting like an irate father responsible for a teenage daughter ever since he'd rushed in, all querulous bustle. While she valued his interest, she didn't appreciate his acting as if she needed his intervention in order to be safe. "Kane, really. Ease up. I told Nick he could stay until he felt better, the weather improved and he perhaps had a lead on who tried to kill him. You do recall my telling you that he took quite a fall and you are aware that we've been snowed in? Besides, his truck was blown to bits. He has no transportation."

Kane wasn't mollified. "There are car-rental agencies listed in the yellow pages." He wasn't trying to be unfriendly, just cautious. Kane had no prejudice against Nick because the man was white. He'd have felt the same about any man who moved in with Sara and was vague about how long he intended to take advantage of her hospitality.

Nick's eyes narrowed. Did Kane perhaps have more interest in Sara than that of a friend, and therefore he saw Nick as a threat, though she wasn't aware of his deeper feelings? "I take it you object to my being here." He said it as a statement, not a question.

Kane's dark eyes slid to Sara, then back to the P.I. "Not you, personally. But you must be aware that Sara is unmarried and therefore vulnerable to rumors and censure. Our community is tight knit and—"

"Oh, for heaven's sake, Kane." Sara all but flew off the couch at his idiotic statement. So much for keeping her cool. "I am almost thirty years old, not seventeen. And perfectly capable of handling myself. If anyone in our *tight-knit* community wants more information, let them come to me."

Seeing that he was fighting a losing battle, Kane stood and changed the subject as he looked at Nick Dean. "Would you like me to take a look at your shoulder or the cut on your head?"

"Sara's taken care of both to my satisfaction. But thanks for the offer." He also stood, relieved to see he was quite steady on his feet. "Please be assured I won't imperil Sara's reputation in any way."

"Tomorrow, weather permitting, I plan to take Nick around the reservation and introduce him to people so they can see him for themselves." It was something they'd talked about at dinner, and Sara had been greatly surprised at his eagerness to tour the area. "I want him to meet Jackson and Maggie and the Thunderclouds. Then I'll take him to the trading post to pick up a few things and show him our day-care facilities and the community center."

Shrugging into his heavy jacket, Kane frowned as he walked to the door, slipping his arm around Sara's waist.

"Are you sure that's wise? He'll be gone in a few days. Why drag him all over?"

Stepping back, Sara crossed her arms over her chest. "He wants to look around, Kane." Although she had misgivings about spending the upcoming weekend sequestered with Nick, it was because of her disturbing attraction to him, not because she didn't trust him as an individual. "Why do you object?"

Kane lowered his voice, glad that Nick was bending to stoke the fire. "You know how some of our people react to whites. How are they going to feel about having one living here, especially with you?"

"You've known me a long time, Kane. Do you think any man would be able to get to second base, or even first, if I didn't want him to?"

He studied her eyes, so fierce with determination. "And do you want him to?"

Sara turned her head, too annoyed to answer as she looked at the ceiling, wishing she could think of a good retort. Was she angry at his interference or because he'd hit at the heart of the matter? she asked herself.

"Sorry, but I've never seen you so quick to come to the defense of a total stranger." He busied himself putting on his gloves, then leaned down to kiss her cheek. "I just care about you, that's all."

And she believed he did, which was why she turned back and gave him a smile. "I care about you, too. But I wish you'd trust me."

"All right, I will. Call you tomorrow." And he was gone.

Locking the door, she went back to the couch and sat down to stare into the fire. After a lengthy silence, she looked over and saw that Nick seemed absorbed in the flames, too.

Finally, he spoke. "I suppose Jackson Hawk's going to climb all over my case, too."

"Probably. You have to understand, those two are like brothers to me. Especially since my own brother left the res."

"The what?"

"The reservation. We call it the res." With her fingers, she shoved back a long fall of her hair. "Kane didn't mean to be rude."

Nick smile was rueful. "Sure he did. He was warning me that you're off-limits. I don't think he's looking at you as a brother at all."

Sara shook her head. "You're wrong. Kane's not interested in me. I don't think he's ever really gotten over Moriah Gilmore."

Interested, he angled his body on the couch so he could see her better. "Does this Moriah live on the reservation or in Whitehorn?"

"She used to live in Whitehorn. She's white, and from what I've heard, Moriah's mother didn't want her involved with Kane. So she took her daughter out of state when Moriah was still a teenager. The desertion devastated Kane. Poor Homer Gilmore, Moriah's father, became quite eccentric."

"Why didn't Kane go after Moriah?"

She shot him a look that indicated he truly didn't understand. "He was a young Indian, wanting desperately to become a doctor. What could he have offered her, especially if her mother was intent on keeping them apart?"

"Are you so sure Kane's never gotten over her?" The doctor's concern for Sara seemed genuine and far more than brotherly.

"I don't think so. Oh, he's dated others, recently a nurse at the hospital named Lori, but sometimes he still mentions Moriah."

"And you believe the breakup was because her mother couldn't accept the fact that he's an Indian? Surely that sort of thing wouldn't happen today."

The man must have just dropped off Mars. She drew up a leg and shifted to face him. "Of course it could, and does every day. You don't appear to be the sort who hides from the truth. Prejudices against cultural and ethnic differences are alive and well and living in every country in the world."

"I guess you're right. I saw some examples of it at State."

He'd seen it; she'd lived it. Sara swung back to gaze into the fire, struggling to keep her memories buried.

But Nick's curiosity had been awakened. "Why do you suppose Kane wasn't keen on having me tour the reservation?"

A harder question to answer. "Maybe because he thought you'd get an even colder shoulder from some of our residents. We don't get many whites here, except delivery men and an occasional government representative. Certainly not any that stay overnight or longer."

"None?"

She shrugged. "A few, I guess, over the years."

"Like your father?"

So he'd figured that out. It wasn't difficult. Lewis was definitely not a Native American name. "Yes, like my father."

"How did he manage to fit in?"

"He never quite managed it."

Go carefully here, Nick warned himself. "Then why did he stay?"

"He loved my mother, even though they fought all the time."

"About the Indian-white thing?"

"No, about his drinking." Why hadn't she stopped this conversation when he'd asked the first question? Now that they'd come this far, Sara felt compelled to explain, so he wouldn't judge her family too unkindly. To understand was to forgive, or so her mother had told her repeatedly. "From the beginning, they were mismatched. They met, believe it or not, at a church bingo. Aaron Lewis had been a problem teenager, came from a broken home and had had several minor skirmishes with the law. One of the priests at the church took him and several other young truants under his wing and tried to straighten them out. One requirement was working the bingo, the same one where my mother was a volunteer."

"Here on the reservation?"

"Yes. The Catholic Church is not very far from the tribal center. At any rate, they met, fell in love and wanted to get married. My mother's parents weren't thrilled because they felt my father wasn't very stable and that he might coax my mother off the res. But he had no family elsewhere and surprised them by moving here."

"I guess there must have been problems or he wouldn't have started drinking."

"Oh, yes. See, there aren't a lot of occupations that provide jobs on Laughing Horse, especially for the unskilled. We have no industry. Back then, unemployment was even higher than today, and far too many men were undereducated. When the kids come along and there's no money, a man loses heart if he can't find work to support his family."

"Why didn't he look for work in Whitehorn?"

Leaning back, she absently threaded her fingers through her hair. "I wondered about that myself. Later, when I was older, my mother told me that my father was like a man without a country, so to speak, unable to find real acceptance anywhere. The whites wouldn't hire him even for entry-level jobs such as pumping gas because he'd married an Indian. This was over thirty years ago, when prejudices were even more open. And people on the res wouldn't take a job away from a Native American and give it to a white man. So my father turned to the bottle for solace."

"And got sick and died?"

"Not quite. He left us finally. Not long after we heard that he'd been killed in a head-on collision. Probably never knew what hit him. He was drunk."

She said it so quietly, so calmly, without emotion. Yet Nick knew that inside she had to be hurting. "Is that why you don't keep alcohol in your home—because your father drank and you're afraid you might become an alcoholic?"

Her eyes shifted to his face as she tried to read his thoughts. He was more intuitive than she'd guessed. However, she doubted that he was getting the message yet. She was glad to shift the focus, since she'd already revealed more than she'd intended. "That's not it at all. If you'd grown up as Paul and I did, heard the quarreling, witnessed the fighting, saw how alcohol changed a basically sweet man into an incoherent, blubbering mess, you'd stay away from it, too. Alcohol is banned from most Indian reservations, since it kills more Native Americans than all other diseases put together. Although my father was white, he was no different from other men on the res who have too little education, are scarcely employable and therefore without hope. And if we don't do something to change it, still another generation will follow in their footsteps.''

Although he'd lived around or near Indians all his life, Nick had never truly thought about their economic problems. He'd known that many drank, but not why. ''What's the answer?''

Sara sighed. ''Education, for starters. Money appropriated by the government to further education for Native Americans. Maggie Hawk's doing a wonderful job now that she's crusading for funding and implementing social-reform programs. She used to be an aide to a pretty corrupt Montana congressman before her marriage to Jackson. She's getting things done, but there's so much more that needs doing.''

''You have a school right here on the res?''

''Of sorts, as part of the community center. But our kids have to go into Whitehorn for high school. And that can be a problem. Some poor families can't afford the right clothes for their teenagers, much less typewriters, schoolbags, money for lunches. We've had some equipment donated by Maggie's stepfather, but much more is needed. The dropout rate is very high. The crime of it is that many of these kids are really bright and want to learn. They'd do well, probably even go on to college. If only.''

Nick couldn't take his eyes off her. She was excited and animated when talking about something she believed in passionately. He couldn't help wondering if she carried that same passion to bed. He swallowed at the thought as she turned to look at him.

''Aren't you sorry you asked?''

''No,'' he answered honestly. ''And I agree that education is the answer. Not just educating the kids, but educating people outside the reservation about conditions here. Then maybe you'd get more action.''

He wasn't stupid, so he had to be merely naive. "Just how would you go about that?"

Nick took a minute to consider that. "Newspaper articles—get magazine journalists to tour the area. Write letters to your congressmen. Surely they aren't all corrupt. Do fund-raising to equip and perhaps enlarge the school. Solicit donations for scholarships. Get an athletic program going for young men. Nothing like sports to teach a guy clean living."

She had a gleam of admiration in her eyes. He'd given a very thoughtful, comprehensive answer. Certainly not one off the top of his head. She began to think there might be hope for him. "That's very good and all those suggestions are valid. But who's going to initiate them, follow through, get funding, organize and work like a fiend to see that they happen? There are a handful of young Native Americans like Kane and Jackson and Maggie who stay and do things for the tribe. The rest either leave or hang around and slip into the downhill slide of either drugs or drink. The others remaining are mostly the elders. And they've pretty much lost hope."

She watched Nick scratch his head thoughtfully, causing strands of blond hair to stick up at random and a thick lock to fall onto his forehead. Why was it that, even disheveled, she found him so appealing? Why was she sitting here debating old issues when what she longed to do was to move closer, inhale the clean, soapy scent of him and slide her fingers into his thick hair? Averting her eyes, she shifted to study the fire, wondering if she was losing her mind.

"I guess there are no simple solutions."

"You've got that right."

"Still, there's got to be an answer. You can't just sit back and accept the status quo of an intolerable situation. We have to start somewhere, even if only a little bit of progress is made with each step."

Raising one eyebrow, she looked at him. "We?"

He made a dismissive gesture. "I'm not arrogant enough to think that any one person can fix such a monumental problem, one that's been going on for years. But that doesn't mean we shouldn't try. There's power in numbers." Maybe tomorrow, he'd go talk to this Jackson Hawk. He was a Native American attorney and his uncle was tribal-council chairman, so Sara had told him. Tossing out a few suggestions couldn't hurt. Since he was confined to the reservation, he might as well be doing something worthwhile.

"Power in numbers. Just who are you teaming up with to *fix* the problems?"

She was making fun of him and he would let her. For now. "I'm not sure yet. Let me think on it." Easing fractionally closer, he trailed his fingers along her outstretched arm. "Your skin is the most beautiful color."

Perhaps it was time to change the subject. She searched his face and saw that he seemed to mean every word. "And quite a bit darker than yours."

"You should see me after working outside all summer without a shirt. I'm the color of mahogany from the waist up."

"Our differences are more than the color of our skin. We come from vastly different backgrounds and cultures." Their discussion had just pointed out how very different.

He stared at her until she made eye contact. "You just can't let go of it, can you? You make it sound as if we came off two separate planets. Is it because your parents' marriage didn't work out that you're afraid to get involved with me?"

"No." Actually, that was only a small part of it.

"Then tell me what it is."

Her sigh was a ragged sound. How was it that close-mouthed Sara was telling this man so much? "I cared about another white man once, in college."

"What happened?"

"We couldn't get past our—our differences."

"And you think that *we* can't get past any so-called differences? Sara, *what* differences?"

She was growing exasperated. "Why do you persist in this? Do you just want to add an Indian woman to the notches on your belt? Is that it?"

It was all he could do not to bunch his fists. "You're not just an Indian woman. You're a woman and I'm a man. I've watched you and you can't deny there's an attraction between us. I don't want to take over your life. I'd just like to follow up on the attraction and see where it might lead us. Damn it, Sara, what's wrong with that?"

Needing to move about, she stood, unable to come up with a good answer. "Do you know that it's a misdemeanor for a man to swear in front of a woman in Whitehorn?"

He rose and stepped to her. "To hell with that. Sara, give us a chance. I want to kiss you and have you kiss me back. I want to show you how I feel and find out how you feel." Remembering her earlier rebuke about her grandfather's saying, he chose his next words carefully. "Do you want to give me a kiss?"

He was a quick study after all. But just because he'd asked kindly didn't mean she'd jump at the chance. "We can't always have what we want. Besides, I don't want you." The lie felt uneasy on her lips, but once said, she couldn't back down.

The control he'd forced on himself all day snapped. "Oh, you want me, all right. But you won't say it or reach out or allow yourself to even think it. Not Sara, the original drugstore wooden Indian. See no emotion, *feel* no emotion. Reserve your passion for issues and turn from people. Stoicism at its finest."

Shocked, she just stared at him.

Clamping down on his temper, he towered over her. "You're lying to me and to yourself. Admit it."

Anger, frustration, desire—she felt them all. "Damn you," she muttered.

He straightened, feigning surprise. "It must be at least a felony if a woman swears in front of a man."

"Oh, shut up." Rising on tiptoe, she let her mouth seek his. She'd show him, by God, that she wasn't unfeeling, that she had plenty of passion and not just for issues.

By the time she realized her mistake, she was so caught up in the kiss that she was helpless to do anything but put all she had into it. His mouth, as she'd somehow known it would be, was incredibly soft as it pressed against hers, yet hard with purpose. Her blood swam hot and furious as her mind clouded over. Without half trying, he'd found the key to unleash all her dormant desires.

A log in the grate sizzled and crumbled, throwing sparks. The old floorboards beneath their feet creaked as they clung to one another. Sara was only peripherally aware of any sound except her own labored breathing and the thrum of her wildly beating heart. His rugged, masculine scent wrapped around her and she was lost, lost.

The kiss was everything he'd been imagining, and so much more. She was tall, yet her bones were small and infinitely feminine beneath his traveling hands. Her taste was ripe with needs he recognized as mirrors of his own. She smelled like velvet nights drenched in moonlight, like a summer meadow rife with wildflowers. There was the aspect of the forbidden about her, which drew him even more.

It seemed as if he'd wanted this woman in this way all his life instead of a mere twenty-four hours. The explosion that had shattered his Blazer hadn't been half as potent as her effect on him. His fingers thrust into the lustrous thickness of her hair where they'd been longing to be, and he felt the room tilt. He slipped his tongue tentatively past her lips and felt hers mate with him boldly. Shaken to his shoes, he devoured.

The seducer was being seduced, Sara thought with the hazy part of her brain still able to function. She'd sought to show him and instead was being shown just how few defenses she had against this man. Trembling, she stepped back, breathing hard.

Eyes locked, they studied one another as opponents might, assessing weaknesses, gauging strengths. Then, almost simultaneously, he felt the loss and she murmured low in her throat. They came together again, as if to see if the first encounter had been just a fluke.

It hadn't. Sara felt her breasts grow fuller, awakening as his large hands at her back pressed her closer to his hard, broad chest. Her hands slid up his shoulders and thrust into his hair as her lips drank from his. Never had she felt such a burning need, such a fierce longing. Her body of its own accord molded to his as if fashioned just for this purpose.

How could that be?

Her mouth was addictive, inviting. Nick eased her closer, wondering how he'd ever lived without experiencing this intoxicating feeling. The satin column of her throat, the silkiness of her skin, the soft sound she made as he deepened the kiss—could he ever let her go now that he'd known this?

When finally he released her a second time, she had trouble catching her breath. And even more difficulty finding her voice. "There," she said, her words barely above a whisper. "I just wanted to show you."

Stepping back, his arms limp at his sides, Nick blinked to clear his vision. "Yeah, you showed me, all right."

Five

"It took awhile to find all the bones," Jackson Hawk said as he leaned back in his desk chair. "The area where the remains were discovered is near our old burial grounds, and at first it was thought that some of those bones had shifted from a grave site. It wasn't until the FBI sent Tracy Roper, a forensic anthropologist, to examine the skull that the identity was confirmed. You might have met Tracy. She married Whitehorn's sheriff recently."

Seated across the desk from Jackson, Nick consulted the small notebook he always carried. "No, but I've had several discussions with Sheriff Hensley."

Jackson's dark eyes studied the blond man intently, then shifted to Sara, seated next to him. She looked a bit tense today, he thought. He'd been more than a little surprised when Sara had dropped in this morning with a strange white man, but not in the least amazed to hear that she'd taken in someone who'd been hurt. When they'd been kids, Sara was the one who'd always been finding wounded birds and starving cats, taking it upon herself to make them strong and well.

But before him sat a man, not an injured animal. From what they'd just told him, Nick Dean was staying with Sara, a fact that didn't sit too well with Jackson. He needed to know more about this stranger. "I'd heard there was someone new in Whitehorn asking questions around town about Charlie Avery. You're from Butte, right?"

"That's right," Nick answered. He'd been expecting the third degree and apparently Jackson wasn't going to disappoint him, even though they'd just told him how he'd come to be on the reservation. He'd say this for Sara, she had her share of watchdogs. "Melissa Avery hired me to find out what happened to her father."

"Judd wants Nick to go to his office and give him a list of everyone he's talked with since arriving in town, in case they might have had something to do with the explosion of his Blazer," Sara offered.

Jackson frowned thoughtfully. "You sure you want to do that? Seems to me if someone had tried to put me out of commission, I'd sure think twice before giving him a second chance to finish the job."

Sara smiled, pleased that despite Jackson's misgivings about a stranger staying with her—and a white man, at that—he was also concerned for Nick's safety. And she was amused that he had phrased it exactly the way she and Nick had. "Just what I told him. Judd can't touch him here."

Jackson raised a curious brow. "Of course, I'm not sure how the sheriff will react to your not doing as he asked."

Nick crossed his long legs. "I've already told him and he's not happy, but he doesn't know where I am so he's going to have to be content with my phoning him with a list of the people I've talked with so far."

As always, Jackson thought of Laughing Horse first. "Any of our people on your list?"

"No." Nick turned to look at Sara. "Your people took me in when I was bleeding and disoriented with a concussion. *One* of your people, that is."

Smitten. The man was already smitten with Sara, Jackson thought. And why not? She not only had a heart of pure mush for the wounded and downtrodden, she was beautiful to boot. And though Sara wasn't even looking at Nick, Jackson could tell she wasn't unaffected. This might mean trouble and he didn't need any more right now. Perhaps it was time to step in.

"Well, Nick," he began, "never let it be said that the Northern Cheyenne aren't a hospitable people. My wife Maggie and I have a big house out aways. Why don't you come stay with us until you're mended and ready to resume your investigation? I'm sure Sara has her hands full with her job and her volunteer work on the res."

That was one he hadn't been expecting. Nick opened his mouth to answer, but before the words were out, Sara jumped in.

"That's very kind of you, Jackson, but we've got things worked out just fine." Her dark eyes bore into Jackson's, as if warning him to stop interfering. She hadn't planned on Nick staying for an extended period of time when she'd picked him up. But since learning that someone had tried to kill him, she felt differently. She'd offered him her hospitality and she resented those who questioned her decision. She was a big girl and didn't need constant protection from Jackson, Kane or anyone else.

Jackson had seen that look before. He stumbled, feeling awkward. "It's just that—that your place is rather small and I—"

"Is Jackson trying to run your life again, Sara?" came a feminine voice from the doorway.

Nick looked up and saw a lovely woman with short black hair and dancing dark eyes in the doorway, her smile loving yet scolding as she looked at the attorney.

Sara swiveled in her chair and smiled at Maggie Hawk. "I'm afraid he is. Time to sit him in the naughty chair like we do with the little ones at the day-care center."

Laughing, Maggie walked to her husband and leaned down to hug him. "Oh, just leave him to me. I'll think of a way to make him leave you alone."

Reluctantly, Jackson gave up his effort not to smile. Ever since their marriage, Maggie had that effect on him. "I'll just bet you will."

Warmed by their affection, Sara felt the tension in the room ease. "Maggie, I'd like you to meet Nick Dean. He's—"

"He's the man you picked up the night of the storm." Still smiling, she held out her hand. "A pleasure to meet you, Nick. You're the talk of the res."

It was impossible not to respond to the woman's friendliness. "The same here," Nick said, shaking her slender hand, wondering how word had spread so rapidly when he hadn't left Sara's house till a few minutes ago.

Sara was wondering the same thing. "How did you hear about Nick?"

"From Kane, of course." She winked at Nick. "He's checked you out and couldn't find any skeletons in your closet, so I guess you're off the hook, temporarily."

"Knowing Kane, he'll keep looking," Jackson added, thinking that wasn't such a bad idea. After all, an unknown woman had died in that burning Blazer. How did they know this guy was on the level with his story?

"It's fine with me if he does," Nick said. "I haven't got anything to hide and I've told all of you the truth, as far as I know it."

Nick had wanted to come here, Sara reminded herself. She'd hinted that Jackson might be rough on him, but he was handling it pretty well. "I must warn you, Maggie," Sara said as her friend settled herself on the corner of Jackson's desk, "we're both fugitives according to Sheriff Henley." Quickly, she brought Maggie up to date on what had happened to Nick's Blazer, the hitchhiker and his injuries. "So it just makes good sense that Nick should stay on the res until he learns who's trying to harm him. He's safer here than anywhere else right now."

It hadn't escaped Maggie's notice how quickly Sara had sprung to the man's defense. She hadn't known Sara but a few months and didn't know if she had ever been seriously involved with a man. If she was inexperienced, the situation would bear watching, just in case Nick Dean wasn't as "all-American clean-cut" as he looked.

Unlike her husband, Maggie felt she could best do that by being noncritical and yet let Sara know she was available to talk if her friend needed her. "How exciting. Outlaws together, eh? What do you plan to do when Sara goes back to work, Nick? This snow isn't going to last forever."

He'd been thinking about that himself. The snow was melting rapidly today in the warmth of an October sun, the early storm disappearing as quickly as it had come. His shoulder was better and his cuts were healing. He couldn't just sit in Sara's house and wait, especially since he didn't know just what he was waiting for. "I'm not sure. Rent a car, I guess, and do some quiet snooping in town."

Maggie's mischievous side surfaced. "Maybe we could work up a disguise so no one would recognize you."

Nick couldn't figure out if she was making fun of him or simply had an offbeat sense of humor. "That has possibilities."

But Sara was on another track as she turned to Nick. "The museum's closed Mondays, so I won't be going to work until Tuesday. You can drive me to work and use my car. No one will think to look for you in my Volkswagen."

That brought Jackson into the discussion. "And have someone plant a bomb in your car? Too dangerous. I think Nick's right. He should rent a car."

Sara sent him another narrow-eyed look. "Thanks for the input, but we'll work out the details when the time comes."

Nick decided it was time to get control of the conversation with a change of subject. As Sara had said, they'd work out the car situation later. "So other than the FBI identification of Charlie's remains, you don't know anything more about why he'd have been on the reservation some twenty years ago, Jackson?"

The tribal attorney shook his head, his two braids shifting on his big shoulders. "It isn't common, but whites come on the reservation occasionally. The spot where the bones were found is about ten miles from my house, and it's very rural out that way. There're acres of grazing land and sections of wilderness. The fencing isn't real good. Anyone could wander into the area and we'd probably never know. Does Melissa have any theories?"

"Not really. She's given me a few names, men who reputedly didn't get along all that well with Charlie, but she was only a child at the time. The main thing for her is that she's always felt abandoned because her father disappeared so abruptly. Now that we know he was murdered, we can surmise that he might not have left voluntarily. She feels better knowing that, but understandably, she wants to know who did him in."

Jackson had been in his teens at the time of Charlie's disappearance and had paid little attention to the news. But the finding of his bones on his res had him interested now. "What names did she give you?"

Nick consulted his notebook again. "Unfortunately, two of them are already dead. Cameron Baxter and Jeremiah Kincaid."

Maggie looked surprised. "Jeremiah? What reason would the richest man in town have for killing a ranch hand who didn't even work for him?" She'd heard stories about Charlie Avery since his remains had been found on the res, and most folks described him as having been restless, impulsive and unhappy being tied down with a family and very little money.

Jackson, who'd disliked Jeremiah, felt that the man had thought himself above the law and wouldn't need much reason to kill a man. "We might not know his reasons, but we know that Jeremiah was short on conscience and could easily have justified murdering someone, say if the man had something on him."

Nick jotted that down. "Do you know anything about Cameron Baxter?"

Jackson leaned forward, his elbows on the desk. "I know that the Baxter Ranch at one time was quite prosperous. But Cameron was a conniver and gambler, always dreaming up get-rich-quick schemes. He wound up having to mortgage off his land little by little to pay off his gambling debts and poor business investments. There was bad blood between the Baxters and Kincaids, especially after Kincaid bought up much of Baxter's land. But how Charlie fit into the picture, I wouldn't know."

That pretty much confirmed what Nick had gathered from folks in town. "Anyone left of the Cameron family?"

"I don't think so. Cameron's wife died even before he did. They had a daughter who was rumored to be pretty wild as a teenager. Then she disappeared, and as far as I know, no one's heard from her since she left town years ago."

"Not much to go on." Nick glanced at his notes again. "The only other possible suspect I have so far is Ethan Walker. Melissa tells me Ethan and her father quarreled publicly more than once. I tried to get him to talk with me, but when he found out what I wanted to know, he left the Sundowner Saloon, where I'd approached him, without finishing his beer."

Jackson thought that over. "I've heard that Ethan's reclusive and antisocial, and that he gets into fights occasionally. He was in Vietnam, so he might be familiar with bombs and weapons. But I've also heard that he's honest and hardworking. He was still a teenager when Charlie disappeared. What would be his motive?"

"I don't know. I need to convince him to talk with me, and hopefully I can interview some of his friends and neighbors." He closed his notebook and put it in his shirt pocket. "Whitehorn's a pretty closemouthed town."

"Yes, and they're not crazy about strangers," Maggie threw in. "Most especially not Native American strangers."

"But you set them straight, didn't you, sweetheart? And impressed them to boot." Jackson sent her an affectionate smile, then turned to Nick with an explanation. "When my wife worked for the government, she 'persuaded' the school superintendent to treat the Indian kids more fairly and she shook up the town fathers a bit. They don't call her 'The Little Fed Who Actually Listens' for nothing."

Nick looked puzzled. "The little Fed who actually listens?"

Maggie liked her name and was pleased to explain. "That's what they call me on the res, my Indian name."

"Aha." Nick looked over at Sara. "And what is your Indian name?"

"Never mind. It's time we got going." She stood, buttoning her jacket.

Nick rose, but wasn't going to let it go. "Come on, give." When she shook her head, he turned to Maggie. "Is it so terrible?"

Maggie laughed. "Of course not. Sara is 'The Little Lamb Who Thinks Too Much.'"

Sara sent her friend a mock scowl. "I do *not* think too much, nor am I a little lamb."

"More like a roaring lion these days, I'd say," Jackson said, then pretended to flinch as Sara shook a fist at him. He, too, got to his feet and decided to lighten up and take Nick Dean at face value. The guy seemed all right. But he'd still keep his eyes and ears open. "If there's anything I can do to help your investigation, Nick, let me know," he said, walking to the door with them.

"Thanks, I appreciate that." The overprotective 'big brother' had calmed down since his wife's arrival, Nick thought. Like beauty taming the beast. The two men lingered as Sara and Maggie walked ahead arm in arm. Nick stopped, turning to Jackson. "I want you to know I wouldn't hurt Sara. She came to my rescue in a way few would have. I owe her."

Jackson studied the man's vivid blue eyes a long moment and decided to believe him. "Glad to hear you say that," he said, clapping Nick on the shoulder. At the door to the tribal office, they caught up with the women.

"I was just saying that it would be nice to have Sara and Nick over to the house for dinner one night, Jackson, since he's going to be around for a while," Maggie said, looking up at her tall husband. Before her marriage, she'd lived with Sara for a while and had grown to respect and admire her. Besides, she was curious as to how things between Sara and Nick might develop.

A good way to keep track of their relationship, Jackson thought as he nodded. "Fine with me."

Maggie smiled her thanks. "I'll call you, Sara."

"Great." Carefully, Sara stepped out into slippery slush as the noonday sun melted the drifts. She felt Nick grab her arm as her booted feet sunk further into the mess. "I liked the fresh snowfall better than this stuff." They'd opted to walk over, since the day was warming, but Sara wished now that they'd taken her car.

"Didn't I see a restaurant on the other side of this building as we came around?" Nick asked.

"The Tribal Center Restaurant, yes."

"Good. I'm hungry. Let me take you to lunch, since you've been feeding me for quite some time now."

She wasn't sure that was such a dandy idea. The small restaurant was a gathering place as well as an eatery, and the patrons were unused to white people. Still, how could she explain that to Nick without sounding as if the entire res was prejudiced? Perhaps it would be best to let him find out for himself. "Lunch sounds fine."

The bell above the door tinkled in greeting as they entered, wiping their boots on the thick mat. There were clusters of tables throughout the restaurant, a small counter at the rear with six stools and half a dozen red vinyl booths along the outer wall with its low picture windows. All but two tables and one booth were occupied, with three and four people at each and only a couple with two diners. As one body, the occupants looked up and stopped talking.

Only the clink of dishes from the kitchen could be heard as Sara led Nick to the far booth, smiling at several people along the way and greeting most by name. Nearly there, she stopped to hug a small girl of perhaps five and speak a few words to her parents. Then she slid into the booth and began unbuttoning her jacket as if nothing unusual had just happened.

He wasn't one to feel awkward often, Nick thought. Yet that silent walk across the room had definitely done something to shake his confidence. Clearing his throat, he picked up the menu, though his eyes were on Sara. "I took a shower this morning, even combed my hair. What do you suppose it is? I haven't said a word and they don't like me on sight?"

"Many of our residents aren't used to white people on their turf. Some rarely even go into town. Give them time." He looked so taken aback that she felt sorry for him. However, she'd been through this exact scene more than once herself, only in the reverse. Some places even around the college had made her uncomfortable, even after living on campus for four years.

Nick stared at the menu, but couldn't concentrate. Well, he'd wanted to see the reservation up close and it seemed he was. He'd traveled a great deal, been many places, yet he'd never once felt this...this out of place. Like a foreigner. No, more like a little green man who'd just popped off a distant planet, an interesting species one should be wary of.

Running a finger around his collar, he dared to glance around. The adults dropped their eyes and went back to their food, but the children openly stared as if he were that visiting alien. Sara had been right. The differences he'd so readily dismissed did make him stand out among her people. Surely, though, they'd get used to him.

Wouldn't they?

"How long does it take a white man who lives on the reservation to be accepted?" Maybe he'd be better off returning to the motel and taking his chances. He wasn't used to such a collectively hostile environment.

"I wouldn't know. My father never quite made it and he lived here ten years. There's been no other white man who's ever come to live here permanently." Surely this incident told him more than she ever could in words. They were vastly diverse and not just in skin color. In his hometown or in Butte, she'd likely be feeling as he now was if he'd take her into a restaurant there.

No, it would never work. Despite their strong attraction and the power of those two kisses she'd lain awake most of the night reliving, an involvement was out of the question. People who stuck to their own kind were happiest. She must keep that in mind.

Sara opened the menu she already knew by heart. "Have you ever tried Indian fry bread?"

"Sure, lots of times. There's a shop in Red Lodge that sells it."

"Along with Indian jewelry and pottery?" She'd seen those typical shops, often in touristy areas. Most weren't even run by real Indians.

He heard a hint of criticism in her voice. "Yeah. What's wrong with that?"

"Nothing." Sara closed the menu as the waitress approached. "Hi, Gretchen. I'll have a cheeseburger and fries. And coffee, black."

"Oh, you mean the usual?" Gretchen's wide face split in a big smile. She wrote the order on her pad, then looked to Nick hesitantly, her smile fading. "And for you?"

Nick gave her his most dazzling smile. He would show them, by God, that he wasn't taking their snub to heart. "The same, please." He was a bigger man than that. He knew it took time to win strangers over. But he was good at it. Real good. As the waitress turned to fill their order without responding, he looked around the room, still wearing his smile. Only one small boy even made eye contact.

He shifted his gaze out the window. "If I make it out of here alive, where are you taking me next?"

He was hurt and trying to hide it. Sara felt a softening inside that she didn't want to acknowledge. She didn't want to like him, to empathize with him as few others could. It would be so much easier to handle his leaving if she didn't care at all.

Why hadn't she let Jackson and Maggie coax Nick to stay at their much larger home? He'd have been more comfortable, and more accepted as the guest of not only the tribal attorney, but a man and his wife, rather than remaining with a single woman. She'd been asking herself why ever since leaving Jackson's office.

And she was all too afraid of the answer.

"If you feel like marching through the slush, I'll take you to the day-care and the community centers. And you said you'd like to pick up a few things at the trading post."

"Yeah, fine."

He looked so dejected that she wanted to reach across the table and squeeze his hand in reassurance. But Native Americans frowned on public displays. She was certain her gesture would be misinterpreted by the people seated nearby pretending not to watch them. She groped for a subject that would distract him, wondering when his happiness had become important to her. "Did anything Jackson said about the suspects on your list help in your search for Charlie's killer?"

Nick shrugged, then ran a hand across his face in a weary gesture. "Hard to tell. I need to get back to Whitehorn, to interview more people. At this point, I still don't have much."

"Would you want me to go with you?" An impulsive offer, but Sara rather thought she'd enjoy helping. "To drive you, I mean. Surely the mad bomber wouldn't take on two of us."

He couldn't keep his surprise from showing on his face, nor his other feelings. "That's—a very generous offer." He reached across the table and took her hand. "I thank you, but I can't let you do that. It's far too dangerous and I wouldn't involve you."

Gretchen chose that moment to bring their order. Sara pulled back her hand and placed it in her lap as the waitress silently set down their food. Her fault, she told herself as she caught disapproval in the eyes of an elderly woman two tables over. She hadn't told Nick about some of the important traditional Indian customs that he needed to know if he were to remain on the res, even for a few more days. If she didn't, she'd soon have a scandal whirling about her head.

Nick pumped catsup onto his burger, unaware of her uneasiness. Picking up the generous sandwich, he took a big bite, savoring the juiciness. "Mmm, this is really good."

Sara tasted a french fry. "I suppose you're a junk-food junkie and I've been plying you with healthy soups and salads."

"No, I love what you've been fixing. But once in a while I get a craving for a greasy old burger."

"Me, too. I got hooked when I was in college." She took a bite of her cheeseburger, feeling better. He hadn't seemed to notice her earlier discomfort. She'd enlighten him in private.

They ate, chatting easily, about Montana winters, and then he asked about her work at the museum. The subject was near and dear to Sara's heart, so she told him about her love of ancient artifacts and their accompanying history. By the time the check arrived, Nick was convinced that he'd like to visit the museum.

He also insisted on paying for both of them. Leaving a generous tip, he took her elbow as they left, again amidst a watchful silence. Outside at last, Nick pulled up his coat collar against a cool wind. "You know," he couldn't help commenting, "even with the wind-chill factor, I think it's warmer out here than in there." He took hold of her arm again, hoping to take the sting from his words, since her neighbors' attitude was hardly her fault, as he followed her around the building to the trading post.

Summer Lewis was behind the counter just as Sara had told Nick she would be. Sara smiled and hurried over to hug her mother. "Hello, Mama."

The woman could have passed for Sara's older sister, Nick thought as he watched the two embrace. Summer was as tall as her daughter and as slender, her black hair pulled back from her face and wound into some sort of bun, with only a few strands of silver showing. The big difference was that the mother's skin was about two shades darker and her eyes reflected a kind of tired wisdom.

"I've brought someone I'd like you to meet," Sara said, motioning for Nick to come closer. "This is Nick Dean, a private investigator from Butte looking into who killed the man whose bones were found on the res recently. Nick, this is my mother, Summer Lewis."

He smiled warmly and held out his hand. The older woman hesitated, as if she rarely touched strangers, but finally placed her hand ever so briefly in his, then quickly withdrew it. "It's good to meet you, ma'am. You have a daughter to be proud of."

Summer's black eyes warmed as they returned to her daughter. "That is not news to me." She reached to touch

Sara's long braid. "You didn't tell me you had a new friend." Of course, she'd heard about the white man on the res from Kane's visit and from others who'd come into the store. But not from her daughter's lips.

Sara heard the unspoken part, a new *white* friend, and felt the slight rebuke. She rushed to explain about Nick's Blazer and how she'd happened on him. Although her mother's eyes widened when she realized that Nick had spent two nights at her daughter's house, to her credit she didn't mention it.

"It was good of you to take him in. I taught you well." The smile finally came, but slowly.

Sara knew she was forgiven, but that her mother would want an in-depth explanation when they were alone. "Nick's interested in purchasing some shirts and jeans."

"Men's clothes are at the back," Summer said. "Come with me."

There was no one else in the store at the moment, but Nick still sent Sara a don't-leave-me-alone look, so she trailed after them. Summer asked him questions as to size, then pointed out the stacks of flannel shirts and denim pants. Sara watched him select two of each, then turn to the packaged underwear and socks. She'd told Nick she'd drive in to the motel and pick up his luggage, but he'd said he didn't feel she'd be safe and therefore wouldn't let her go. As casually as he purchased replacement clothes, she had to assume he must do fairly well in his business.

"Sara," Nick said, handing his choices to Summer, "those moccasins you wear look so comfortable. Did you buy them here?"

She pointed to the far wall, where boxes were stacked in neat rows. "Right over there. Let's go see if they have your size."

"How is my grandmother?" Sara asked afterward as Nick paid for his purchases.

"She is well. You should go see for yourself. She misses you." With nimble fingers, Summer rang up the charges on the old cash register.

"She is home?"

"No. She sits with Tommy Running Deer's newborn. You know where that cabin is?" She slid the clothes and moccasins into a large paper bag and held them out to the man. But her thoughts were on Sara, on how frequently her eyes drifted to this white man, on how easily they'd laughed together as he'd tried on the moccasins.

That is how it so often begins, Summer remembered—a man and woman laughing easily together. She tried to keep from frowning, recalling the summer Sara had come home after her college graduation, filled with a lingering sadness instead of anticipated joy. She sent a swift prayer to *Maheo* that her daughter would not fall prey a second time.

"Of course I know where Tommy Running Deer lives. Perhaps I will go." Her mother was broadly hinting that she visit her grandmother, and Sara wondered why. Summer was concerned about the white man, that Sara could see in her eyes. Did she think by showing Nick a more realistic Indian cabin, he might be shocked enough to leave and never return? That had to be it.

Moving to her mother, she embraced her again. "You worry too much," she whispered in her ear, then listened as Nick thanked Summer for helping him. As they made for the door, the bell above tinkled again and two middle-aged Indian women entered, each carrying a satchel. Sara greeted them in Cheyenne, knowing that neither spoke much English, then walked outside, keenly aware that two pairs of dark eyes as well as her mother's watched Nick follow her.

On the slippery walk, Sara nearly fell, but Nick's strong arm caught her to him and held her upright. "Thanks," she said, her voice trembling not from the near fall but because she knew both women and probably her mother had witnessed this strange white man rushing to assist her. They would not openly criticize her, but the disapproval would be in their eyes.

Why was she opening herself up to so much censure? Sara asked herself. She who led a nice orderly life, was liked and accepted by nearly everyone both on the res and at work, respected, admired and loved by the young people she tried to help. Why was she tossing all that aside for a man who would walk out of her life just as soon as he was finished using her?

Nick felt her deep sigh. "Is something wrong?" he asked, genuinely puzzled.

She stopped, turning to look up at him. The weak winter sunshine turned his hair golden and the capricious wind tossed it about, rearranging it even more boyishly. But there was nothing boyish about the way he so often looked at her, stirring her in that indefinable way that both excited and frightened her.

Maybe her mother was right. Maybe she should expose Nick to a hard dose of res reality, the kind that separated the men from the boys. A glimpse of actual Indian life had sent Jackson's first wife scrambling back to her comfortable white world. Sara couldn't help wondering if Nick was made of sterner stuff.

"Would you mind if we went to visit my grandmother? We could go to the community and day-care centers tomorrow."

"That'd be fine. You said she's eighty, and she's actually baby-sitting a newborn? She must be something."

"Manya is definitely one of a kind."

"Is *Manya* grandmother in Cheyenne?"

"No. It means revered one. As long as I can remember, my grandmother's been called Manya."

Anxious to meet the lady, Nick gripped her arm as they made their way back to the house and Sara's car.

The lady was barely four feet tall, with pure white hair worn in a long braid down her back and a corncob pipe stuck between her lips. "Child, it's good to see you," Manya said, pocketing her unlit pipe as she stepped back from the old wooden door. But when Sara bent to hug her and she was able to see the tall white man behind her, the old woman stiffened.

"I've brought someone to meet you, Manya," Sara said, standing aside and drawing Nick closer. Watching her grandmother's wrinkled face, she introduced them.

Delighted by Nick's warm greeting and firm handshake, Manya smiled. "He reminds me of Aaron, only his hair is lighter."

"Yes, a little." Sara actually didn't think that Nick resembled her father other than by skin color, but she didn't want to contradict the older woman. "We've come to visit with you and see the baby."

"Come in, come in. It's bitter cold out." Turning, she walked back to her rocker by the fireplace alongside a small wooden cradle, while Nick and Sara removed their jackets.

Sara went over and pulled back the blanket, revealing a fat-cheeked baby with coal black hair sleeping soundly. "Oh, he's adorable. Is he good?"

Manya nodded. "Very good. He was so small, not even four pounds, but he's growing now."

The baby still seemed awfully small to Nick, who viewed him from a safe distance over Sara's shoulder. "A preemie, eh?"

"Yes," Manya answered, "and we almost lost him along with his mother."

"His mother died?" He saw the old woman nod as he straightened. "It's pretty rare these days, a woman dying in childbirth. Was she ill?"

"Not ill, just unlucky. A breech birth. She lost too much blood." Manya shook her head sadly. "Tommy grieves daily."

"Didn't the doctor give her transfusions? Lots of babies are born breech and—"

"There was no doctor. She had him here in this cabin."

Nick felt a strange rush of déjà vu. Only this time, the mother had died. Reliving remembered pain, he glanced around the cabin, finding it far more primitive than Sara's simple house. He'd noticed as they'd arrived that the small structure was made of logs, and from where he stood, he could see daylight creeping through in several places. There was no insulation and the coldest weather had yet to come.

The floor was rough planking, with only two thin braided rugs in the large room. The kitchen area was at one end and a pine bed stood in the corner. He could see no bathroom, no door leading to one. Clothes hung on hooks on the far wall and the two small windows in front seemed ill fitting. All of it, however, was spotlessly clean. Lord, how could anyone survive a Montana winter in this cabin, especially a tiny baby?

He turned back to the old woman, who was wearing a shawl and sweater over a dark dress, and caught her studying him. He had to know, had to ask. "Did the baby come too quickly so there was no time to make it in to the hospital or even the clinic?"

Manya chewed on the stem of her pipe. "The labor went on for hours, the medicine woman told us. There was no money for the hospital, even if Katrina would have gone."

"But it might have saved her life."

Sara saw a concern on his face that surprised her. "A lot of Native Americans don't trust hospitals or city doctors, Nick."

He couldn't let it go. Guilt revisited, he knew. "Then why didn't she call Kane Hunter? Doesn't he deliver babies?"

Manya saw his agitation, too, and the tight look on her granddaughter's face. "Tommy has no phone and Katrina wouldn't let him leave. She didn't think she would die. She feared more for her baby. By the time he finally came for me and I reached Kane, it was too late."

Too late. Two of the saddest words in the English language. Nick became aware that his face was damp. He'd stepped too close to the fire, he thought as he wiped his brow.

Sara turned from him and touched the silky softness of the baby's cheek. "At least Tommy has his child. That's more than some have."

Manya felt the heaviness of Sara's old sadness, the one that would never leave her. "I will make us a hot drink," she said, rising slowly from her rocker.

"I—I think we should go," Nick said, wanting to get outside, to breathe fresh air. He took the old woman's small, work-worn hand in his much larger one, intending to thank her. Instead, he got caught up in another memory. "My grandmother had hands like yours," he said, his voice low. Why was it that being with this lady and seeing that child had dragged him back through his own past?

"She lived with us when I was growing up." He met the old woman's dark gaze. "When her hands held me, I used to feel safe. The baby's lucky to have you."

The old woman squeezed his fingers. "Come back one day. We will talk."

Nick nodded. "Thank you." He turned to Sara. "Ready?"

Sara had watched the interchange between Nick and Manya silently and felt stunned to see a suspicious moistness clouding the blue of his eyes. Perhaps he, too, had painful memories best left buried. Ironic that Summer had thought Nick's visit to this place would send him running from the res. Instead, he'd found an affinity with Manya that transcended age or racial differences.

Quickly, she leaned to kiss her grandmother's leathery cheek. "Stay well, Manya."

Outside, the air had grown cooler and dark clouds had moved into the sky. "I think it's going to rain," Sara commented as she gazed upward.

Nick took several deep breaths, trying to shake off his sudden depression. Turning back, he studied the cabin with a practiced eye. Several others a short distance away along a winding path looked to be in equal disrepair. "Who built these homes? A structural inspector would condemn them."

Hands thrust into her pockets, Sara followed his gaze. "No one will come to inspect. No one in city government cares about anything on Laughing Horse."

He swung about. "Can't Jackson or his uncle do something?"

"They try, but they keep running into red tape and brick walls. Besides, where would the money come from to repair the homes, or to build better ones? Where would these people live in the meantime?"

Where, indeed. "Does Tommy have a job?"

"He works part-time on one of the ranches near town. Employers don't have to pay benefits to part-time employees." She tried to keep the anger, the injustice from her voice, but didn't know if she was succeeding.

He caught it. "It *isn't* fair." With his chin, he indicated the row of shabby houses. "None of it's fair."

She hadn't thought he'd notice or care. She'd been wrong. "You're right."

"There ought to be something that can be done." Walking to the car, he opened the passenger door.

Sara climbed in behind the wheel, turned the Volkswagen around and had gone only a short way when she saw a woman carrying two heavy bags walking slowly along the edge of the road. She stopped and wound down the window. "Can I give you a lift, Alice?"

The young woman shook her head, then peered curiously at Sara's companion. "I'm almost home, thanks."

"Alice Thundercloud, meet Nick Dean. He's investigating Charlie Avery's murder."

Alice's smile was friendly. "Yes, I heard. Hello."

Nick smiled. "Nice to meet you. Those look heavy. You sure you don't want to get in?"

As Alice shook her head again, Sara frowned. Nearly three months pregnant with her first baby, Alice shouldn't be carrying weighty packages nor walking in ankle-deep slush. "Where's John?"

"At the museum. Something about unpacking stock."

Sara hid her reaction to that piece of news. John Thundercloud worked part-time at a ranch near town and after that did maintenance work at the Native American Museum. But it was Sunday and the museum was closed. Of course, he could be doing a side job somewhere. "Well, if we can't give you a lift, then we'll be on our way. Bye, Alice.''

Returning her friend's wave, Sara drove to her house, her mind first on the Thunderclouds, then on the mood of the man beside her. Something was bothering him, some memory that had been triggered inside the little cabin, and she wondered if she should mention it. As she pulled up in her drive, she decided to ask. ''Nick, did you ever lose a child?'' She saw a muscle in his jaw clench, but he didn't look her way, just sat staring.

Finally, he answered. ''A long time ago.'' Sara had never married, had never had high hopes for a baby on the way. Not yet, anyway. How could she relate? ''You wouldn't understand.'' He got out, closed his door and walked toward the porch.

Sara let out a trembling breath. ''Don't be too sure,'' she whispered.

Six

A slow, steady dripping sound woke him. Nick opened his eyes and realized the threatening rain had finally arrived. With luck, it would wash away the dirty snow. Rearranging his pillow, he settled back down in the comfortable bed.

But the dripping continued, and it sounded as if it were inside rather than out. Shoving back the quilt, he rose and snapped on the bedside lamp. It took him but a moment to locate the problem. The roof was leaking from a crack in the ceiling just over Sara's desk. Walking over, he saw from the accumulated puddle that the rain must have been splashing onto the oak top for some time.

Quickly he pulled on his jeans and stepped into his new, fur-lined moccasins. Moving past the fireplace on his way to the kitchen, he noticed that the fire was only smoldering embers. He turned on the kitchen light and opened the cupboard beneath the sink. Rummaging around, he found a bucket toward the back, but no rags. He grabbed a kitchen towel and headed back to his room.

Hurrying along the shadowy hallway, he almost collided with Sara, who was walking toward him, tying the sash of her long green robe. "I didn't mean to wake you," he told her, hardly able to take his eyes from her long hair cascading down her back. He much preferred it loose and flowing rather than in the braid she usually wore.

"I'm a light sleeper. What's going on?"

"Your roof is leaking onto the desk in your guest room." He moved past her and into the bedroom. The towel soaked up the rain easily. "I don't think the finish has been damaged." Wiping down the front of the desk where some water had trailed to the floor, he next felt the wood. "We caught it in time." He placed the bucket under the drip and stared up at the ceiling. "Were you aware of this crack?"

Sara followed his gaze and let out a frustrated sigh. "No, it's a new one. I had several leaks patched this past summer. The repairman said he thought he'd gotten them all."

"Roof leaks are often hard to find and to track to the original crack, especially in houses with no attics or substantial crawl space. My dad and I once tracked one in the ranch bunkhouse on and off all summer until we finally tagged the point of entry." Nick adjusted the bucket slightly to better catch the leak. "I noticed you have a ladder in your utility shed. I'll go up and check this out in the morning, provided the rain has stopped."

Sara thrust her hands deep into her pockets. "I can't ask you to do that."

He turned to her and paused to watch the lamplight dancing in the ebony of her hair. "You didn't ask. I volunteered." She was standing too near, and the big, inviting bed was causing mind pictures that had him clearing his throat and reaching for his discarded shirt.

Thank goodness he was putting something on, Sara thought. She'd had to hide her hands to keep from reaching out, the desire to explore that hard chest matted with blond, curly hair still making her pulse erratic. She couldn't stay in this room another minute with his things scattered about and his masculine scent making her light-headed. "Thanks for catching the leak," she said, walking to the door. "Good night."

"Mind if I pump up the fire?" Nick asked, following her out. "Suddenly, I'm not sleepy."

"No, go right ahead." Sara feigned a yawn. "See you in the morning." She started down the hallway.

"Is it okay if I have a glass of milk?" He stood in the archway and waited for her to turn his way. He smiled. "Might help me sleep."

"Help yourself." She moved to her own bedroom doorway.

"Would you care to join me in a glass?"

Slowly, she swung to face him. What game was this? He certainly hadn't faked the roof leak, yet this seemed a ploy to get her to stay up with him. But why?

He'd been lost in his thoughts and unusually quiet since they'd returned from visiting her grandmother. She'd seen him wander to the bookcase, pick up a book and try to read. He'd given that up and had sat staring moodily into the fire most of the evening. Then he'd gone to bed early. She'd left him alone, wary of pursuing the subject of the child he'd said he'd lost a long time ago. It was really none of her business.

Sara had always disliked it when people tried to pry information out of her, so she tried not to do it to others. She valued her privacy and respected Nick's. Yet she had to admit to a certain curiosity. All he'd said that first night about his marriage was that it hadn't worked out. Had it failed because he and his wife had lost a child?

The death of a baby was often a catalyst in finishing off a shaky marriage. The loss left both parents shattered, unable to forget and forgive. The knowledge that Nick had suffered a loss somehow shifted their relationship for Sara. It humanized him more, which unnerved her. She didn't want to think warm, sympathetic thoughts of him. She wanted to be detached, friendly from a distance, uninvolved.

But was that even possible?

Catching the hopeful glint in his eyes, she found herself walking back to join him, wondering if perhaps she'd been a fool to think she could corral her feelings in the face of this riveting attraction Nick Dean held for her. Maybe what she needed to do was play it out, face it down, check into it. Perhaps she'd be happily surprised to discover that once she'd satisfied her curiosity, the feeling would die a natural death.

In the kitchen, Nick opened the fridge and poured two glasses of milk. She'd come up beside him and he handed her one. "What we need with this is chocolate-chip cookies."

"Sorry. I rarely buy cookies."

"You don't *buy* chocolate-chip cookies. You *make* them from scratch. Tomorrow we'll go get the ingredients and make some. What do you say?"

She couldn't help smiling. The man could charm the birds from the trees. "You honestly want to bake cookies?"

"You bet. And eat them when they're warm." He closed his eyes and rubbed his stomach. "Mmm. Nothing like it."

Carrying her glass, Sara left the kitchen and went to sit on the couch. "I suppose we could take the extras to the day-care center. The kids would love it."

Nick set down his glass and bent to stoke up the smoldering fire. "If there're any left."

Sitting back, she watched him, that fine yellow hair falling onto his brow, the way the shirt stretched over his broad back as he tossed wood chunks onto the grate. He really was a beautiful specimen, she decided, trying to think of him clinically.

Dusting off his hands as the blaze caught, Nick backed up and sat down next to Sara. Not at the other end of the couch, but near her, though not touching. He turned to her, studying her profile until she finally raised her eyes to his.

The look held as each tried to read the thoughts of the other. The only light in the room came from the fire, the only sound the crackling and hissing of the flames licking at the wood. Nick could smell some kind of lotion on her skin mingling with her clean, feminine scent. He drew in a deep breath as she shifted her eyes to her hands, laced together in her lap.

"I've been thinking about what you said in the car," Sara began, needing to talk, needing to know, for what reason she was uncertain. She looked back and saw the vulnerability in his eyes. "Will you tell me what happened?"

Nick turned, stretching out his long legs toward the fire, leaning his head on the couch's back. She hadn't talked very freely about her own failed relationship in her college days, and he had to admit to a relentless curiosity about her past. Perhaps if he shared with her, she'd open up to him more.

But even after eight years, it was still so damn difficult to talk about. He searched for the right words. "I married Beth shortly after graduating from the police academy in Butte. I was twenty-four and she was twenty-one. Both of us so damn young."

It hadn't seemed so at the time. He'd been out of college three years and had traveled all over, taking ranching jobs, working on construction crews. "It didn't take me long to make sergeant, and then I was transferred to vice.

It's rough duty, long hours, undercover, frequent stakeouts, dealing with a lot of people you wouldn't invite to dinner."

She could only imagine and that was bad enough. Shifting, she saw that his eyes were closed, as if he were watching the past roll by on the screen of his mind.

"Beth hated my work. She was a teller in a bank and was always after me to quit the force and get a nice, safe job. But I wanted adventure, I guess. A taste of life, or whatever." He heard the bitterness in his tone, but he couldn't help that. "When she found out she was pregnant, she stepped up her campaign to get me to quit. I wouldn't listen, kept putting her off. After the next bust, and the next." He swiped a hand across his face, wishing he could wipe away the guilt as well.

This was too hard. "I shouldn't have asked, Nick," Sara said softly. "I had no right."

He seemed not to hear, lost in his memories. "Beth was in her seventh month. I was on an important stakeout, thirty miles outside of town. I had a beeper and told her to call me if she needed me. She went into premature labor and tried to reach me, but something went wrong. My beeper didn't go off. She finally called a friend, who drove her to the hospital. By the time I got home, found her note and raced to the hospital, it was too late." He swallowed around a huge lump. "Too late. A little boy. He didn't make it."

Sara reached out to him in an instinctive gesture of comfort, her fingers wrapping around his. "I'm so sorry."

"Yeah, me, too." Nick sat up, watching their intertwined hands. "Beth was understandably bitter. She never went back to our apartment. She went to her parents' house and filed for divorce."

"Why did she blame you? Chances are it would have happened even if you'd have gotten her to the hospital sooner. Babies two months premature can have many things wrong with them."

"The doctor said something about the baby had been deprived of oxygen too long. Because—because Beth had struggled to hold the baby back, waiting for me."

Sara squeezed his hand. "It's unfair to lay the blame all on you."

"It was my work. Beth blamed my job, and me for not quitting it, for not being there for her." He gave a painful laugh. "The irony is that, after that, I lost my enthusiasm and left police work."

Sara was not a toucher, not with people she didn't know well. Yet the urge to touch him, to reach through his guilt, overwhelmed her. She pressed her hand to his cheek and turned his face to her. If ever there was a subject she understood, it was this one. "Years later, you're still blaming yourself, and you mustn't. Even today babies still die under the best of circumstances. And occasionally mothers in delivery, like Katrina. Who knows if Tommy's wife would have made it even at a top-notch hospital? Someone bigger than us sets our fate. You call Him God, we call Him *Maheo*. Either way, He calls the shots. We can never control all aspects of our lives, much as we'd like to think we can."

He heard her, but the guilt ran too deep, the self-condemnation was a habit too ingrained. "I wish I could believe that."

Of their own accord, her fingers stroked his face. "You should. You're a good man, Nick."

"Good men make mistakes, too. Mistakes that damage other people. Some things you can't make up for, like a life lost before it's had a chance to grow."

His words hit home and she shivered in reaction. "I know, but we can't go through life dragging all that guilt. What adult hasn't made some mistakes, mistakes that they'd do anything to go back and fix? But we can't. Dwelling on regrets is for the weak. I think of you as strong. Very strong. My grandmother recognized your strength, your worth. She asked you to come back and talk with her. I've never heard her make such a request to a white man, not ever." Manya had been wary of Aaron Lewis from the beginning, she'd been told. And had had no use for him once he'd started drinking.

Nick needed to pull himself back together, to shift the focus. He covered her hand with his own, drew it to his lips and placed a gentle kiss on her palm before meeting her eyes. "How did you get so wise? A wise Indian is a cliché." It was his turn to stroke her face. "And how did you get so beautiful? Is it because you're so beautiful inside?"

Sara eased back a fraction, her nerves tensing. "You don't really know me."

"Oh, I think I do. You're a bright, educated, refined woman who chooses to live in far less comfort that you deserve, because you have this need to give, to share, to do for others. I watched you with your mother and Manya, your friends and your neighbors at the restaurant. You're compassionate and caring. I know you've loved someone once and were disappointed, even deeply hurt, as I was." She tried to ease back farther, but he held her steady. "You don't want to talk about him, and that's all right. I won't press you." He remembered how he'd thought her cold and then had discovered her warmth. "You have a buried passion you want to deny for some reason. Like you want to deny that you're attracted to me." He tipped her chin up. "How am I doing?"

Close. Way too close. "Conjecture. All of that's conjecture." She put a hand to his chest to push him away, to give herself some breathing room. Only his shirt was open and her hand touched the soft hair there. She made a small, helpless sound deep in her throat, fascinated at the sight of her darker fingers twining in the wiry blond curls. She felt his heartbeat pick up its rhythm, thrumming beneath her touch. Slowly, she raised her eyes and found his deep blue and aware.

"Still think I'm conjecturing?" And then he was wrapping his arms around her and crushing his mouth to hers.

Desire didn't creep in on little cat feet. It didn't steal through her quietly like the drizzle of fine wine on the tongue. It exploded, rocketing through Sara's system like a flash of lightning followed by a clap of thunder.

Her hands on his chest tightened, then went exploring along hard muscles. Beneath his shirt, they moved to his back so she could gather him closer. She allowed his tongue entry to her mouth and tasted a hint of the milk he'd sipped, the innocent flavor, incongruous yet oddly exciting. As if from a distance, she heard the rain pounding on the roof, the sound keeping time with her galloping heart.

She shouldn't want him like this, shouldn't be pressing her body so eagerly against his. She knew in the vague recesses of her mind that this had nowhere to go, that getting involved with this man was a dead-end street. Yet she could no more have pulled back than she could have walked on water.

She had his head spinning and his thoughts whirling out of control. He wanted her desperately, wanted her hot and throbbing beneath him, warm and welcoming. He wanted her flesh-to-flesh with him, no barriers between them. He wanted her hands on him, touching him, pleasuring him.

Nick knew he had to have felt all this before. Since the divorce, he'd known his share of women who'd meant something to him briefly. He liked it that way—to part friends, no hard feelings. But he'd never felt this kind of fire with anyone before, never felt the need to make a woman his and his alone. The thought had him nervous and edgy. Yet when Sara made a soft sound and tilted back her head, his lips burned a trail down her satin throat and his hands went wandering.

Quicksand. She was sinking in quicksand and sensed the danger. She'd given in to similar feelings before and had lived to regret it. All the accumulated doubts, the buried fears resurfaced and had her trembling.

"Nick," she said, her voice shaky. Her hands, which still wanted to drag him closer, were suddenly pushing him away as her mind took charge of her emotions. "Stop, please."

His breathing was choppy as he drew back. Needing a moment, he touched his forehead to hers, letting his nerves settle. "I didn't mean to push. It's just that I touch you and I want more. Lots more. I've never had a problem quite like this before."

His admission, such a parallel of her own thoughts, almost had her reaching for him again. She steeled herself to move farther back. "This can't keep happening. If it does, you'll have to go stay with Jackson and Maggie." Still a bit unsteady, she stood nonetheless.

Fighting a rush of anger, Nick rose, touched her arm and turned her toward him. "What are you so afraid of— that you'll commit the cardinal sin and fall for a white man?"

Her eyes heated. "Only fools make the same mistake twice." Pulling free, she rushed down the hall to her bedroom and closed the door behind her.

Picking up his empty glass, Nick struggled against an urge to smash it into the fireplace. Instead, he took it out to the kitchen and slammed it down on the counter.

The childish gesture didn't make him feel one bit better.

Nick hung up the phone with a muttered oath. He'd just spent an exasperating half hour talking with Sheriff Hensley, giving him a detailed list of everyone in Whitehorn he'd interviewed in connection with his investigation. And it wasn't enough.

Judd wanted him to go in to the sheriff's office or tell him where he was staying so they could talk in person. When Nick had refused, the sheriff calmly said that if he didn't cooperate, he'd issue an All Points Bulletin for him. On what charge? Nick had wanted to know. No charge, just wanted for questioning in the death of an unknown female who'd died in the Blazer fire. When Nick had pointed out that he'd answered every question Judd had put to him, the man still continued to insist that he show up at the sheriff's office.

That was when Nick had hung up.

Rising from the kitchen table, he walked to the counter and poured himself the last cup of coffee from the pot. But when he took a sip, he found it bitter and poured it into the sink. Or perhaps it was just his mood.

He and Sara had been tiptoeing around one another ever since awakening on this cloudy Monday morning. Their emotional conversation last night and the stunning kisses were hard to avoid thinking about. The memory hung between them, thickening the air with tension, as did her warning that it had to stop.

A subdued Sara had busied herself doing laundry. So he'd taken her toolbox into the bathroom and reattached the towel bar he'd pulled from the wall. Then he'd gone outside to the storage shed and propped the ladder against the house. The ground was soggy from melted snow and rainfall, but a slight warming trend appeared to be doing its best to do away with any excess moisture.

He'd climbed up to the roof over the spare bedroom, but hadn't been able to spot a specific section where the leak might have begun. It seemed unlikely that a thorough repair could be done until the spring thaw, after the long winter. However, he'd found some shingles in the shed, probably left over from last summer's patch job, and nailed them down, overlapping a dozen or more in the vicinity of the suspected leak. He hoped that would take care of the problem temporarily.

He'd gone back inside just as Sara had been putting on her jacket. She told him she was leaving to help out at the day-care center. Though he waited for her to invite him along, she hadn't. He understood, though. She needed some space, and perhaps he did as well. Yet as he'd watched her drive off he'd felt strangely abandoned.

So he'd stayed in and made some calls. To his partner in Butte, to Melissa Avery and finally to the sheriff. He'd learned nothing new from the first two and had been frustrated by the third. It was this confinement, Nick told himself. He was an outdoor man and unused to staying in so much, especially in a small house with a woman who set his teeth on edge. And he hated not having his own wheels.

Through the kitchen window over the sink, he watched a sparrow flit from one barren tree branch to another, envying the bird's freedom to go wherever it pleased. For the first time ever, Nick found himself a prisoner of circumstances, and he didn't much care for the situation. Someone had tried to kill him, and probably that someone was still out there somewhere, possibly waiting to try again. That alone could make a man nervous. He'd happened on a safe place where any white resident of Whitehorn who came looking for him would stand out like a sore thumb.

Yet keeping safe meant staying put, being restricted. Nick was certain he wouldn't be able to maintain the status quo much longer. Hiding out went against the grain. His makeup was far more confrontational than evasive. Regardless of the risks, he'd have to take his chances soon because he was beginning to feel cowardly hiding out rather than hunting down Charlie's killer, probably the same person responsible for planting dynamite in his Blazer.

Tomorrow he would take some action.

That decided, he felt better. A weak sun was trying to break through the cloud cover, Nick noticed as he peered out the window. What he needed was a walk to clear his mind. Sara hadn't said how long she'd be gone. It didn't matter, actually, since she would probably stay late in order to avoid being alone with him.

If he left tomorrow, he was certain she wouldn't weep over his departure. She wanted him, of that he was sure. But something in her past—more correctly, *someone*—was causing her to turn from her feelings. And from him.

So be it, Nick thought, shrugging into his jacket. He'd learned the hard way that you couldn't make someone care if something in their mind or heart stopped them. Beth had turned off her feelings for him the night their baby had died. It had taken him longer, much longer.

Which was why it was best to remain uninvolved, unattached, he reminded himself as he stepped out into the brisk, early afternoon air. That's the way he'd played it for a long time now, and that credo had kept him from getting hurt deeply again. Little did Sara realize that he didn't want a serious relationship, either.

He wanted friendship, a caring, intimate friendship. All right, so maybe he'd entertained fleeting thoughts of how good it would be to have Sara there at night when he came home from a long day. How comfortable it would be to talk together by the fire and share their days with one another. How pleasant it would be to have their meals across the table from each other, morning and night. How wonderful it would be to crawl under her grandmother's quilt together in the big four-poster bed.

How easily she chased away the loneliness he hadn't recognized until she'd come into his life. But she was right. They *were* very different. She was committed to helping her people on the reservation. He needed to be free to come and go as he pleased. The two life-style choices would never mesh.

It was best that he found out now, wasn't it? Before he fell really hard, before he began to think of her during the day and dream of her at night. Before she got a real stranglehold on his feelings.

Stepping off the wooden porch, Nick realized there was a loose board underfoot. He'd have to fix that next. Provided he was around long enough. Whistling to affirm that his mood had improved, he started off down the crooked path.

Nick felt a little foolish standing outside the day-care building peering first into one window, then another. But he'd wanted to catch Sara with the children when she didn't know he was watching. He walked on to the next one, keeping low.

He'd spent several hours wandering the main streets of the reservation, checking out the buildings. Most of them were in need of repair or, in some cases, of being torn down and rebuilt. But the people had impressed him more this time.

He'd walked into the rehab center and introduced himself to Earnest Running Bull, the crusty old Indian who ran the place. Earnest had been suspicious at first, then had warmed to him when he'd mentioned Sara's name. Everyone, it seemed, knew Sara. Two thousand people lived on Laughing Horse, and by the time he'd finished his walk, Nick was certain each and every one he'd met had something good to say about Sara.

Clyde White Feather, the tribal police chief, had been most interested in talking with him about the investigation. He'd been a bit cool and hostile until he'd heard the whole story, then had wound up saying that Nick was welcome to stay on the res until he felt it was safe to leave. Again, Sara's name had come up several times, and undoubtedly she was the reason for the chief's friendliness.

Then he'd walked along some of the streets, many little more than rutted, muddy paths, and viewed the houses, some from a distance, some up close. So much needed doing. An infusion of money wouldn't hurt, either.

He'd strolled on, running across an older Indian named Henry Raintree, and had stopped to talk with him about horses for some time. He'd spotted Maggie Hawk strolling arm in arm with a tall, thin older woman she'd introduced as Annie Little Deer, her grandmother. They'd taken him into the grocery store and helped him find the ingredients for chocolate-chip cookies, which now rested in a sack on the front porch of the day-care center while he searched for Sara.

Finally, at the third window, he got lucky.

She was apparently in charge of the preschool kids today. There had to be over a dozen boys and girls ranging in age from two to five or so. They were seated on the floor in a half circle facing Sara, who was kneeling, her full, multicolored skirt arranged around her, a battered guitar in her hands. They were rehearsing a song she'd evidently taught them before, for she'd point to a twosome, who'd chime in with their part, and then three others, who'd jump in with theirs. Then she'd beckon to the back row, obviously the chorus, and they'd all but shout out the next line or two.

Through the window, Nick could see that each small head was turned toward Sara, some expressions intent and others smiling from ear to ear. A couple of the smaller children were sucking their thumbs and several squirmed restlessly. A round-faced boy kept scooting closer to her and she'd reach out to touch him affectionately, then inch him back into his space.

The song was loud and somewhat off-key, or so it sounded through the ill-fitting window. But the children were loving every minute of the sing-along. And so was the woman in the bright turquoise top with the long braid hanging down her back and the warm smile lighting up her face.

His first thought was that she looked very much at home, a woman meant to have a whole passel of kids. As he watched, the song ended. Sara set down the guitar to wild applause from the children, and picked up the round-faced boy, plunking him onto her lap. Her free hand reached to still one of the wiggly girls, who giggled as Sara ruffled her short bangs. Nick wasn't sure why he felt a sudden thickness in his throat.

"Hey, what are you doing over there?" came a deep, bellowing voice from behind him.

Surprised, he swiveled about and saw a huge man in the uniform of a tribal policeman coming toward him, dangling a stick attached to a leather strap from his hand. Over six feet tall and more than two hundred pounds, he wasn't a man to be on the bad side of, Nick thought, turning on his smile. "Hi. I'm Nick Dean. I've come to see Sara Lewis."

The big man frowned. "You that detective fellow, the one working on that old murder case?"

Their communication system on Laughing Horse was better than AT&T. "Yes. I've just been over talking with Chief White Feather."

The man's frown disappeared and he nodded. "I'm Al Black Bird, the first one on the scene when they found those bones."

"That's good to know, Al. Maybe you can spare some time this week and tell me about it."

The man's substantial chest swelled importantly. "Sure." He glanced at the window and back at Nick. "Why don't you just go inside?"

Nick gave an embarrassed laugh, wondering how he could explain his impulse to be a Peeping Tom. "I think I will. Thanks." He walked back to the front and entered through the double doors just as Sara and several other adults were helping the little ones into their outerwear.

Straightening from zipping up a small jacket, Sara spotted him. She didn't smile, just stared, wondering why the sight of this one man could make her pulse scramble as no one else ever had. She'd tried to stay annoyed at him since last night, although her conscience told her that what had happened was as much her fault as his. But after what she'd heard this afternoon from no fewer than three sources, it was difficult to maintain even a cool expression.

She watched as he walked slowly toward her, a hint of wariness in his blue eyes. He stopped in front of her as two of the children stepped behind Sara, unsure about being around the tall white man. "I hear you've been busy," she said casually.

"A little. I went for a long walk." He nodded toward the doors. "I've got a surprise for you on the porch. Chocolate chips."

She didn't think he'd forget that. But cookies weren't what she wanted to talk about. Scooting the children over to the other adults, she grabbed her jacket and walked outside with him. "I understand you met Henry Raintree," she began.

Nick nodded. Did she get a report on his every move? "And Chief White Feather, Earnest Running Bear, plus Annie Little Deer."

"Did you capture a runaway horse for each of them?"

So that's what this was about. "Who told you?"

She stood buttoning her jacket, watching his face. "Three of the parents who dropped off their children. They say you saved Henry from being trampled to death."

"Oh, hardly that. I happened to be walking past his fence and saw him trying to get this black stallion into the corral. The stubborn cuss knocked Henry over and was about to take off."

And he'd run over, jumped on the stallion bareback and gotten him under control and inside the gate, then had helped Henry up. "The way I heard it, you risked your neck for someone you don't even know." For a white man to disregard his own safety to save an Indian was uncommon enough to have half the reservation talking about the incident by now.

"Henry's a nice man. His wife died not long ago and he's lonely. But I guess you already know that. He invited me in and we had a drink." He made a face. "I'm not sure what was in the drink, but it sure had a kick to it."

"Why'd you do it, Nick?" Sara needed to know, needed to fit the variant puzzle pieces that made up Nick Dean into a nice, neat picture she could understand.

"Why'd I drink it? Because I was cold and I thought it would warm me. Besides, it would have been rude to refuse."

"I'm not talking about the drink. Why did you help him?"

His brow wrinkled in a genuine frown. "Why is this such an issue with you? The man needed help and I was there. No big deal. Do you think I should have passed on by and ignored someone in trouble?"

"A lot of white men would have." She searched his eyes and saw the goodness there. The surprising, genuine goodness.

Nick's frown deepened. "I don't understand."

"I honestly think you don't."

"Are we arguing about this Indian-white thing again?"

"No, we're not arguing at all." This time she took his arm and didn't care who was watching as she smiled up at him. "Come on, let's go make those cookies."

Seven

Some sort of unspoken barrier between them had disappeared suddenly, Nick thought on the ride home. Sara was friendlier, warmer, even chatty. Once inside, she poured a glass of apple cider for each of them while he built a fire. Wanting the mood to continue, Nick asked about the preschool program. Sara's eyes were lively as she told him stories about the children, some funny, some a little sad.

"I took a course last summer through the university extension program and modified it to fit our small day-care center. The idea is to learn while having fun. On weekends I've been teaching some of the younger women how to conduct the classes, so that the parents of the children are free to work in town when possible. The older women help out by baby-sitting the infants. It's not all it could be, but it's improving."

"I watched you through the window for a while," he confessed. "You're great with those kids. You should have half a dozen of your own." The words were no sooner out of his mouth than he saw her back stiffen and the dreamy smile she'd been wearing fade. He saw a hint of sorrow in her eyes before she turned away and quickly stood.

"It's time I made dinner." She headed for the kitchen.

Annoyed with himself that he'd inadvertently spoiled another pleasant spell, Nick followed her. He found her peering into the open refrigerator. "I said something wrong. Although I don't know what, I'm sorry." He touched her shoulder lightly. "Please don't be angry with me."

His apology was almost her undoing. She leaned on the door a moment and took a calming breath. "I'm not angry. Sometimes I overreact." She needed to change the focus. "Do you like chili? I think I have everything we'd need."

"Only if you let me help."

They made a pot of chili together and Sara's somber mood lifted, though Nick couldn't forget how quickly one careless statement had unnerved her. He'd pursue that again at a better time.

They wound up laughing through their tears as the onions made their eyes water. Sara let the melancholy memories recede and found she couldn't recall a time when cooking had been such fun.

Fun. Something she didn't have a lot of in her life. Odd how she hadn't even realized that until... until Nick had moved in. He made her laugh, she who was known around the res as fairly serious. For once, he made her smile and forget to think too deeply or analyze too thoroughly. Later, however, as she watched him mix the thick cookie dough, she wasn't sure if all the changes he'd brought about were for the good. This constant physical awareness was playing havoc with her state of mind.

Studying his face, she saw him grimace as he pulled the wooden spoon through the batter, then try to mask his involuntary reaction. "I think you strained that shoulder again, either when you were pounding on my roof or when you were wrestling with that stallion. Are you always this careless?" Bending to the lower cupboard, she removed two large cookie sheets.

"My shoulder's fine and I'm not careless." The last thing he wanted to do was argue with her, since dinner had gone so well and she'd even been enthusiastic about making cookies. "I'm ready for the chocolate chips."

She dumped the whole bag into the bowl he held out and stood watching him blend the chips into the contents.

After several silent minutes, Nick decided he'd held off as long as he could. He dipped a finger into the batter, came up with a gooey cluster and popped it into his mouth for a taste. "Mmm. Want some?"

Sara frowned as she opened a drawer. "That's raw dough. It'll make you sick."

"Nah. I used to eat this when I was a kid, and I'm still here." He dipped his finger back in, scooping some out on the tip and holding it out to her. "Come on. Try it."

His look challenged her, so Sara bent her head and closed her lips around his fingerful of batter. Drawing gently, she got most of it off. Still, he held the finger up, indicating she should return for the rest. Eyes locked with his, she swirled her tongue around his finger, cleaning off every speck of the dough. Sara felt the color seep into her face, knowing exactly what he was thinking, for she was thinking it, too. Swallowing with difficulty, she straightened.

She was the most unconsciously sensual woman he'd ever known, Nick thought. He felt like circumventing the counter between them and pulling her into his arms, the desire to kiss her so strong that his hands were shaky. As she averted her heated gaze and began dropping teaspoonfuls of batter onto the prepared cookie sheet, he grabbed the towel and wiped his hands.

The phone rang just then, a welcome interruption of the sudden tension in the kitchen. Sara reached for it, dragging the cord over to the counter, hoping her voice wouldn't betray her unsettling emotions. "Hello."

"Sara? This is Alice Thundercloud. Are—are you busy?"

The young woman sounded worried. "Is something wrong, Alice?"

"I think so. It's my first pregnancy so I'm not really sure."

Sara set aside the bowl, her heart skipping a beat. "Is something happening?"

"I've had some spotting and a little pain. Sort of like low pressure. John's not home yet and I can't locate him. Do you think you could come over? I'm—I'm a little scared."

Alice was so young, only twenty-one. Her parents were both dead and she didn't get along well with her in-laws. Of course she'd be frightened. Sara felt a rush of déjà vu, the memory flooding her mind. Alice had to get to a doctor quickly. "Have you called the clinic?"

"I phoned, but they told me Dr. Kane's at the hospital in town tonight."

Sara was already turning off the oven and refrigerating the cookie dough. "I'll be right there to take you to the hospital."

"Wait, Sara. I've heard stories about the Whitehorn hospital. My grandmother told me—"

"Alice, those things happened years ago. Kane wouldn't practice there if problems still existed." She could hear the fear in the young woman's voice and tried to make her own sound strong and reassuring. "You trust Kane and so do I. I promise I'll stay with you and make sure no harm comes to you or your baby."

"All right, Sara. If you say so."

"Get into your coat. I'm on my way." Sara hung up and headed for her own jacket, praying that they'd make it in time.

"What's happening?" Nick asked, although he'd heard Sara's end of the conversation. A chill had raced up his spine as he'd guessed the rest.

"Alice is spotting and John's not home. I've got to get her to Kane." She stepped out of her moccasins and tugged on her boots.

"It sounded as if she's not anxious to go to the hospital. Why would that be?"

She didn't have time to pretty up the truth, even if she'd wanted to. "Years ago, white doctors often sterilized Indian women after they delivered their first child. It happened to Maggie's mother, for one. The stories circulated and, even though we now have our own Native American doctor in Whitehorn, some women can't forget the tales of horror they've heard."

He felt the outrage the Indians must have experienced. "That's barbaric! It's inhuman!" Coming to a decision, he reached for his own boots. "I'll drive."

"No. You can't leave the reservation." She grabbed her jacket. "I'll manage just fine."

Nick stepped to the door in front of her. "*I'll* drive, I said. You'll have your hands full with Alice. Especially if things get worse on the way over."

She looked up at him, exasperated. "It's too dangerous, Nick."

"That's my decision to make, Sara. This is important. Very important." He opened the door.

She saw the determined set of his jaw and knew there was no arguing with him. She also knew why this hospital run was important to him. "All right. Let's go."

He didn't think about blowing his cover as he drove Sara's Volkswagen as fast as he could without endangering their lives on the thirty-something-mile trip to Whitehorn County Hospital. He didn't think about the possibility that the person who'd tried to kill him might be out and about and spot him, then perhaps try again. All he thought about—and it was more a prayer, really—was that Alice Thundercloud must not lose her baby.

This time he'd make sure they weren't too late.

In the back seat, where he'd helped her lie down minutes before, Alice was tight-lipped and obviously fearful, Nick realized as he glanced in the rearview mirror. He couldn't blame her. With all the medical knowledge available in these modern times, so much could still go wrong.

Beside him, Sara had her hands clasped in her lap in a white-knuckled grip, the only outward sign of her anxiety. She was a good friend to Alice, taking on the younger woman's fear for her unborn child as if it were her own. That trait, more than anything he'd learned about Sara, was what set her apart from so many women he'd known. Sara genuinely felt other people's pain.

At eight in the evening, Route 191 wasn't heavy with traffic. Nick kept their speed at five miles over the limit, almost hoping a sheriff's car would happen by. Compared to this crisis, his problem with Judd Hensley didn't matter, and they'd be able to open up the sirens and escort them to the hospital more quickly. But none were in sight.

The drive seemed to take forever, though Nick knew he'd made good time. At the emergency entrance he pulled to a halt, and Sara was out of the car almost before it had stopped. He turned to reassure Alice, while Sara ran inside to get help. Two men were out with a gurney in short order, reaching in to help the young woman out of the back seat.

"She's Alice Thundercloud, a patient of Dr. Kane Hunter's," Sara told the desk clerk. She'd phoned from

Alice's house and knew that Kane was at the hospital waiting for them. "Would you page him, please?"

The young woman at the admitting desk busily snapped her gum as she indicated the waiting room through an archway. "Have a seat. I'll call the doctor."

Just then the gurney came through the double doors, with Alice looking pale and nervous under a dark blue blanket and Nick trailing after.

"I want to stay with her until Dr. Hunter arrives," Sara told the admitting clerk.

The woman behind the counter shook her head. "Against the rules. You can wait in there."

Sara had known this might not be easy. "I'm *staying* with her until Dr. Hunter arrives!" Turning, she hurried after the gurney, which the two men in white were wheeling down the hallway.

Obviously annoyed, the redhead spotted Nick. "Are you the husband?"

"No, ma'am," he told her, then rushed after Sara.

Wrinkling her brow in dismay, the desk clerk stood. "Wait! You can't go with her, too. It's against the rules." She leaned across the counter and saw that no one was paying the least attention to her. Frustrated, she picked up the phone to page Dr. Hunter. Every time Indians showed up, there were problems, she thought, chewing her gum while she waited for the page to be answered.

Kane was with Alice, Sara told herself as she gazed unseeingly out of the waiting room window into the parking lot. It would be all right. She was in good hands. Kane would assess the situation, stabilize her, order complete bed rest, if necessary. Alice would *not* lose her baby. First thing tomorrow, Sara would phone her mother and others on the res. She'd organize help for Alice so she could rest, so the baby would grow and be strong.

So this baby would live.

Sara closed her eyes a moment. She felt rather than heard Nick come up behind her, then pause, letting her regain control. She'd almost lost it several minutes ago when the silly woman from Admitting had come after her, demanding she fill out paperwork, insisting that Alice's husband or some other responsible party had to come in and sign forms. Sara had almost told her exactly what she could do with her precious papers.

And just where in hell was John Thundercloud? Sara wondered. She'd phoned his home, the ranch where he worked and even the private number to the museum, hoping to catch him somewhere. Here it was nearly nine and Alice had said he'd left at seven this morning. Sara knew that John wasn't a drinker, nor did he run around. Where was he then? How could he leave his pregnant wife alone for over twelve hours without even phoning?

"Are you all right?" Nick asked finally.

Her face once more composed, Sara turned to him. "I'll feel a lot better when Kane tells me everything's okay with Alice and her baby."

It was the eyes, Nick realized. Her eyes gave her away even though her features were calm and her body almost relaxed. Once you knew her, you could see in the dark turmoil of her eyes how deeply she was affected.

He didn't want to mutter platitudes like "I'm sure they'll be fine," when he wasn't sure of anything. So he slid his arms around her and eased her closer, rubbing her back, offering comfort. But he felt her stiffen at the contact and pull back.

Sara glanced at a white couple also waiting in the room, the woman pretending to leaf through a magazine, but the man openly staring at them. "Not here, Nick," she said, keeping her voice low. "It's...so public."

He felt a flash of irritation, then a hurting sensation. He was aware his jaw clenched as she stared up at him, but he didn't say a word.

Damn. Now she'd hurt him, and she hadn't meant to. It had been a godsend having him available to drive them here. Her own nerves had been frazzled enough to welcome his help. She knew how concerned he'd been about getting Alice to the hospital on time, because he'd been too late to save his own baby. He'd been patient with Sara herself, too, even though he had no idea why Alice's problem was hitting her so hard.

And she'd hurt him because she didn't want the two others in the room—people she knew by sight but not name—to see an Indian woman allowing a white man to comfort her. She flushed with shame as she realized how hypocritical that was. To hell with what others thought, Sara decided, reaching for Nick's hand.

"I'm sorry," she whispered, then let her eyes say the rest. Apparently it was enough, for he squeezed her fingers in response. When he led her to the far end of the room, she let him draw her down to the two-seater couch, his hand still firmly gripping hers. Together, they waited.

That was the way Kane found them minutes later. His brow wrinkled as he realized that Sara's hand was enclosed in Nick's. His practiced eye told him that these two were more than just friends, and the knowledge didn't please him. "Alice is fine and the baby, too. For now."

Sara sagged with relief. "Thank goodness," she whispered.

"I'm going to keep her here for a day or two," Kane went on, "just to make certain the danger has passed." He glanced around the waiting room. "Where's John?"

"I've been trying to find him, but no luck so far." Sara nodded toward the admitting desk through the archway. "They want paperwork filled out. I don't suppose John has insurance. I can sign if—"

"I'll take care of it." Hands thrust into the pockets of his white coat, Kane shook his head. "You go on home and keep trying to reach John. Alice is going to need to stay off her feet for a while, not do any lifting. Generally take it easy. I want to talk with John, make sure he understands."

Sara stood, as did Nick. "I'll round up some help for her." She touched Kane's arm. "Thank you."

Kane's dark eyes studied Nick's face for a moment, then moved back to Sara. "Is everything all right?" he asked pointedly.

She almost smiled. Kane never changed, which was a comfort in itself. "Fine. Can I stop in to see Alice for a moment before we leave?"

"Sure. Come with me." Without a word to Nick, he turned and started down the hall at his usual brisk pace.

"I'll be right back," she told Nick, then hurried after Kane.

Wearily, Nick sat back down. They hadn't been too late. Thank God.

He held a cup of tea sweetened with honey and wished it were a snifter of fine, aged brandy. It was a perfect night for a heady drink, with the chill wind whistling outside while wispy clouds floated past a midnight moon. He stretched his moccasin-clad feet toward the fire he'd rebuilt and absorbed the welcome heat.

Sara had been very quiet on the ride back to her house, and he'd respected her need to be alone with her thoughts.

He sensed something had upset her tonight beyond Alice's problem and wondered if she'd tell him about it.

Only a few days of living on the reservation had shown him that Sara's hesitancy about their relationship was not without cause, for the Indians on Laughing Horse were as suspicious of whites as the residents of Whitehorn and other cities were about Native Americans.

It was all so damn silly, Nick thought, as he took a sip of tea and set down the cup. But he'd seen the way Sara had reacted to his touch in front of the white couple in the waiting room, yet she'd reached out easily enough to Kane. Of course, Nick had noticed that she'd regretted rejecting his comfort, but she'd still been uncomfortable holding his hand.

He was beginning to care for her far more than he'd thought he ever would, he admitted to himself. And in such a short time. A woman, a relationship, certainly hadn't been in his game plan when he'd left home. He liked his life just fine the way it was. And yet...

There was something about Sara. She'd managed to get under his skin, though he knew she didn't want an involvement. She fought her feelings for him every step of the way. Yet she felt them, and they were growing, he could see. He'd thought she'd come home and say goodnight, go straight to bed saying she had to get up to go to work in the morning. But she hadn't. She'd asked him if he wanted tea, had made it and then excused herself to freshen up.

It helped a little to know that she was fighting the same losing battle he was. Because, if he were totally honest with himself, he'd have to admit that he was falling for her in a big way. And that thought had his nerves jangling.

Nick heard footsteps, looked up and almost stopped breathing. She'd changed into well-washed jeans and a soft, furry white sweater, then brushed her hair out of its long braid. As she sat down on the couch and it settled around her shoulders and down her back, he felt his mouth go dry. He swallowed with some difficulty. "I thought you'd be tired."

She took a sip of her tea, which had been waiting on the end table, before answering. "Tired, but not sleepy." She turned to him, saw that his eyes were dark and aware. "You risked a lot to drive us tonight. I admire courage." All the way home she'd been checking the side mirror, praying no one particular car had been following them. The nameless, faceless person who'd planted the dynamite was out there somewhere and she'd felt the threatening presence as keenly as if he were after her.

Nick shrugged off the compliment, knowing he didn't deserve it. "It wasn't courage. I didn't want you driving that far at night with a woman who could start hemorrhaging any moment. And I couldn't stay here in a safe place while still another baby was at risk."

She'd known that that was what had motivated him. In a small way, he'd been trying to make up for not being there to save his own child. "I know I've said this before, but you have to let go of all that guilt. You can't spend your life trying to make amends for something that wasn't your fault."

He let out a frustrated sigh. "That's easier said than done. Haven't you any aspects of your life that you can't control?"

Did she ever, and one was sitting beside her and inching closer. Did he really think she hadn't noticed that the space between them was slowly disappearing? "A few," she said in answer to his question. "But I know my weaknesses and I try to avoid temptation." Except tonight.

Tonight, she'd deliberately arranged this time alone with him. She was feeling particularly vulnerable and in need of comfort, perhaps because of the emotions of the past few hours, when they hadn't known if Alice would lose her baby. She'd walked through the mine field of her memories and felt wounded anew. So she'd invited him to sit with her, fully aware of where it might lead.

The truth was, she wanted him to make love with her. It was a hard admission for Sara to make, even to herself. She'd been a virgin when Jack had seduced her, and she hadn't consciously wanted him until he'd shown her that her body liked the way he could make her feel. He'd swept her off her feet and sent her soaring, then dropped her without a safety net or even a kind word. He'd merely said he'd thought a smart girl like her would know the score. Apparently, she hadn't been as smart as either of them had thought.

Making love with Nick wouldn't be that way. Sara could tell that he was kinder, more honest. Besides, she wasn't the naive girl she'd been then. She'd vowed that summer after graduation when she'd returned home and managed to live through the pain of Jack's rejection that nothing and no one would hurt her like that again.

Perhaps she and Nick could share something special, without promises made that neither could keep—because he was a man who needed his freedom and she was a woman devoted to this place. But they were both adults, neither tied to another, obviously yearning to express their attraction physically. It had been so long and she felt so needy. Wasn't taking a chance on temporary happiness better than turning from the possibility altogether?

Nick had been watching the play of emotions on her expressive face and wondered what she was thinking. "I believe your Indian name suits you. You are a little lamb who thinks too much."

She surprised him by agreeing. "You're probably right. A bad habit I should try to break."

He eased closer, his body almost touching hers now, her scent teasing him, making him crave what had so far been forbidden. There was something different about her tonight, and he liked the difference. "So, then, what temptations are you trying to avoid?"

Her eyes as they met his were the dark brown of rich chocolate. "You," she said simply.

It was exactly what Nick needed to hear. He slipped an arm behind her and brought her nearer. He felt her heart begin to pound beneath the soft sweater and saw her tongue lick her lips as her nerves reacted. Then he took her mouth.

She didn't hesitate even a fraction of a second, her lips parting and inviting intimacy. He felt her arms go around him as if she, too, couldn't get close enough. He heard his own heartbeat thundering in his head, then shifted his hands to thrust them into the rich silk of her hair. And he drank from her with the intensity of a desert wanderer who'd stumbled across an oasis.

Right. This felt so right, Sara thought. The feel of him against her body, already beginning to soften in welcome. The masculine scent of him, clean and sharp and sensual. The taste of him on her tongue, achingly familiar, as impossible as that seemed.

His lips were softer than she could have imagined in a man—so lean and hard, yet agile and seeking as they left her mouth and skimmed down her throat. She tipped back her head and gave him access, then felt wet kisses trail lower into the open V of her neckline. A shiver took her as her hands bunched in the material of his shirt.

His breath coming in heated puffs, Nick deliberately slowed, raising back to look at her. Needs raced through his bloodstream like a quick shot of expensive bourbon. Crazy, wild thoughts whipped through his mind, things he'd like to do to her. Pick her up, carry her to her bed, bury himself deep within her and make love until neither of them could move. Stay with her, hold her, love her all night long.

But he knew as he met her eyes that this was not a woman to rush but to savor. And this might not be the night to do either. She'd invited, but how would she feel in the morning? After the adrenaline high of the evening they'd spent, was she just reacting or did she really want him? He couldn't chance hurting her, wouldn't touch her without finding out.

He framed her face, her beautiful face, with hands that trembled. "I want you. I have since that first night when I woke up and saw you sleeping in the chair, making sure I was all right. But I need to know that this is what you really want, too."

Sara felt a little funny talking about it this way, and dropped her gaze to his second shirt button. "I wouldn't have said what I did if I didn't."

He placed a gentle kiss on the tip of her nose while his hands caressed her back lazily. "I need to hear you say the words, to be sure." Leaning in, he kissed both of her eyes closed and heard a sigh escape from her.

She'd never played the game this way, and wasn't quite sure what to make of him. "I'm not a casual person, Nick. I think you should know that."

"Casual isn't how I feel about you, Sara. Tell me how you feel."

He was forcing her to verbalize her feelings, and she hadn't been prepared for that. Edgy with nerves, she struggled to think while his warm mouth worked its magic at her left temple. "I—I want you, too. I have from the beginning. I tried to fight what I feel, but it's not working." She couldn't be more honest than that.

What would it be like with him? She'd wondered for days now, and long, restless nights. Just minutes ago, she'd decided to act on that need. Yet she worried that once she shared herself with him so intimately, could she keep from wanting more? Could she guard her heart this time?

He saw the indecision in her eyes, yet saw the desire, too. He would do away with the first and satisfy the second. Slowly, he let his lips roam her face, tasting the honeyed flavor of her skin. His hands at her back snuck beneath her sweater and began their own journey of discovery. His fingers trailed a burning path as they moved to the front. When his hands closed over her breasts, she moaned low in her throat and sought his mouth.

The kiss was deep and desperate as passion ignited. His head was beginning to spin as his mind fragmented. No other woman had ever made him so helpless so quickly. He kneaded her flesh, then fussed with the bra's clasp, freeing her breasts to his grateful hands. He brushed his thumbs over the points and heard her release a cry she couldn't hold back.

Shifting the material of her sweater, he lowered his mouth to her and felt her hands move into his hair and press him closer to her yearning flesh. She was so responsive, so sensitive to his touch.

Breathing hard, he raised his head, needing to know. "Are you on the pill?"

It took Sara a moment to come back from the wondrous place where he'd taken her. "No. I...it's been awhile and there's been no need. Don't you have...?"

He shook his head. "Not with me."

She felt the disappointment first, then the concern. Moving back, she found herself trembling. "We can't, then. I get . . . that is, I have a feeling I could get pregnant easily. I can't risk that." She began moving away, straightening her sweater.

Frustrated but far from finished, he shifted, then lifted her, leaning her back against his chest, trapping her between his spread legs. "There are other ways."

"But I—"

"Shh," he said, already nuzzling her neck. "I won't get you pregnant. I promise. And you can stop me anytime you want if you're worried."

Her back was to him and he buried his face in her neck beneath the heavy fall of her hair. His lips feasted on her ear next and felt the shivers race through her. He sent his hands back to worship her breasts, then angled around to capture her mouth with his.

As his hands and mouth aroused, she became restless, her fingers fidgeting along his arms. When his hand trailed down to the waistband of her jeans and loosened the catch, she made a soft, mewing sound. His fingers roamed lower to discover her most intimate secrets and she jerked, as if startled. Nick waited for her to settle, his mouth still locked to hers, making the kiss quietly persuasive.

Before she could gather the strength to protest, he was arousing her beyond belief—perhaps because it had been so very long or maybe because he knew just how to touch her. Sara no longer knew which, nor cared. She crested with such a fierce explosion of feeling that she thought her pounding heart might burst from within her. The tremulous waves went on and on, until she finally sagged against him, totally replete.

And still he didn't turn from her, but held her as aftershocks shuddered through her. Lying in his arms, Sara felt a rush of emotion for the man who could give so much without taking, an emotion she feared putting a name to.

Finally, she craned her head so she could see his face and found him smiling at her. She felt no embarrassment, but rather a spreading warmth. Yet she felt bad for him.

Reaching up, she stroked his cheek. "I loved what you did, but it's a lonely way to make love."

He dipped his head and gave her a very long, very gentle kiss. "I enjoy touching you. Tomorrow, I'm going into town to find a store. Then we'll climb the mountain together."

Tomorrow. He was already making plans for tomorrow. She hadn't the strength, nor the desire, to argue.

Eight

"It's about time you turned yourself in, Dean." Sheriff Hensley's expression was not friendly.

Nick settled his long frame in the chair across from Judd's desk. "I wouldn't exactly call it that. I'm not a wanted man, except in your eyes. It was my Blazer blown to bits. I'm the victim, remember?"

Judd chose to ignore his remarks as he picked up a piece of paper. "Are you sure you didn't leave anyone off this list of people you talked with since arriving in town?"

"I'm sure."

"What makes you and Melissa Avery think that you'll be able to find her father's killer all these years later when we haven't been able to?"

They'd been over this ground before, on his first visit before the explosion. Apparently the sheriff was still annoyed that Melissa hadn't left the unsolved murder up to his department. "What can it hurt having one more person investigating? You and your staff are busy with other things, but I'm focusing in on this alone."

Sitting back, Judd frowned. "Why did Melissa wait so long to put someone on this?"

"Because until Charlie's remains were found, she wasn't sure her father hadn't just taken off on his own. When she learned he'd been murdered, she felt compelled to find out who did it."

"Why? She was a little girl when Charlie disappeared. From what I've gathered, Charlie wasn't really close to anyone in his family."

Nick shrugged. "Guess you'll have to ask her."

Judd already had and had gotten nowhere. He intensely disliked having a P.I. nosing around. Civilians, even licensed investigators, tended to muddy up his own work. And added to his workload when they wound up irritating someone enough to have them plant dynamite in a vehicle. "Who do you suppose tried to kill you?" He indicated the list. "Someone on there?"

"Your guess is as good as mine."

"You're taking all this rather lightly, I'd say."

Nick straightened. "No, I'm not at all. I've apparently got someone in Whitehorn worried with my inquiries about something that happened twenty years ago. My guess would be that it's the killer. I've had other attempts on my life in my line of work, and I never take them lightly. What would you have me do, turn tail and run back to Butte?"

"Some might think that's wise." The sheriff nodded out the front window of his office. "You're driving Sara Lewis's car. Just how did you get involved with her?"

Reluctantly, he told the sheriff the story of how Sara had found him wandering about on Laughing Horse Reservation the night of the explosion, dazed and bleeding. Whitehorn was a small town and Nick knew Judd would find out sooner or later, if he hadn't already, and was just testing him for veracity. He felt the best path to follow was to be up-front.

"So you've been hiding out on the reservation, knowing it's off-limits to us?"

Nick's jaw clenched, but he forced himself to relax, realizing the man was just doing his job. "I wasn't hiding out as much as recuperating from a dislocated shoulder and other injuries." He still had a small bandage near his temple where the deepest gash hadn't quite healed. "Sara and her neighbors have been very good to me."

Judd studied him thoughtfully as he toyed with his pen. Nick Dean seemed honest enough, but who could tell in this bizarre case? He would bear watching. "Now that you're back at the motel, what are your plans?"

Nick held on to his temper, though barely. Judd Hensley was treating him as if he were a suspect. "I've checked out of the motel. As to my plans, I intend to finish the job Melissa hired me to do."

Tossing down his pen, Judd leaned forward, his ancient desk chair protesting under his sudden weight shift. "In other words, you're going to march around town inviting this killer to take another crack at you."

He'd about had it with this small-town lawman. "Look, Sheriff, I don't want to get hurt again and I certainly don't want to get myself killed. But I've made a commitment. I'm not leaving until I find the person responsible for Charlie's murder, but I'm not stupid enough to offer myself up as a sacrifice to flush him out. I worked vice in Butte for some years. I know what I'm doing."

"Maybe if you saw the remains of your Blazer, you'd reconsider."

"Doubtful, but I'd like to take a look."

Hensley got to his feet and reached for a ring of keys. "Come with me."

It wasn't a pretty sight. Fire hot enough to fuse metal was an inferno. Again, Nick had reason to thank his lucky stars that he'd been thrown free.

"Have your people learned anything about the cause of the explosion? Was it dynamite for sure? Was forensics here?"

"Yes. Some fragments were found. Not a lot to go on."

The man surely didn't seem eager to find the person or persons responsible. Nick knew small-town lawmen moved slowly, but this seemed almost purposeful.

Watching Nick's expression, Judd continued his own questioning. "Did you remember anything else about the hitchhiker that might help us identify her?"

"I told you all I know." He struggled with an involuntary shudder, thinking of what a torturous death the poor soul had endured.

The sheriff led the way out of the garage. "Who are your main suspects so far?"

Nick named the three men who appeared to have motives to kill Charlie. "But two of them are dead, and though Ethan Walker hasn't been cooperative, I haven't come up with enough evidence to implicate him. I plan to interview some people who knew Cameron Baxter and Jeremiah Kincaid well back then. And I'm going to corner Ethan again." He met Judd's dark gaze. "Have you got any leads you'd be willing to share with me?"

"Not so far. Has it occurred to you we may never find the person responsible?"

Nick turned up his coat collar as a chill wind sent a gust of cold air down his neck. "I'm not one to give up easily."

"Where can I reach you if I need to?"

He wasn't about to tell the sheriff he was staying with Sara. "I'll check in with you periodically." He could see that Judd wasn't pleased with his answer. Without another word, he turned and walked back toward his office.

Nick headed for Sara's Volkswagen. He had a number of stops to make before he picked her up at the Native American Museum at five.

Nick slid into a booth by the window where he could keep an eye on Sara's car. He wasn't paranoid. Just careful.

It was nearly noon and the Hip Hop Café was busy with the lunchtime crowd. It was a landmark eatery, a throwback to the fifties with a long chrome counter, mismatched tables and chairs, colorful wall posters and hanging baskets of ivy at odd intervals. The air was welcomingly warm, heavy with the sweet scent of syrup and the aroma of coffee, rich with the greasy smell of fried bacon and burgers. An old jukebox thrummed out a Patsy Cline ballad as three waitresses zigzagged expertly through the makeshift aisles with heavy trays.

Melissa had seen Nick enter and give the waitress his order. She walked over to his booth, a cup of coffee in her hand. "Well, the prodigal P.I. returns," she said with a smile as she slid in opposite him. "I hope you're fully recovered. I feel terrible about your injuries and the loss of your Blazer."

"Yeah, me, too. Did you give some thought to the woman I described to you on the phone, the hitchhiker who died in the explosion? Ever see her in here?"

Melissa shook her head. "From your description and Judd's, she doesn't sound familiar, and I have a good memory for faces. They still don't know who she was?"

"Afraid not."

"Have you learned anything new?"

"This is my first day out after the accident. I plan to talk with a couple of people this week." His lunch arrived just then, barbecued beef on a bun and a beer. Nick waited until the smiling waitress whose name tag read Daisy refilled Melissa's coffee cup before he leaned forward. It wasn't likely anyone would hear over the loud music, but he wasn't taking any chances. "Have you run across anything I can use since we talked on the phone?"

Melissa took a sip before answering. "There's been a lot of talk and speculation in here, but nothing concrete. People are wondering how it came to be that my father's remains were found on the reservation, of all places. It's not an area most townsfolk frequent. And, of course, about your Blazer catching fire and a stranger dying. A few have heard the sheriff say it wasn't an accident."

Nick had been aware of several interested looks coming his way as he'd sat down—especially from the couple two tables over. "Who are those two?" he asked, indicating the almost delicate looking blonde picking at a salad alongside a tall, pale man who'd already finished his lunch.

Melissa took her time glancing over before answering. "That's Dugin Kincaid and his wife, Mary Jo."

So that was Jeremiah's son. Nick saw the man's pale blue eyes dart around the restaurant nervously. "From what I've heard, he's not much like the old man, is he?"

Keeping her head averted and her voice low, Melissa leaned closer. "You can say that again. Dugin's always been wimpy, but since Mary Jo popped up on the scene, he's led an interesting life."

Nick took a long swig of beer. It tasted good, perhaps because he hadn't had a glass in ages. "What do you mean by interesting?"

"Well, one of the guests at Dugin and Mary Jo's wedding—a man named Floyd Oakley—was found dead. And just before that, a baby had been found abandoned on Dugin's doorstep."

"A baby? No kidding!" But the dead man interested him more. "Who was this Floyd Oakley?"

"That's the odd part. No one claimed to have invited him." Melissa waved as one of her regular customers walked in, then returned her attention to Nick. "And no one knows where the baby came from, either. This little town has more than its share of mysteries."

Nick finished his sandwich. "So it would seem." Wiping his mouth, he saw that Mary Jo Kincaid had dropped all pretense of politeness and was openly staring at him, her eyes curious. He smiled at her, then shifted his gaze out the window to check on the Volkswagen.

Melissa followed his gaze. "Are you nervous since the accident? Not that I blame you. I want you to know, Nick, I never dreamed you'd be in actual physical danger. Maybe we should drop the whole thing."

He took a moment to study the woman who'd hired him. Nick knew she was planning on marrying rancher Wyatt North soon, and she'd told him they were very happy. Melissa was an attractive woman around Sara's age, vibrant and full of life. But she couldn't hold a candle to Sara's dark beauty and the most gorgeous black hair he'd ever touched. "Is that what you want, Melissa—to have me back off?"

"Not really. But I also don't want you to lose your life trying to help me."

Nick glanced at the check, noted the amount and placed a bill on top of it with a generous tip for the hardworking Daisy. "I appreciate your concern, but I'll be all right."

Melissa reached for the check. "I'll take care of this."

He took it back from her. "Thank you, but no." Nick had always preferred paying his own way. He slid to the end of the booth, very aware of Mary Jo Kincaid's eyes still on him as Melissa rose and walked to the door with him. "I'll be in touch. Keep your ears open."

"I will. And Nick, take care, please."

With a nod, he headed for the Volkswagen.

Ethan Walker had a lived-in face, as if the man had seen his share of pain. Right now, his wide forehead wore a deeply furrowed frown. "I thought I made it clear I didn't want to talk to you," he said to Nick, turning back to the fence post he was twisting barbed wire around.

Nick had spotted the stoic rancher from alongside his barn and had walked out to where Ethan was working, hoping to break through the man's reticence. "I suppose you did. I'll only take a few minutes of your time. If your father had been gone for over twenty years and suddenly someone ran across his bones and it was learned he'd been murdered, wouldn't you want to know what happened to him?"

The expression on the weathered face didn't soften as Ethan straightened and adjusted the thick gloves he wore. "My father ran out on us when I was young. If he didn't want to be with me when I needed him, I don't give a damn what happened to him."

A hard man, Nick thought. Or was he coming from a position of being hurt by his father's abandonment and never quite getting over it, much like the woman who'd hired him? "Well, Melissa Avery doesn't feel that way. She wants to know what happened to Charlie. And word around town is that you argued with her father fairly often. Is that right?"

Ethan squinted into the afternoon sun, as if trying to decide whether to answer Nick or throw the man off his property. Finally, he swung back. "Yeah, we argued. That doesn't mean I killed him."

"What did you argue about?"

"I just didn't like him." He picked up his wire cutters.

Like pulling teeth, Nick thought. "What was it about him that you didn't like?"

"Everything."

"Could you be more specific?"

Ethan let out a whoosh of disgust, then tossed down the cutters and straightened again. "You just aren't going to quit, are you?"

"Not until I learn the truth. If you have nothing to hide, you have nothing to fear from me."

Removing his gloves took some time. Then Ethan ran one rough hand over his unshaven face. "Charlie was selfish. He cheated on his wife and he didn't give a damn about Melissa or her brother, not that you should go and tell her that. He doesn't deserve all her worrying."

It wasn't enough. "What specific gripe did you have with him that made you openly threaten him, an incident several people overheard?"

Ethan's face took on an annoyed look. "When Charlie got to drinking, he got meaner by the minute. He'd brag, and didn't have anything to brag about. He was always complaining, always criticizing. I was just a teenager, but he got on my nerves whenever I saw him. And sometimes he seemed to be sniffing around some of the girls in my school. He was older than them and a married man! I told him it was wrong and he didn't like it. I told him to stay away from them or he'd be sorry. That was all there was to it."

Nick doubted that. "What did you mean when you told him he'd be sorry if he didn't stay away from the girls?"

Temper fairly crackled in the rancher's eyes. "Not that I'd kill him, if that's what you're getting at. I meant we could meet and settle our differences, man-to-man. But he never had the guts to take me up on that because he knew I'd win, hands down. Even then I was bigger than him— something he couldn't deal with.''

"I heard you got into more than one fight back in your younger days."

"So what if I did? After I got home from Nam, I had some problems. Lots of guys did." He started putting his gloves back on.

"Did you know Charlie's wife?"

"Some. Not well. I felt sorry for her. I don't like to see men take advantage of women."

"Did Charlie ever cut in on some girl you did care about?"

Ethan's scowl was awesome. "Look, you're on the wrong track here. I didn't like Charlie because I didn't care for the kind of man Charlie was, not because he'd done something to me personally." But Nick noted something evasive in Ethan's eyes.

Nick removed a small notebook from his pocket and flipped through it till he found the page he wanted. "Fellow named Arnie McDonald says he was on the Kincaid ranch one day when you and Charlie fought. Do you recall that incident?"

Ethan ran his ungloved hand through his hair, looking exasperated and cornered. "That wasn't a fight. Charlie tried to take a swing at me. He was drunk. I hit him, knocked him out. Then I left."

"You didn't stick around to see if he was all right?"

Ethan grunted, as if it should have been obvious. "He was coming around before I left. Listen, I've had enough. Go bother someone else. Lots of guys didn't like Charlie Avery. He was a no-account loser."

"Then you were hoping he'd disappear." It wasn't a question.

Now the man's eyes became flinty. "Yeah. But I didn't *make* him disappear." Turning his back, Ethan returned to his fence.

His gut instinct told Nick that Ethan wasn't telling him everything. Arnie McDonald had been very sure that the fight between Ethan and Charlie had been about a woman. However, Nick didn't think he'd get any more out of the hostile rancher today. "Thanks. If I need more, I'll be back."

Nick didn't wait for Ethan to respond, but instead walked back toward the barn, where he'd left the Volkswagen in plain sight of where they'd been talking. He felt it was best to err on the side of caution.

He glanced toward the big barn and wondered if Ethan kept dynamite on hand, as so many ranchers did. He couldn't risk taking a look today.

Nick had just a few more stops to make before it would be time to pick up Sara. He hadn't really made much progress on Charlie's case, but he was smiling nonetheless as he got behind the wheel.

The evening stretched before him, sharing dinner with Sara, talking over the day with Sara and hopefully making love with Sara. His body's quick reaction to that thought had Nick hurrying as he pulled out of Ethan's drive and onto the road.

He was trying to concentrate on Sara's recital of her telephone conversation with Alice Thundercloud as he drove. The traffic on Route 191 was rather heavy during rush hour so he kept his eyes on the road. "So she's going to be released from the hospital tomorrow?"

"Yes. Kane says the immediate danger has passed, but she still has to be careful." Sara paused, remembering the rest of what Alice had told her. "She told me that John is now working three jobs trying to make ends meet, and that he was at this third place last night when she needed him. Naturally, she can't stay angry with him, since he's working so hard for his family.''

''Do you believe that's where he was?''

''I *want* to. Alice never did say where the new job was, only that John said it was going to pay well. As I've mentioned before, most of the men from the res who work in town can scarcely get minimum wage, and they never get benefits. Small wonder they have to work two and three jobs just to live at poverty level.''

Nick had seen examples of that in his walks around the reservation. Unemployment was widespread, with too many able-bodied young men hanging around the gas station or coffee shop with little to do. ''They need to be trained. Vocational schools, maybe. Classes in plumbing and heating, carpentry, electrical. Not only could they keep their own places in repair, but they could hire out if they were skilled.''

Sara sighed. ''Exactly. But how do we entice instructors onto the res to teach our people when they can't pay?''

Nick changed lanes, then zipped around a white truck. There'd been a dark sedan directly behind the Volkswagen for several miles and it was making him tense. ''That is a problem,'' he answered, keeping up his end of the conversation so she wouldn't guess his concern. ''Otherwise, how was your day?''

She told him, animated and excited about the acquisition of some valuable textile hangings, some of them priceless. ''They're fantastic. You should come early the next time you pick me up and meet our head curator. Jason Eagle's very nice and quite knowledgeable.'' But as she thought about what she'd just said, she decided she might have been too presumptuous. "Oh, but you're probably not interested in artifacts."

Nick pulled his eyes from the rearview mirror. The dark sedan had indeed followed his lane changes. "What makes you think I'm not?" he asked Sara. He sent her a quick look as he took her hand. "I'd like to see where you work."

She didn't want to be pleased at his remark nor warmed by his touch. Just like she hadn't wanted to think of him nearly all day nor look forward to seeing him this evening. She was heading for danger, Sara warned herself. But after the night she'd spent in his arms on the couch, the warning was probably too late.

No man had ever made love to her as unselfishly as Nick had last night, then held her until they'd both fallen asleep. Jack had always sought his own satisfaction greedily while hers had been incidental. It had taken time, distance and a bit of experience before Sara had realized that. Remembering Nick's touch, she felt her face flush.

Nick pressed down on the accelerator and the little car jerked forward. Maneuvering quickly, he zigzagged around a slow-moving horse van, passed a station wagon and then dipped back into the right lane before slowing down. In the side mirror, he saw the dark sedan with the tinted windows stay to the left, keeping the Volkswagen in sight. Only another couple of miles to the turnoff to the reservation. Surely whoever was driving wouldn't try anything on a crowded highway.

"What's wrong?" Sara asked, sensing his tension and watching him frown into the rearview mirror. Twisting in her seat, she could see only a lumbering station wagon behind them.

"Don't look back. It's the black sedan left of us. They've been on our tail for some time now. It may be nothing, but—"

She felt a flash of fear race up her spine. It was one thing to hear about this sort of thing and quite another to experience it. "The res isn't far."

"I know. We'll be all right." But his hands gripped the wheel tighter. If only Sara wasn't with him, he wouldn't be so concerned. Now, by using her car today and apparently catching the wrong person's attention, he'd exposed her to danger as well.

In minutes, they came to the turnoff, and Nick quickly zoomed to the right and onto the road bordered by thick pines. Of course, nothing could prevent the sedan from following them, but the occupants had to know that a strange car would stand out on Laughing Horse and perhaps even invite questions by the tribal police. Without breaking his speed, he kept his eye on the road behind and saw that they were no longer being followed. "They didn't turn," he told Sara. "I was probably mistaken."

"I doubt that. Where all did you go today?" Perhaps she could figure out who might have seen him.

By the time he'd given her a rundown on his visits with Judd, Melissa and Ethan, they were parked in her drive. Nick shut off the engine and turned to her. "The car was always in my sight, but any number of people could have seen that I was driving your Bug. Especially at the Hip Hop. Jackson and Kane were right. I should have rented a car. That way, they couldn't have connected us."

"Then you'll just stay on the reservation from now on. They won't come after me alone." She got out of the car.

Nick didn't agree, but didn't argue. He took several packages out of the trunk and followed her inside. He set down his bundles on a chair while she snapped on the light.

Then, before she had time to slip out of her jacket, he pinned her arms to her sides and pulled her to him. "All day I've been thinking about you." He watched awareness leap into her dark eyes. "While I was talking with people, when I was driving along and even shopping, you were on my mind." He raised his hand to capture a dark strand of hair that had escaped from her long braid. "Your wonderful hair." He kissed each of her eyes. "Your beautiful eyes." He buried his face in her neck. "The way you smell."

Her mind beginning to spin, Sara put a hand to his chest. "Nick, I—"

"The soft sound you made last night when I—"

On tiptoe, color flooding her face, she pressed her mouth to his, not wanting to hear out loud what she knew he was about to say.

The kiss began slowly, but warmed quickly. His lips were so soft, so giving. His tongue met hers in a mating dance that stole her breath away. Her hands dove into his hair as she pulled his head down to her.

This. This was *exactly* what she'd been dreaming of all day. This race into passion, this rush into madness. He wasn't the man she needed, but he was the one she wanted. Here, inside her small home where no man before Nick had ever kissed her, he now kissed her as if there were no tomorrow. Tomorrow was not something she would think about tonight. For this night, he was here in her arms where she'd longed for him to be, and he was hers.

Nick heard his own heartbeat echo inside his head, or was it hers? He no longer knew where he left off and she began. No woman had ever aroused him so thoroughly, even dressed in layers of clothes and her hair sedately braided. Breathing heavily, he eased back from her and found her eyes already misty with desire.

"Let's go to bed," he suggested, his voice thick.

Sara's brows shot up. "Bed? It's barely six in the evening. We haven't even made dinner."

"I bought dinner. We can reheat it later."

She tried to think calmly, rationally. No one had ever suggested making love when daylight had barely disappeared. "But—but what if someone comes to the door?"

"Are you expecting anyone?"

"No, but—"

He reached over and slammed home the dead bolt. "Let them knock. We won't answer." He bent to kiss her again, his hands slipping her jacket from her, then starting on the buttons of her pale blue sweater.

Sara placed her hands over his, then shivered as he shifted his attention to kissing her ear. "The sun's hardly gone down and—"

"Are you so conventional you can't make love unless it's dark outside or the middle of the night?" His fingers closed over her breasts and he heard her struggle with a soft moan.

There could be only one answer to his question. She wasn't sure how much longer her knees would hold her upright. "Do you want to go to my room?"

"You have to ask?" Bending, he picked her up in his arms as if she were no heavier than a child and he hadn't had a dislocated shoulder only days ago. He carried her to her room, reached to flick on the low bedside lamp, then let her slide down his body before he captured her mouth in another stunning kiss.

He was right, Sara thought. It seemed a foolish waste of time to wait when they both were so needy. The time of day meant nothing, nor which room they were in. All that mattered was that finally, at last, they would come together.

Plenty in the outside world would not approve, some in her own circle of family and friends. Most certainly his people would not, if they knew. But no one need know, for they were behind locked doors, safe from weather and prying eyes and strangers with bombs that could kill. For this sweet moment in time they would be free to explore and enjoy each other.

From behind his back, Nick brought out a long cellophane bag he'd grabbed on the way to the bedroom. In the soft light, he watched her draw out the single, long-stemmed red rose, her dark eyes widening with pleasure as she inhaled the heady fragrance. He'd had to drive forty miles to find a store that sold roses, but the look on her face was worth it.

"Romance?" she whispered, for she hadn't believed such a sexy man would also be romantic.

"Perfection deserves perfection," he answered, his hands going to her braid. "Undo it, please."

Sara did, setting aside her rose and watching him all the while, noticing his breathing grow shallow as she shook out the final strands. Could there be anything more thrilling than seeing such open desire in a lover's eyes?

Swallowing, Nick took off his jacket and hurriedly removed his boots before pulling off hers. Then he turned down the quilt and leaned toward her, his hands at his sides, only his lips touching her. He kissed her long and lazily, his mouth toying with hers, his tongue dipping in for a thorough, lingering taste. Deliberately teasing, he saw her eyes close as he trailed his lips over her face, along her jawline and the base of her throat. He felt her pulse pound there, pound for him.

She was floating, drifting, tingling. She'd wanted his hard, clever hands learning her, she'd thought, never dreaming this slow onslaught would shatter her more quickly. She felt her blood racing, churning. When slowly she opened her eyes, she saw him watching her.

"I want to see you," he said softly, "to look at you." But his hands were trembling and he wasn't sure he could free the tiny buttons of her sweater.

She did it for him, very slowly, drawing out the anticipation. Two could play this game, Sara thought, knowing the waiting would sweeten the reward. She stepped out of her slacks and skimmed off her hose, a little worried that the contrast of her white bra and panties against her dark skin might give him pause. But she saw only approval and a hint of impatience in the blue of his eyes as he examined her.

When she tossed aside the last two items, she heard his breath catch, then whoosh out as she stood before him in the dim light. She almost smiled as he rid himself of his clothes in record time. It was her turn to admire. And to tremble.

Hesitantly, she reached out to run her fingers through the thick patch of blond hair on his chest. It felt so good, so right to touch him freely. Closing her eyes, she let herself feel.

He'd never seen a more responsive woman, nor a more natural one. She unfurled like the petals of a rose as his fingers skimmed along her shoulders and down her arms, then moved back up to caress her breasts. This time she didn't bother to suppress the moan that came from deep in her throat.

He eased her onto the mattress and followed her down. A breath shuddered from her as his lips closed over flesh begging for his attention, first one side, then the other. His hand skimmed along her rib cage to her narrow waist and the gentle flare of her hips.

"Tell me what you'd like me to do," he said, wanting to please her in every way.

"Whatever you want," she managed to gasp. "Just don't stop."

An aching pleasure wound its way along her nerve endings as, with teeth and tongue, lips and hands, he tasted and teased, doing delightful, delicious things to every part of her. The fragrance of the rose mingled with his intoxicating male scent, the combination dizzying. His warm breath skimmed along her sensitive skin and had her shivering. For always she would remember this, their first time.

She was exquisite, to taste, to hold, to kiss. Restless now beneath his questing fingers, she arched into his touch. His head swam with the wonder of being able to love her at last, to love her slowly and freely.

But his control was nearing the breaking point. Days of desiring her, last night holding her and loving her, hours of dreaming had him strung tighter than a barbed-wire fence. And he could tell she was running out of patience, too, as her hand settled nervously on his hard stomach.

"Touch me," he said, guessing that she wanted permission. And when her fingers closed around him, it was his groan of pleasure that filled the room.

He took a moment to put in place the protection. Then, as if they'd been waiting for this moment forever, he slipped inside her effortlessly. She rose to meet him in welcome. Like old lovers, he found the rhythm quickly and they moved together. The sweet friction built as, locked in his arms, she kept her eyes on his. His control unraveled as he moved them to a fierce finish. When he felt her explosion begin, he tightened his hold on her. Just before his mind fragmented, he whispered her name.

* * *

Sara lay perfectly still in a euphoria of satisfaction. She wasn't absolutely certain she could ever move again. Despite Nick's weight pressing on her, she was content to lie just so. And to relive the wondrous thing that had just happened.

She wasn't naive enough to think that making beautiful love meant that two people were destined to be together. Remembering her mother and father, her brother and his wife, Jackson Hawk and his first wife, she knew that attraction didn't necessarily guarantee happiness.

But oh, it had been glorious. Why did it have to be that when at last she'd found a man who could make her feel so much, he was the wrong man?

Nick stirred, shifted his weight and looked into her eyes. He saw a sadness there that instantly upset him. "Are you all right?"

"Mmm," she murmured, rearranging her expression and putting on a smile. "More than all right. Wonderful."

But still he frowned. "You're sure?"

Dropping her gaze, she toyed with his chest hair. "I never knew it could be like that."

He felt that, too, yet hesitated to tell her. His fingers moved to tangle in the silk of her hair. "It sure beats the *moo shu* chicken, fried rice and sweet-and-sour pork waiting for us in those cartons in the living room."

"You picked up Chinese for us?"

"I figured after working all day you wouldn't feel like cooking."

No, she'd felt like lazily loving instead. Stretching, she reached for her rose, drawing it to her nose. "You were busy today, shopping for surprises."

The reminder had him frowning. "Uh oh. I forgot about something."

"What?"

"I also bought a quart of fudge ripple ice cream. It's probably a soggy puddle on your chair by now."

She laughed. "I guess you got distracted."

"A little." He nuzzled her neck, took her rose and trailed the soft petals along her throat, then circled her breasts. He saw her skin quiver and jump, her stomach muscles tighten. Smiling, he gathered her to him. "What the hell. It's already melted. What's another hour?" And he took her mouth in a soul-shattering kiss.

Nine

Hammer in hand, Nick sent the nail home with his third swing. It was a cold Saturday afternoon, but the air was dry, the sun shining. He felt good, useful and productive. Physical labor always made him feel like this—tired at the end of the day but pleased with results he could see.

Lining up another nail, he found himself wishing investigations worked that way. He'd spent the past week hunting down people to interview in connection with Charlie's murder, and though he'd found a few, the results weren't exactly promising.

Tex Barlow was in his sixties now, a ranch hand working on a small spread off Whispering Pines Road. But years ago he'd worked on Cameron Baxter's place, until the rancher had had to sell it to pay off his gambling debts. Tex had thought his employer to be a mean old cuss at times, but Tex was the sort who kept to himself, got his work done and didn't stick his nose where it didn't belong.

However, Nick had found the man's memory wasn't all that bad. Tex had overheard Cameron ranting about Charlie Avery several times, mostly to his daughter, Lexine, the wild one who'd apparently left town in her youth. Of course, Cameron, according to Tex, had raved on about several men his daughter had known, often shouting so loud that his voice carried through the open windows of the big house into the yard and beyond. Tex's own daughter had run away at an early age after his wife had died, which was one reason he lived in a bunkhouse now. He empathized somewhat with Cameron's difficulties with his own high-strung girl.

It boiled down to nothing concrete that could be pinned on Cameron Baxter about Charlie's death.

Nick climbed down from the ladder, reached for another wide board and maneuvered it into place. The large stack of lumber his father had had shipped to the reservation after his call was slowly disappearing. Nick had told Bill Dean that many houses here were in need of shoring up and insulation for the colder winter days ahead, and like the man his son knew him to be, Bill hadn't hesitated in sending enough supplies to keep him busy for some weeks.

Not that he'd probably be staying that long.

He'd started on repairing Henry Raintree's place first, because the old man had quickly agreed to accept Nick's help. He knew how prideful the Northern Cheyenne were and he didn't want to insult that pride in any way. So he'd begun with Henry, a man who seemed to like him, and hoped that when the others saw he was doing repairs not only because they were needed but because he needed to keep busy, and that he wanted to repay the folks who'd befriended him when he'd been hurt, they'd allow him to assist more. And if he could round up a few of the teenagers, he could teach them basic carpentry skills they'd be able to use on their own homes.

Nick climbed back up and reached for another nail. He was itching to get to some of the worst ones. Like Tommy Running Deer's home, with the newborn child inside. Then there was the Thundercloud house, with the sagging porch and leaking roof. And Summer Lewis's place, with such poorly fitting windows that the wind whistled in constantly, something Sara had let slip recently.

Squinting into the sun, Nick glanced over at Sara's car, which was parked in her mother's drive. She'd left this morning to work half a day at the museum and had told him she'd be dropping in on Summer afterward. The side windows of the small house looked out on to where he was working on Henry's place. He couldn't help wondering if he was Topic A in the mother-daughter conversation today.

Finished nailing the board in place, Nick went down for another, wiping his damp brow with his handkerchief before climbing back up. All along this rutted road, cabins and dwellings that could only be called shacks badly needed attention. The only home he'd visited so far that was truly sound was Jackson Hawk's residence, about ten miles from the reservation center.

Maggie had had Sara and him over for dinner last night and, though Nick had been a little uneasy about going, he'd wound up enjoying the evening. Maggie was a good cook and Jackson had inexplicably warmed to him. Earlier, Nick had run his idea of asking his father to donate materials for housing repairs past Jackson and, after thoughtful consideration and quiet questioning, the tribal attorney had accepted Nick's offer. He'd also wanted to know how the Avery investigation was shaping up.

Nick had told him about the little he'd learned from Tex Barlow about Cameron Baxter's relationship to Charlie. And he'd revealed that he'd located a widow named Mattie Finn, whose husband had worked for Jeremiah Kincaid twenty years ago. She'd described Jeremiah as handsome and flashy, a man who ran his ranch with an iron hand. He was also ruthless and selfish, liked by very few.

Mattie knew who Charlie was, had even seen him on the Kincaid ranch a time or two, but didn't think he'd had a deeper relationship with Jeremiah than any other drifter looking for work in those days. Personally, she hadn't liked Charlie because she'd heard stories that he stepped out on his wife and neglected his young children.

But she'd offered no motive for Jeremiah to want Charlie out of the way.

After listening, Jackson could come up with no other suspects for Nick to talk to, though Nick had said he planned on questioning Arnie McDonald about Ethan Walker again next week. They'd ended the evening having coffee at the big oak dining table and playing Scrabble, a homey touch. Nick had driven back to Sara's house feeling mellow.

But alone with her, his mood had changed to barely restrained passion, one she'd matched willingly, eagerly. Once they'd made the leap into physical intimacy, they couldn't seem to keep their hands off one another. Even at the Hawks's place, Nick had made sure he sat next to Sara, within touching distance. He knew she wasn't ready to reveal their close relationship to anyone at this point, but his own churning needs had him finding a dozen excuses to pat her hand or brush back her hair. Each time, color would move into her face and she'd put a bit of distance between them. Not to be outmaneuvered, he'd scoot closer. Nick was certain, despite keeping up a lively conversation, that their hosts hadn't missed the little interplay.

And he knew their knowing bothered Sara.

Nick picked up the last board he'd cut for this side and shoved it into place before going back up the ladder. Why, he wondered, did she want to keep their alliance a secret?

He was falling in love with her and wanted to shout it from the rooftops.

Correction: *had* fallen in love with her. He whacked the nail in place, realizing how far he'd come in such a short time. He'd arrived on the reservation with not a thought in mind about a woman or a relationship or permanency of any sort. He'd neatly avoided anything resembling commitment since his divorce.

But it was different with Sara.

She was so beautiful, for starters. Such a cool facade that hid a passionate nature, the kind he'd only dreamed of before meeting her. She was intelligent, funny, warm. She cared about people, genuinely cared. From the youngest to the oldest, people were drawn to her. As he was.

Yet he hesitated in telling her. There was something in her eyes that stopped him even at their most intimate moments. She surrendered her body to him freely, but her mind was full of secrets and her heart was kept under guard. Unavailable, unreachable, remote.

Would she ever come around?

Nick's jaw tightened with determination. Yes, she would. He would see to it that she did. He would wear her down, win her over, make her see that it could work between them.

It was the Indian-white thing gnawing at her, he knew. Even more than he, she was aware of the way her people had regarded him in the restaurant that day, of the shocked hostility of the white couple in the hospital waiting room when Nick had taken her into his arms. She focused on their differences, whereas he saw only their similarities. He felt she loved him, but was afraid to admit it. To him, perhaps even to herself. How could he convince her that they were meant to be together?

Pounding in the last nail, Nick realized he didn't know the answer to that important question. But he would, by God, find it, he decided as he slowly climbed down.

Sara stood by the kitchen window and stared out past her mother's starched white curtains. Nick was starting on the other side of Henry's house, nailing thick boards over insulation he'd already put in place earlier today. He'd told her this morning he had to hurry to finish in case another storm hit. Henry had a bad cough he didn't like the sound of and was treating it with that rotgut whiskey he'd probably made himself. So far, Nick hadn't been able to convince the old man to go to the clinic and let Kane take a look at him, but he was working on it. Each day she spent with Nick, he amazed her more.

And then there were the nights.

"He is a good man," Summer said, peering over her daughter's shoulder as she chopped vegetables for soup and quickly finding what was fascinating Sara so. "Did you know that he asked your grandmother to talk with Tommy Running Deer about letting him insulate his house? For the baby's sake, he said."

Sara tried not to let the thought warm her. "I'm not surprised."

"He was here yesterday, you know." Summer had opened the door to the tall blond man and experienced such a rush of déjà vu that she'd almost reeled. Nick Dean didn't really resemble Aaron Lewis all that much. Yet there were similarities that had dragged her back more than thirty years.

This time Sara was surprised. "Here?" She'd been at work at the museum, of course, having driven the compact car Nick had asked Jackson to rent for him the day after the incident with the dark sedan. Nick had insisted she take that one and that he'd use her Volkswagen, since he'd already been seen around town in her car. She knew he'd been in Whitehorn part of the day tracking down nebulous leads, but he'd been home when she'd returned. "Why was he here?"

"Manya invited him. He'd visited her at Tommy's and she'd promised to make him fry bread. The three of us sat at the kitchen table, eating and talking, for half an hour." Summer twisted the leafy green tops off a bunch of carrots and watched her daughter's eyes return to the window. Her next statement wasn't a question. "You love him."

Sara didn't answer, her eyes fixed on the tall, lean man who'd hoisted a heavy board onto his good shoulder and was marching over to where he'd propped the ladder. How had she let this happen? she wondered. How had she let this blond giant steal her heart in so short a time?

Summer could see that her daughter didn't want to care, though she did. "We can't choose who we love, Sara." Hadn't she told herself that very thing a million times?

Sara sighed, recognizing the truth. "There's much about me he doesn't know."

"Will you tell him?"

"I don't know."

Summer wished she could take away her daughter's sadness, the sadness that lingered in her eyes. "There is no shame to what happened to you, Sara. It was never your fault."

She knew that, in her head. But her heart reminded her that perhaps she'd been punished for loving so foolishly, so unwisely. Was she doing that again? How did a person know? "He lost a child once. He still blames himself."

"Then he will understand. He's not like the other man you knew, is he?" The man Summer had wanted to hunt down and punish for hurting her vulnerable, trusting daughter.

"No, he's not." Sara watched Nick finish the corner piece, then turned to face her mother. "He sees no difference between us."

Summer's capable hands finished cleaning the carrots and set about rinsing them. "Perhaps love blinds him. Or perhaps he's a fool." Grabbing a towel, she met Sara's eyes. "Or perhaps he's genuine and you're afraid to believe."

She was afraid, Sara thought. And with good reason. "You think I should give in to my feelings for this man? How can you, after what happened between you and my father?"

Summer could feel the heavy regret in her chest as she dried her hands. How much harm had she and Aaron done to their children? she wondered, not for the first time. So much that both were now unhappy. One of her brothers, Paul, was denying the fact that his marriage wasn't working and Sara was afraid to love. How could she fix it? Setting down the towel, she took Sara's hands in her own. "By the time you were old enough to see and to know, there was only pain and bitterness. But Sara, once there was love between your father and me. So much love."

"But it wasn't enough, was it, Mama?"

"Because he was a weak man." Summer nodded toward the window. "I don't think the man out there is. Do you?"

Sara leaned to hug her mother, again not answering. "I have to go. Tell Manya I'm sorry I missed her." Grabbing her jacket, she rushed out into the winter sun, heading for Henry Raintree's house, where Nick was climbing down the ladder.

* * *

Sara squinted up at Nick, who was sitting astride the black stallion. "I don't know. I've never ridden bareback."

His eyebrows shot up. "An Indian who's never ridden bareback?"

"An anachronism, right?"

"I'd say so." He reached a hand down to her. "Henry doesn't have a saddle, or another horse. Come on. You'll be fine."

Sara wasn't convinced, watching the restless horse fight the bit as he pawed the ground. "Is this the same stallion that almost trampled Henry that time you came to his rescue?"

"He'd been spooked by a rabbit that day." Nick patted the horse's sleek neck. "He's a little jittery, but not mean." Again he held out his hand to her in invitation.

She'd taken to wearing her hair loose when not at work because Nick had repeatedly told her how much he liked it that way. Now she tossed her head as the wind whipped dark strands about her face. Here goes nothing, she thought. Taking his hand, she let him pull her up onto the stallion and settle her between his thighs.

Immediately, even through the denim of his jeans and her wool slacks, she became aware of him snuggled tightly against her back. Blood rushed to her face and she hoped he hadn't noticed. His hands adjusted the reins as his laugh rang out in the cold air, letting her know he'd caught her reaction and it amused him. Playfully, she punched him in the ribs with an elbow as his heels nudged the stallion forward.

Henry had suggested often that Nick could ride his horse anytime he felt like it, not only as thanks for the work on his house but because the restive beast so seldom got a workout. Judas wasn't a young stallion, but he was powerfully built even though he carried a bit too much weight. Released from his corral, he eagerly raced across the field, expertly avoiding the occasional patch of hard snow.

Nick had to lean forward and press his cheek to Sara's to keep her hair from flying into his face and blocking his view. He inhaled her familiar scent and almost purred like a big cat. He breathed into her ear and felt her involuntary shudder, then laughed aloud again.

"Don't you ever think about anything else?" she teased, turning her head so he could hear her. She was unused to this constant sensual awareness. Though she loved knowing he wanted her, she couldn't help wondering how she'd adjust to the loss when he left.

"Yeah," he said into her ear. "Sometimes I think about dinner." But he'd postponed their evening meal many times, more anxious to feel her beneath him than to feed his stomach. "Are you complaining?"

Sara placed her hands along his arms, deciding to enjoy the moment and not worry about the future just now. "Never."

Smiling, Nick let Judas have his head as they hit the open field alongside the woods that ran for miles.

It felt good to walk hand in hand, holding the stallion's reins as the beast cooled down. The sky was such a piercing blue at three in the afternoon that it almost looked as if an artist had painted it, streaking in a few wispy clouds for effect. Welcome sunlight splashed over the mountains. Nick breathed in cold, clean air and the scent of pine. In the distance, cattle bawled intermittently. He'd always loved Montana and had never really wanted to live anywhere else. "It's beautiful here, isn't it?"

Sara stepped gingerly over a protruding rock. One short ride and her legs ached, while her thighs tingled from gripping the horse. "Parts of it are." She gazed upward. "This section unspoiled by man certainly is."

"You're kind of quiet today." He looked down at her. "Anything the matter?"

She shrugged. "Maybe, maybe not. Do you recall my telling you about the textile hangings the museum got recently?"

"The ones that were so valuable some were priceless? Yes. What about them? Did you discover they're fakes?"

"That problem might be easier to solve. We discovered this morning that two of the blankets that date back four generations to the era of Chief Strongheart are missing."

"Missing? As in misplaced, never unpacked, hung on the wrong floor, maybe?"

Sara shook her head. "Jason Eagle and I searched everywhere. That's why I was late getting back. Yesterday, they were exactly where we'd put them on display in a glass case under lock and key. Today they're nowhere to be found."

"What does Jason think happened?"

"The only conclusion is that there was a theft between yesterday's closing time and this morning's opening." She ran a hand through her hair, frowning. "Jason's just sick about it, naturally. This sort of thing has never happened before. He feels responsible."

Nick's detective mind was already considering possibilities. "I assume all the doors and windows were checked for possible break-ins?"

"First thing. The door locks were undisturbed. The windows are permanently sealed, since the museum is climate-controlled to protect the artifacts."

Nick stopped their progress, letting Judas mosey over to drink from the edge of a glittering stream. "Has to be an inside job unless one of your visitors somehow managed to smuggle those blankets out inside a roomy coat or a bag of some sort."

"That would be hard to do, since the case locks weren't broken, either. Only a few of us work on Saturdays, so not everyone was in today. Jason's planning to call everyone over the weekend to tell them he's holding a Monday-morning meeting, then question each one separately."

"You have any hunches?"

"Not really. I know everyone who works there, most for years. I can't believe any one of them is a thief. Of course, someone may have lost their keys and the person finding them could have made duplicates. Or perhaps keys were stolen."

"Or someone slipped a duplicate key to someone, for a price."

"It's difficult for me to believe that." She looked up into eyes as blue as the overhead sky and, as always, felt that funny little hitch in the vicinity of her heart. "I know you're pretty busy right now, but do you think you might find time to go in with me Monday and see if you can help Jason? He's really worried. His job may be on the line."

"Of course I will." Nick bent to place a kiss on her nose. Then, unable to resist any longer, he drew her close into an openmouthed kiss that had his heart thundering in moments. He didn't want it to end and could sense she didn't, either. "What do you say we climb back on Judas and go home? I want you naked on your grandmother's quilt in front of a roaring fire."

"My grandmother would turn purple if she heard you say that." But her pulse was pounding at the mere thought.

He smiled down at her. "I doubt that. Manya's some lady. I'll bet, in her day, she wasn't always staid and proper. She's got this kind of lusty laugh."

"I understand you've been seeing quite a bit of her."

"Yeah, I'm crazy about her. Almost as crazy as I am about you." He took a deep breath and decided to tell her. "Do you know what she asked me yesterday?"

Sara came down off her tiptoes. "I'm afraid to hear."

"She asked when I was going to marry you."

Sara felt a chill wind come up quite suddenly. "It's getting cold. We'd better be getting back."

Avoidance. She was a master at it. Positioning Judas so he could mount him, Nick decided that very soon Miss Sara Lewis was going to have to face a few facts.

Like he was the man she was going to marry.

He'd bought her a gift—a nightgown in the palest shade of peach, with tiny straps, the silk fabric caressing her every curve and ending midthigh. Sara gazed at her reflection in the mirror and felt more feminine than she ever had before. She'd never had money to indulge in beautiful nightwear. She'd brushed her hair after her bath and now reached for her fragrant lotion.

Nerves skittered along her spine as she rubbed moisturizer into her skin. She was doing something she'd never truly done before, not like this. She was preparing for her lover.

Lover. The very word had her blood warming.

They'd ridden Judas back to Henry's place, then stayed and talked for a little while to the lonely old man. After Henry's second shot of his potent whiskey, Nick had gotten him to agree to see Kane at the clinic tomorrow morning, since the doctor usually stopped in on weekends, donating his time to the res. It was remarkable the way old Henry had taken to Nick.

They'd walked over to her car then and had driven to her house. Nick had seemed to want to take over the evening plans, so she'd let him. While she'd made a salad, he'd taken a shower, then he'd grilled catfish fillets along with hush puppies that he'd picked up in town earlier. After they ate, he'd given her the nightgown and asked if she'd put it on while he built a fire.

Sara put the cap back on the bottle of lotion, wondering why she was suddenly so nervous. Then it came to her. The whole evening orchestrated by Nick smacked of a goodbye scene. Had he narrowed down his suspects in Charlie Avery's murder to one viable guilty person? Was he about to go to Judd and arrest the responsible individual, then be on his way next week? Was this to be their farewell weekend?

She felt a jumble of emotional reactions. From the beginning, she'd known they were opposites, wrong for one another. Despite all the good things he was doing on the res, he would leave. And, though she knew he wanted her, love was another whole subject. She hadn't had the courage to ask him what he'd said to Manya when her grandmother had mentioned marriage. He'd been smiling as he told her. She prayed he hadn't laughed at Manya's question.

Even if, wild though the thought was, Nick did love her and wanted her to marry him, he'd also want her to leave Laughing Horse, to live in Butte or elsewhere with him. She couldn't do that. She belonged here, among her own people, where she could do the most good.

So it was hopeless. He would go, as she wanted him to. Didn't she?

Hands trembling only slightly, she opened the bathroom door and turned off the light. If he wanted a night to remember before he left, she would give him one, in spades. It was the least she could do. Squaring her shoulders, she walked into the living room.

She absolutely took his breath away.

Nick straightened from leaning against the mantel and just stared. He'd set the scene—built the fire, poured them each a glass of chilled apple cider and spread her grandmother's quilt on the carpeting in front of the raised hearth. He stood there wearing a pair of his new jeans and an unbuttoned flannel shirt.

And couldn't speak.

Seeing him nonplussed gave Sara the courage she'd lacked before entering the room. Slowly, she walked to him, stepping barefooted onto the quilt where he was standing. Stopping directly in front of him, she raised both arms and slid her hands over his chest, lingering to feel crisp hair and hard muscles as she inched upward. She kept going past his shoulders, her fingers reaching to caress the curls at his nape. Rising on tiptoe, she offered her mouth.

Nick took what she offered.

He came out of his trance, slipped his arms around her and pulled her to him, his mouth taking hers. His hands on her back tightened and bunched in the silky material, then slipped beneath to touch flesh already heated. He inhaled her freshly bathed scent and thought he'd die from the sweet pleasure.

But Sara wasn't going to let him lead, not this time. As her mouth made love to his, her hands shoved his shirt off his shoulders, then drifted down to the waistband of his jeans. She felt his stomach muscles quiver as she tugged the clasp open. Her tongue slipped into his mouth and mated with his as her fingers slowly slid the tab of his zipper downward. She felt more than heard his tremulous intake of breath.

With a sureness of purpose, she shoved his jeans down, then pressed a hand to his chest, indicating she wanted him to sit down on the quilt. Her eyes on his, she knelt and tugged off his pants. But when he reached to pull her to his side, she evaded his hand and instead stretched out on top of him. With her long, shiny black hair curtaining her face, she returned to plunder his mouth as his arms tightened around her.

His fingers moved up to grasp handfuls of her silken hair as his tongue dived deep inside the delicious hollows of her mouth. He hadn't thought she'd ever play the aggressor, yet he gloried in it. He hadn't known what it felt like to be wanted with such fervor, and he reveled in it. He hadn't known that the conqueror could be conquered so effortlessly.

Hot, wild desire coursed through Sara's veins with the speed of light as her mouth rained kisses over his face, the strong line of his throat, the muscular width of his chest. She heard the crackling of the fire as if from a distance and smelled the woodsy scent of the logs mingled with the heady fragrance of man. Her hands raced over him, frantic to touch everywhere, to know everything about him. Sensations piled on top of sensations as dark passions took over.

For tonight, he was hers.

He needed to get some control back, Nick thought as his hazy mind tried to concentrate. He felt his breath hiss from him as she shifted and her small, clever hands moved beneath the waistband of his briefs and shoved them off. Her mouth was back on his as her fingers closed around him.

And he was lost.

He wanted to see her wearing only firelight. With unsteady fingers, he reached for the hem of her gown. "This is beautiful on you. But I want to look at you without it."

Slowly, Sara maneuvered until she was astride his waist, then she paused. Taking her sweet time, she inched her gown up and over her head, tossing it aside, her dark fall of hair settling around her. Her bronze skin glistened in the light from the flames as her dark eyes met his. She saw desire there and admiration. And something else that had her frowning, trying to read it.

Then it was gone and he was skimming the backs of his fingers over first one breast, then the other. They both watched as her skin warmed, with heated blood rushing to the surface. His blue eyes darkened as his arousal deepened. Again she saw that strange hint of something resembling anger in his gaze.

"I hate every man who's ever touched you before me."

"No man has ever touched me before you." Her voice was thick, husky. "No man ever will again." She knew that to be true, and could have wept with the knowledge.

The need to possess her, to make her truly his, all but overwhelmed Nick as he tried to ease her onto her back.

"No. Not this time." This time, they'd play it her way. Rising above him, she took him inside her as they both watched, then she shifted and took him deeper. Leaning forward, she touched her mouth to his.

But dark needs inside Nick compelled him to take over. His movements became desperate, frantic, slightly mad. He drove her and himself, desire-dampened skin against tender flesh. He broke the kiss so he could watch her, keeping his eyes locked with hers as they climbed together. He thought he'd remember her beautiful face flushed with passion until he was a very old man. Her eyes were cloudy with desire, but open and aware. Had he ever seen anything as beautiful as the sensual pleasure of watching Sara wanting him? No. Never.

At last he felt her body tighten, then convulse, as her hands clenched on his shoulders. He waited a long moment, watching her eyelids turn pink with a sensual flush. Then he joined her in an explosion that had him losing himself in the sweet wonder that was Sara.

Ten

She lay snuggled close to him on the quilt, warmed by the fire as he held her. She could feel his heartbeat slowing beneath her ear as it rested on his chest. She was quiet, letting her tangled emotions settle.

Nick angled his head so he could see her face. "You surprise me, Sara. That was pretty wild. And wonderful."

"Mmm. I thought so, too."

"I hope I wasn't too rough. A woman like you deserves tenderness and romance."

Oddly, his words broke her mood. Sara eased back, sitting up, reaching for the gown she'd tossed aside, feeling a sudden need for even its skimpy protective covering. Slipping it on, she shook back her hair and met his watchful gaze. "What do you know of a woman like me?"

Nick bent his elbow and propped his head in his hand. "Not enough. Do you want to tell me more?"

Perhaps it was time. "I want to tell you something—something about my past. Maybe then you'll understand a lot of other things, too." Like why a relationship between them would never work.

He'd known she had secrets, could see them in her eyes. He was encouraged that finally she felt like revealing them. It was the beginning of trust. "All right. I'm listening."

It was a difficult subject, made all the harder since he lay before her, totally unselfconscious in his nakedness. Sara twisted her hands and searched for the right words. "I told you earlier that I'd met a man my last year in college. I didn't mention that he was tall, blond and blue eyed."

Just his luck. "And every time you look at me, you see him?"

"At first, it was like that." She studied his facial features one by one, taking her time. "But not anymore." She shifted her gaze to the fire, because it was easier to continue that way. "Jack came from a wealthy family. Ranchers with a huge spread, their own plane, all kinds of holdings—and he was an only son. I didn't know any of that when we started seeing each other. He was so much fun and so romantic. I thought myself desperately in love, as only the very young can fool themselves into believing. And perhaps I was going through a rebellious stage, as well. The Native American who wins the all-American boy."

Nick heard the bitterness creeping into her voice and kept silent.

"We became lovers. I should have guessed what was coming, but I was absolutely blinded by my feelings for him. Jack said he thought keeping our affair secret was exciting, meeting in quiet, out-of-the-way places, driving to distant motels. When I think back, I wonder how I could have been so trusting, so naive."

"Love makes us all behave stupidly at times."

Absently, Sara nodded her agreement. "There ought to be a course taught in school for the very young. Affairs of the Heart 101. Something to warn them how crushing it is to discover you've been in love all alone."

"Maybe they could make it a curriculum requirement."

Sara detected a hint of self-pity in her voice and cleared her throat. "I suppose you've guessed the ending. As graduation approached, my head was spinning with plans, with possibilities. When I finally found the courage to speak them out loud, I got the surprise of my life. Jack was shocked to hear I might actually have thought we had a future, that he'd take me home to meet his family. My goodness, his dear mother, who controlled the purse strings since the money originated in her family, would faint dead away at the thought of the heir apparent walking in with a real live Indian woman."

Nick took her hands then and felt her fingers curl around his. At least now he understood why the differences between them loomed even larger to Sara than he'd imagined. "Not all white families feel that way. Very few, actually. Certainly mine doesn't."

She went on as if he hadn't spoken. "I was devastated and deeply humiliated. I'd been raised to be proud of who and what I am. Certainly I'd run into prejudice before, in Whitehorn and on campus, but I hadn't been expecting it from someone who'd made love with me." She stopped, swallowing, reaching for control. "I didn't stay to attend the graduation ceremonies, much to my mother's disappointment. I moved back home, feeling drained, soiled. And I had another shock coming. I discovered I was pregnant."

He caught the hitch in her voice and squeezed her hands.

"I decided that my baby's father didn't deserve to know his child. The baby would be mine and mine alone. I didn't tell anyone, just went about making my solitary plans. Then one night I started bleeding. Before long, I couldn't walk, the pain was so bad. I had to tell my mother. Kane wasn't a doctor yet and the clinic on the res hadn't been opened. There were no Native American doctors nearby. My grandmother called the tribal medicine woman and she came over. Later that night, I miscarried." She felt her lower lip tremble and pressed her hand to her mouth.

Wordlessly, Nick gathered her to him, cradling her head, smoothing her hair. She didn't weep, but he suspected she'd shed more than her share of tears for the loss of her child over the years. He ran his hand along her arm and her back, offering the comfort of his solid body.

For a long while she stayed pressed against him, absorbing, regrouping. Finally, she straightened. "I thought you probably realized I had more than a passing interest in rushing Alice to the hospital that night. Just as you did. I've always wondered, and probably always will, whether, if I'd been able to get to a hospital, my baby would have lived. We'll never know."

"Your mother didn't trust the white hospital?"

"That was part of it. Everything happened so fast. I started feeling nauseated right after dinner. I thought it was indigestion. When you're young and you've never been pregnant before, you don't know what's normal and what isn't. Then suddenly, there was so much blood...."

"Don't think about it anymore. It's over."

"Is it?" Eyes dark with pain looked into his. "Will it ever be over? Tell me, is it for you? Tell me you can walk down a street, see a child about the age yours would now be and remain unaffected."

It was Nick's turn to stare into the flames. "He'd be seven now," he said softly.

"Mine would be eight. Do you see what I mean?"

Frowning, he turned back to her. "Aren't you the one who told me I had to let go of the guilt?"

"Yes. You shouldn't feel guilty for something you couldn't prevent, and neither should I. It's the sorrow over an irretrievable loss that stays with me, not guilt."

"I feel that, too. But we have to get on with our lives. We've grieved a lot of years." He gripped her hands again, needing to make her see. "The way to get over a disappointing love is to find a new one. I never thought I'd hear myself saying that, but it's true. And one day you'll have another child, one who'll make the loss of the first one easier to live with."

She searched his eyes and saw that he believed what he was saying. "You see only what you want to see, Nick. Here on the res you found openly suspicious looks at first. Now Henry likes you because you've been a friend to him. And Jackson's accepted you. Manya's even asked when you plan to marry me. Manya knows how long I've been alone and sad, and she wants me to be happy. She is old and hopes you're the answer, that she'll see me happy before she dies. But if we were to—to get together, you might find some of these very people cooling toward you. We're polite to temporary guests, but hospitality can wear thin after a while. My father tried for years and couldn't find acceptance."

Nick shook his head. "I don't believe that. Maybe he didn't try hard enough, or maybe he had a chip on his shoulder. People are people—that's what I believe. If you treat them right, they won't turn against you."

"People have certain prejudices pounded into them in their youth. Indians blame the white man for their current situation. Whites don't respect Indians, have no use for them, and, since they're a huge majority, don't have to pretend to be nice or fair or kind. You think that if, for instance, I were to go with you to Butte or the town where your parents live, everyone there would welcome me with open arms?"

"Yes, I certainly do."

Sara rose, knowing they were getting nowhere. "Then you're more naive than I thought you were."

Stamping down his anger, Nick rose and faced her, taking hold of her upper arms. "Let's not talk about other people. Let's talk about you and me. Look into my eyes, *really look,* and tell me what you see."

"Nick, I'm not in the mood for games."

He tightened his hold. "This isn't a game. Tell me."

Sighing, she looked into his eyes. She would humor him. "Desire. I see desire. And I want you to know I love knowing you want me."

"Desire, yes, definitely. Go on. Look some more."

She studied the blue depths, trying very hard now to read his feelings. "I see compassion and understanding. Tolerance. But that's you, not the people you must live among."

"Don't stop." He leaned toward her, very close now. "Deeper now."

She stared, trying to see what he meant. What she saw had her wanting to back away, but he held on to her. "I—I'm not sure."

"Yes, you are." He'd made his point. He knew it and so did she. "You see love. I love you, Sara. I'm not Jack or your father or any other man you've known. I love you just the way you are. I wouldn't change a thing, except possibly your stubbornness."

She wanted to believe—oh, God, how badly she wanted to believe. Moisture formed in her eyes.

"Did Jack ever say those three little words to you?"

She shook her head and two tears trailed down her cheeks.

"I'm going to say them, regularly and often, until you believe them. I love you, Sara. Love you, love *you.*" His hands moved into her hair and his mouth crushed hers, his need to convince her taking over. Before the kiss ended, he scooped her into his arms and headed for the bedroom.

* * *

On Sunday morning, the air was cold and crisp, the sun bright in the sky. Winter seemed to be holding off after its early freak storm, Nick thought, as he offered his gloved hand to Sara. They'd decided that a hike in the semiwilderness area in the northwestern section of the reservation was just what they needed to blow the cobwebs from the brain.

Her booted foot slipped on a patch of frozen snow, but she kept from falling by clutching Nick's hand. "Whew! I'm out of shape." Stopping a moment, she inhaled deeply. "Is there anywhere on earth where the air is cleaner, fresher, than here?"

Nick looked around. "I don't think so. You okay, or do you want to rest?"

She glanced up toward the top of the next rise and saw an eagle soar high above a Douglas fir. "Let's keep going." Her muscles might ache tonight, but she needed the exercise.

Another set of muscles were pleasantly achy, she thought, hiding a smile. Nick was insatiable when it came to making love and, much to Sara's surprise, she'd found she felt the same. Their serious and conflicting discussion the night before hadn't dimmed their desire. Had, in fact, increased it.

Hearing that he loved her had fueled her passion and warmed her heart, though she still had trouble believing it. She knew she loved him, too, with a love much stronger than any she'd known. However, she hadn't told him, and probably wouldn't. They still hadn't had the really important discussion, the one that centered around the question where do we go from here?

Love, as her parents' marriage proved, wasn't always enough. It didn't always overcome economic problems, racial differences, bigotry in the world around them. And then there was the problem of where they would live, should marriage be a serious consideration.

From the beginning, she'd known of Nick's wanderlust, his need to be free, to get up and go. And he knew of her commitment to Laughing Horse. Did he think he could change her mind about that, as he had about so many things?

"You're doing it again," Nick commented as he glanced over his shoulder and saw her introspective expression. "You're moving off somewhere where I can't reach you."

Putting on a smile, she came alongside him. "I'm right here." Rising on tiptoe, she kissed him.

Suddenly they heard the crackling of twigs being trampled, and they jumped apart. "Who's there?" Nick asked, peering through the thicket of tall aspens to their right.

An older man with scraggly salt-and-pepper hair falling to his shoulders stepped out onto the path a short distance from them. His boots were scuffed, his jeans almost threadbare and his brown corduroy jacket ill fitting over his slender frame. His blue eyes flew from one to the other, looking kind of wild. "Who wants to know?" he asked in a croaky voice.

"Mr. Gilmore," Sara said, stepping forward, recognizing the old man. "It's Sara Lewis from the reservation."

Homer Gilmore squinted at her, brushing an unclean hand over his bearded chin. "Who'd you say?"

Sara repeated her name. "I work at the museum in Whitehorn, remember? I'm a friend of Kane's."

At mention of the doctor, the old fellow brightened. "Kane's a good man. I always told Moriah that Kane's a good man." He shifted his narrowed eyes up at Nick.

Sara introduced them. "Nick's investigating Charlie Avery's murder. They found his remains not far from here."

Homer nodded. "Charlie was always shiftless." He bent to pick up a gnarled stick, then poked at the ground with it. "Don't know why so many folks are out here these days. A man can't have any privacy anymore."

Sara had always felt sorry for Homer Gilmore. Since his wife had taken his daughter away, he'd become a hermit, a man who seemed lost and alone. "We're out hiking. It's such a beautiful day."

Homer swiped at a drippy nose. "That's what she said, too. Bird watching." He gave a bark of a laugh. "Endangered species. Ain't no special birds out here. I ought to know. Been living in these parts all my sixty-two years."

"Who'd you run across bird watching, Mr. Gilmore?" Nick asked, always curious. He recalled Sara telling him about Homer Gilmore, his daughter Moriah and Kane.

Taking out a red handkerchief, Homer blew his nose before answering. "Mary Jo, that's who. Told me she got lost, sprained her ankle and couldn't walk back. Asked me to help her." He shook his head. "Don't seem to be the sort who'd climb around on these rocks and watch for birds, do you think?"

Mary Jo had to be Dugin Kincaid's wife, Nick guessed. And he had to agree with Homer that the one time he'd seen Mary Jo in the Hip Hop Café, well dressed and sort of delicate looking, she hadn't impressed him as the sort who'd go hiking or bird watching. "When was this?"

"Couple days ago." Homer scratched at the frozen ground with his stick. "Said she's marking down bird sightings for the Sierra Club. Can't imagine Dugin letting her hang around with that bunch."

Sara didn't think Dugin controlled Mary Jo's comings and goings, but refrained from saying so. "You helped her find her way back then?"

Homer nodded, his eyes on the ground. "I led her out to where she'd left her car by the road. But funny thing. When she left me, she wasn't limping no more." He shook his head. "Can't understand that woman. House like she's got, what's she doing marching around out here?"

A good question, Nick thought. He might just have to satisfy his curiosity by checking out Mary Jo Kincaid. He nodded toward the crest of the hill. "We're going to climb on up there, take in the view."

Homer grunted. "Not much different from down here, 'cept it's higher." Using his stick, he plodded off into the trees without saying another word.

Nick took Sara's hand and started up. "A strange duck, that one."

"I feel sorry for him. He's got no one."

He pulled her into the circle of his arms. "You empathize with everyone. That's just one of the reasons I love you." He saw the doubt in her eyes, and the need. It would take time, he knew. He lowered his head to kiss her.

Jason Eagle was a big man, every bit as tall as Jackson Hawk, but older and leaning toward flab. His dark hair was streaked with gray and worn in two pigtails, and his dark face wore a worried frown as he sat behind the desk in his office at the Native American Museum. "So, what did you learn?" he asked Nick as the investigator sat down in the chair across from him. Sara took the second one.

They'd arrived early, and while Jason questioned each employee individually, Sara had taken Nick on a tour, showing him the cases where the two blankets had been on display, all windows and doors, each room on every floor.

She'd answered his questions and then they'd returned to Jason's office.

"My best guess is that this has to be an inside job," Nick told the head curator. "Did you learn anything questioning your staff?"

Jason shook his head, his frown deepening. "No one knows anything, saw anything or suspects anyone."

"Did anyone not show up for your meeting?"

"No. Everyone showed. All but two of our employees have been with us for many years."

"Who are those two?" Nick asked. Usually thefts from inside were committed by newer employees, often ones who'd secured the job only long enough to size up the place and commit the felony.

"Amos Redfox, a teenage boy who helps out with framing, labeling, cleanup. And John Thundercloud, our handyman. Both are part-time."

"Do both have keys?"

"All our employees have keys," Sara explained. "We have staggered shifts. They have to be able to open up, or lock the doors at night."

"Do any of your employees work alone, say at night or on weekends?"

Jason glanced at Sara before answering. "Amos and John, occasionally. But both are trustworthy. John's a family man with a baby on the way and he works at least one other job. Amos's father is my closest friend. I can't believe either would steal."

Nick leaned back, crossing his legs. "Someone did, Mr. Eagle. I've looked at the other blankets. It wouldn't be difficult to roll them up and take them out wrapped in brown paper or a large canvas bag, even during museum hours. You have only one security guard on duty and he can't be everywhere."

Sara had introduced him to Noah Breedlove, a thin man in his seventies. He'd been the only security guard at the museum for the last ten years. Nick doubted the old man's presence would put off any determined thief. "Are the door keys the same as the keys to the glass cases?"

"No. Those are separate. There are only three. Sara has one and so do I. The third hangs over there." He indicated a keyboard on his side wall, where several labeled keys hung on silver chains.

"Do you keep your office door locked?"

"It's open when I'm here, but locked otherwise. I'm the only one who has a key to it."

"You haven't lost your keys lately, or remember leaving them around at any time?"

Jason stood, showing a large key chain attached to a belt loop of his pants, then tucked into a side pocket. "This is how I have them, always."

Nick propped his fingers in a steeple thoughtfully. "Then someone had to have come into your office when you were on the premises but busy elsewhere, gotten the key to the case and had a duplicate made. Or just plain lifted it, and no one noticed that it was missing."

Again, Jason glanced at Sara, nervously this time. "I don't see how that could have happened. I'm rarely far from my office."

"Jason, what happened isn't your fault," Sara reassured him. "Nick will find out who did it."

Pleased at her faith in him, Nick sat forward. "How difficult would it be to get something new in, either something real or a very good fake, and make it known to one and all that it would be on display soon? When it arrives, you put it in a special case. And then we wait."

Jason raised his brows. "You mean, set a trap?"

"Right. Our man may not be working alone. We'll set it up, and then you and I will find a good place to hide where we can watch the case. See if we can smoke him out. He's gotten away with something now and probably feels fairly confident. If not too big a fuss is made over the first theft, he'll think that the insurance will cover it, so no big loss. I believe he'll try again."

Jason looked skeptical. Trusting a white man, even one recommended so highly by Sara, wasn't easy for him. But the only other alternative would be to call the sheriff. And if he did that, he'd have to notify the insurance company. Their premiums would skyrocket and their budget was already strained. "If only we had the money to have a good security system installed. Or at least to hire more security guards." He walked around his desk and paced the width of his small office.

"Maybe if we catch the thief and recover the goods, we can talk the board into holding some sort of fund-raiser to obtain cash for a security system," Sara suggested. Jason was a good man, one she liked working with. Too bad his hands were tied by lack of money, as was the case with so many Indian-operated facilities. "Maybe we could get some publicity from the newspapers and generate interest in tax-free contributions."

"Maybe," Jason muttered. "And maybe it won't snow anymore in Montana." He was angry and bitter. But he had a job to do. Turning, he stopped near Nick. "Thank you for coming and for your analysis of the situation. I'd like to take you up on your offer."

"Great." Nick stood. "Just tell me when you've got things set up and I'll be here."

"The first robbery took place over the weekend," Jason said, walking with Sara and Nick to the door. "I'll make sure we have something special, advertised as very valuable, in here by next Friday. Maybe we'll catch us a thief." He held his hand out to Nick.

Nick shook his hand, then strolled to Sara's office with her. Inside, he closed the door and drew her into a long, satisfying kiss. "Mmm, you smell good."

"Thank you so much for offering to help Jason. He's taking this all very hard, but you've given him hope."

"If only it works..." He checked his watch. "I've got to get going." They'd driven in separate cars. "I'll see you back at the house. A little after five?"

"Better make it six." She rose on tiptoe for another kiss. How was it she couldn't seem to get enough of kissing him?

"Don't be any later or I'll come looking for you. And I'm picking up dinner."

Sara watched him leave, wondering how she was going to be able to watch him walk away for good one day soon.

The Kincaid house was imposing, with two pillars at each end of a sweeping porch, a separate wing on each side and beautifully kept grounds. Nick parked Sara's Volkswagen in the circular drive and slowly got out. At the end of a side drive, several barns and other outbuildings, a couple of corrals and men at work where visible. The property stretched as far back as he could see. But then, Dugin was the wealthiest man in Whitehorn, so the vastness of his ranch came as no surprise.

What he'd learned about Dugin's wife hadn't surprised Nick, either.

He'd just come from a visit to the local chapter of the Sierra Club and a nice chat with two members. Both of them knew Mary Jo Kincaid by sight if not in person, and had told him she was not now nor had she ever been one of their members. They didn't have anyone assigned to log sightings of endangered species in the wilderness area Nick had mentioned, or anywhere else. He'd come away pleased that his naturally suspicious mind had been right.

Still curious, he'd decided to pay a visit on the lady herself. She'd certainly indulged in studying him in depth at the Hip Hop Café that day at lunch. It was only right he return the favor. He knew that Mary Jo had nothing to do with either the murder investigation or the museum theft. His visit was triggered simply by his inquisitive nature.

Nick stepped onto the porch and rang the bell. Less than a minute passed before the large door swung open and Mary Jo stood before him, wearing an open red coat, high heels and a surprised frown. He'd been expecting a uniformed maid or butler.

"Yes?" she asked, her voice soft.

"Mrs. Kincaid, I'm Nick Dean. I'm new in town, conducting an investigation and—"

"Yes, I know. You're the one who thinks Charlie Avery was murdered." She swung the door wide open. "I have to go out shortly, but you might as well come in for a few minutes." She shut the door as he stepped in, then led him into a large living room with a massive stone fireplace at the far end. "Why, I wonder, won't folks let poor Charlie rest in peace? The man probably fell and hit his head, and here you are, trying to make something of nothing, prying into things that happened so long ago."

"No, ma'am. From the angle of the wound, someone took a good-size rock to his head." Nick said, watching her search through a handbag and come up with a pair of leather gloves.

Mary Jo's hand flew to her mouth. "Oh, my. That's simply terrible. Just awful."

"Yes, I agree." She hadn't invited him to sit on the sofa or the matching love seats grouped by the fireplace, so he stood, one hand in his pocket. "His remains were found in the same area you were wandering around in a couple of days ago."

Her brow wrinkled prettily. "Me? Now, when could that have been? I really don't go out all that much."

Nick wasn't sure why, but something about the way she spoke didn't ring true to him. "I believe you said you were out bird watching when you sprained your ankle and Homer Gilmore helped you find your way back."

"Oh, yes." Her smile was sweet. "I remember now. I often help out the Sierra Club. They catalog sightings of certain endangered species."

"Is that a fact? I was just over there talking with Alex Morris and Pamela Brown. They said you weren't even a member."

Mary Jo fussed at her nose with a lace hankie, buying a bit of time. "No, I'm not, but I give them a hand now and then. My husband, Dugin, is a prominent member of this community, Mr. Dean. As his wife, it's my obligation to help out wherever I can." She waved manicured fingers, indicating the dining room through the archway. "Would you care for a cup of tea? Dugin and I like strangers to feel welcome in Whitehorn. I'm sorry he's not in or I'd introduce you."

"No, thanks. I've got to be going." Yet he hesitated. "How did you sprain your ankle that day?"

"Why, by looking up into the trees for birds instead of watching where I was stepping, of course. Clumsy of me." She walked with him to the foyer and opened the door, ending their visit rather abruptly. "Tell me, how is your investigation going, or have you given up?"

"It's coming along. And no, ma'am, I never give up. Thanks for your time." With a nod, Nick left.

Mary Jo Kincaid slowly closed the door behind him and leaned against the solid wood, fighting a shiver. Face-to-face with a detective—even a small-town investigator like Nick Dean—had her reluctantly remembering a period of her life she'd just as soon forget forever.

But the memories popped up at the oddest times. She and Floyd working together, hopping buses and freighters when times were tough, then cars and sometimes planes when a good con job paid off. Floyd had saved her from the streets and taught her a lot. Nick reminded her of the cop that had arrested her and Floyd once. Fortunately, there hadn't been enough evidence for a conviction. But after that, Mary Jo could always smell a cop a mile away.

Nick Dean had the tenacity of all cops. That's what worried her. The more he poked around, the more chance there was that he'd turn up something she'd just as soon leave buried—literally and figuratively. Too many people around town recalled that Floyd had shown up and been found dead right here at the Kincaid house the day she and Dugin had married. The police still hadn't a clue about what he was or why he'd come, and Mary Jo wanted to keep it that way.

Of course, when she'd thrown Floyd over way back when and had taken up with Frank Travers, that alliance had nearly killed her.

Taking a deep breath, Mary Jo straightened and tugged her leather gloves on. All that had happened many years ago. The Past Should Stay Put, was her motto. Now she was Mrs. Dugin Kincaid, the wealthiest woman in miles.

And she wasn't about to let anyone rock her comfortable boat.

Eleven

The rural strip mall was located on Willow Brook Road in the southern end of Whitehorn. Nick pulled the Bug into the gravel parking lot alongside a chestnut mare tethered to a hitching post. He'd been told this was the largest ranch supply store for miles around. By the looks of the crowded lot filled with vans and pickups, Melissa Avery had been right.

Stepping out, he nodded to a burly cowhand who greeted him in a friendly manner, then went on into the main store. Blinking as his eyes adjusted to the dimness after the bright afternoon sunshine outside, Nick looked around. Horton's Hardware & Feed Store was typical of many found throughout ranching communities, with crowded and cluttered shelves offering a variety of feed, tools and farm equipment. A couple of men in work clothes were wandering the aisles, two were standing at the checkout counter, their purchases on flat carts, and at the back was an open stall where grain sacks could be loaded onto trucks. Hands in his pockets, Nick strolled around until he found the section he wanted.

Again he'd visited the garage where the burnt wreckage of his Blazer was being kept and had talked the police mechanic into allowing him to sift through the rubble. On his first trip there, Judd Hensley had told him that he suspected dynamite as the cause of the explosion. On careful examination of random parts of his vehicle, Nick had found a fragment of one dynamite stick with part of the serial code still legible. He'd copied it down before leaving, wondering if the sheriff was checking out the possible purchaser.

From working in his father's business and at various ranches, Nick knew that dynamite was sold in sticks, available in varying lengths. They were color coded by the federal government, with serial numbers on each stick and box. Purchasers had to produce a driver's license and fill out a form to buy dynamite, the same as for guns or ammunition. Builders often used dynamite to blast out sections of solid rock before digging foundations. Ranchers used it for a variety of purposes, and nearly every ranch had dynamite in its storeroom.

Now if he could only locate the purchaser of dynamite sticks marked with the serial number he'd copied down, chances were good he'd have the name of the man who'd sabotaged his truck and, perhaps, who'd killed Charlie Avery. Nick's examination of the dynamite display revealed that the boxes were arranged numerically. In moments, he found the series he was searching for.

Noticing a lull at the checkout, Nick walked over to the short, balding man behind the counter and introduced himself.

Chet Horton studied Nick's card a moment, then pocketed it. "Heard you were in town. What can I do for you?"

"I'd like to see the book you keep with signatures of the people who buy dynamite here. I assume you list all the serial codes alongside their names?"

"Sure do. This about your Blazer being blown up?"

Nick had realized by now that nearly everyone in Whitehorn knew him, if not by sight then by name, small towns being what they were. Therefore, they'd have heard about the fire that totaled his Blazer. But he'd thought that the sheriff had said he hadn't mentioned specifics, only that he suspected foul play. "How'd you know about that?"

Chet shrugged. "Most folks know. Not much else can cause a fire like that 'cept dynamite. 'Less you're talking incendiary bombs, and I don't know as though anyone around here would know how to put one of them together." He reached toward a shelf beneath the counter and pulled out a well-used ledger. "Judd know you're here asking about this?"

Nick decided to hedge. "Sheriff Hensley and I are working together to find the person responsible."

Horton paused a moment, then turned the book toward Nick. "Guess it's all right." He pointed to a small table near the back as a tall man in overalls moved to the counter to pay for his purchases. "You can go over there."

It took Nick less than ten minutes to find the series of numbers he was looking for. Though the last digit was missing on the scrap he'd located, the numerical order showed that the stick he'd identified had been included in a particular box bought by one specific rancher.

That man was Ethan Walker.

Arnie McDonald wasn't in a friendly mood. Nick had caught up with him cleaning out horse stalls on the Tyler Ranch, where he was currently employed. It was four in the afternoon, with a chill wind blowing outside, hinting at snow in the air. Arnie was behind and still had a good three hours work ahead of him before he could quit for the day, clean up and get his supper. The last thing he wanted was to be answering questions asked by a detective who wouldn't let him be.

"I don't have time for you today," Arnie said, raking a stall with short, rapid movements. "I got too much work to do."

"You can keep on working," Nick told him. "I just have a couple of quick questions. You remember you told me that you'd seen Ethan Walker and Charlie Avery fighting?"

"Yeah. So what?" Arnie grunted as he scooped manure into a pile outside the stall door.

"You said you thought they'd fought over a woman, but Ethan says Charlie was drunk, so he hit him. Knocked him out, even. I'd like to know what really happened."

Arnie moved to the next stall. "Guess you got to decide which one of us you're gonna believe then."

Nick propped his arms on the stall. "Let's say it's you I believe. I need to know if you can remember the name of that woman."

Arnie went on raking, quiet so long that Nick thought he wasn't going to answer. Finally, he glanced up at the detective, leaning on the handle of his rake. "You ever hear folks around here mention Lexine Baxter?"

Nick came to attention, but his expression didn't change. "Cameron Baxter's daughter? Heard she was a wild one."

"That she was." Arnie McDonald seemed to be struggling with his pride, before he continued, "I don't care how many stories Ethan told you or whatever. I heard what I heard and I ain't no damn liar. Them two fought over Lexine Baxter."

"Only that one time?"

Arnie rearranged his hat. "More than once. Ethan was sweet on her and he didn't like Charlie, an older, married man, fooling with her. Charlie laughed at Ethan's warning. That did it. Ethan went for him. Knocked him out with two solid punches. Charlie went down like a sack of flour." Arnie returned to his raking. "Deserved it, too, most of us felt. But Ethan's a hothead. He don't have many friends to this day."

Nick couldn't help wondering if Arnie's dislike for Ethan was causing him to distort his memory, or perhaps his distaste for the philandering Charlie had added embellishments. But still, there was the indisputable evidence that Ethan had purchased the dynamite that had caused the explosion to his Blazer. And if what Arnie said was true, Ethan had had a running dispute with Charlie that gave him motive. Along with the rancher's well-known hot temper, everything added up to a viable murder suspect.

"If it came to that, would you be willing to testify in court about what you just told me?"

Arnie looked up, suddenly nervous. "Now, wait a minute. I don't want to get involved in something that happened twenty years ago. That Ethan's bad news. He'll come gunnin' for me, sure as shootin'."

"He won't be able to if he's arrested. The sheriff will protect you." Nick hoped he sounded more convincing about that than he felt. So far the sheriff hadn't exactly knocked himself out trying to solve either Charlie's murder or his own Blazer explosion.

"I don't know," Arnie said with a worried frown. "I got to think that over."

That part would be out of his hands, Nick thought. Arnie wouldn't be able to ignore a subpoena, not if he wanted to stay out of jail himself. He didn't think this was the time to remind the man of that point of law.

"Thanks for your help." Glancing out the open barn door, Nick saw that the sky was growing darker and it had begun to snow. He would think over what he'd learned today and go to Judd with it tomorrow. "I'll be in touch,"

he told Arnie, then hurried to Sara's car. He still had dinner to pick up and he wanted to beat her home.

"I'm not sure which I love more, making love with you
or lying in your arms all night long." Sara sighed with
contentment, a feeling she was getting all too used to.

"Thanks a lot," Nick said, cradling her against his
body, just cooling down from their sensual lovemaking.

She reached to tug playfully at a tuft of his chest hair.
"Don't let your ego get in the way here. I love how you
make me feel when we make love. But there's a peaceful-
ness when I sleep in your arms, a feeling of being safe, that
I've never experienced before. It's equally wonderful."
And equally frightening, for it would be yet another thing
she would lose when he left her.

"Since you put it that way, I'll forgive you." He snuggled closer. "I feel the same." Beth had preferred twin beds
during their brief marriage. Having spent her growing-up
years sharing not only a room but a bed with several sis-
ters, she liked sleeping alone. "I love to hold you, to have
you close to me." He gazed out the window, where they'd
purposely left open the drapes so they could watch the
snow fall. "Especially on a night like this."

"I wish it would storm all night and tomorrow, too. I
wish the snow would all but bury us here in this little
house, much deeper than on the night we met. I wish we
could stay here and hide from the world." The world that
would separate them. Sara blinked back a rush of tears,
knowing the cause of her melancholy.

Nick had told her he'd be visiting Judd tomorrow and
that they'd likely be arresting Ethan Walker for the murder of Charlie Avery.

His work in Whitehorn was nearly finished. She knew
he'd stay long enough to help Jason trap the museum

smuggler. Nick always kept his word. But after that he'd
no longer have a reason to remain. Stacks of lumber and
insulation sat under a plastic covering in her yard, waiting
to be installed in several more houses, but Sara didn't think
he'd stay to finish fixing up all the places that needed repair. After all, he had a business in Butte waiting for his
return and a partner who'd phoned twice during the last
week to discuss several cases. Nick had a life to take up
again, and she would be left with only poignant memories.

Nick felt the change in her breathing, as if her restless
thoughts were getting her agitated. He wished he knew
what to say that would calm her. "It isn't necessary for us
to hide, Sara. We have no reason to. We can hold our
heads up high wherever we go. If people don't accept us,
that's their problem, not ours. I love you. I wish you'd
believe that."

She wished she could, too. She lay quietly, watching the
snow for several minutes. "Actually, I think I like summer storms better than snowstorms. When I was little, I
used to sit on the covered porch of my mother's house and
watch the lightning flash in the sky, listen to the thunder,
smell the rain. Paul didn't like to be out when it was
storming, but I did. It's exciting, exhilarating."

Shifting, she turned to face him. "Being with you is like
being in the center of a storm. Just as exciting. Even more
exhilarating."

He knew she didn't want to discuss his declaration of
love or the cultural differences. She wanted to avoid it. He
should probably insist, get it all out so they could get past
it. But it was late and it had been a long day. He'd let it go
awhile longer and try to convince her with physical loving
what he so far hadn't been able to convince her of with
words.

Gathering her close, he touched his mouth to hers.

* * *

In Sara's kitchen, Nick dialed the Sheriff's number. He'd gotten word through Sara that Detective Sergeant Rafe Rawlings wanted him to call. Wondering what it was all about, he waited impatiently for someone to answer.

"Sheriff's Department, Rawlings here," came the deep-voiced answer.

"This is Nick Dean. You wanted to talk with me?"

"Yeah, right." Rafe shuffled papers on his desk until he found the one he needed. "I understand that you've traced the dynamite from your vehicle's explosion to Ethan Walker. Is that right?"

"That's right." Apparently, old man Horton from the hardware supply store had notified the sheriff that he'd been there.

"Along those same lines, I've been out to the cave where Avery's bones were found, re-examining the whole area thoroughly. Found a couple of interesting things."

Nick waited for the slow-talking man to continue.

"We found an old and battered lipstick case, a broken compact and some loose change."

Leaning back in his chair, Nick wondered what the detective was getting at. "Sounds like a woman dropped her purse."

"I thought so, too, though we didn't find one. But we did find an old class ring. The date inside goes back to the time of Charlie's disappearance. And the initials on it are EW."

A horse of another color, Nick thought. "And you think the ring belongs to Ethan Walker?"

"Don't know. I've got a couple of yearbooks from the high school for that time period and we're going through them now, seeing how many people have the initials E.W."

He doubted that very many would. "It doesn't look good for Ethan, though everything's circumstantial at this point. By the way, Ethan told me he had some things stolen from his barn recently. Even reported the theft to the Sheriff. Do you know anything about that?"

"Yeah, we've got the report somewhere. It sure doesn't mention an old class ring."

"I don't imagine most people keep their jewelry, old or new, in their barn," Nick answered. He'd never met Rafe Rawlings and wondered if he was as close-minded as the sheriff seemed to be.

"Judd would like you to bring that dynamite report in to us as soon as possible."

"I'd planned on coming by later today."

"Fine. See you then."

Nick hung up feeling inexplicably sad. It looked very much like Ethan was their man. Which meant that his job here was finished. Oddly, he had mixed emotions about that.

"You really think he's the one who killed my father?" Melissa asked Nick, studying him closely from across the booth. It was late morning and the Hip Hop wasn't very crowded, the breakfast diners already gone and the luncheon crowd not yet in. From the jukebox, Dolly Parton was telling the world about her coat of many colors.

"All evidence points to Ethan Walker," Nick said, repeating what he'd told her minutes ago when he'd walked in. "He had means, motive and opportunity. In talking with at least half the people who live in Whitehorn, neither Judd nor I have run across anyone else who had all three. And he's the one who purchased the dynamite used in destroying my Blazer."

"My God! Do you mean he intended to kill you, too?" Melissa's blue eyes were wide with shock.

"Well, he denies both the murder and sabotaging my vehicle. But as the murderer, he's the only one in town who would have benefited from my death, since I'd started asking around about a crime he'd thought he'd gotten away with."

Melissa shuddered. "He's been in here a few times. Not much. The man keeps to himself. He hardly says two words to anyone. Used to bring the newspaper and read it while he ate. He—he doesn't look like a killer."

Nick smiled. "I've been in police work a lot of years, Melissa. There's no certain look to killers. They range from innocent-appearing teenagers to sweet little old ladies, and everything in between."

Melissa drank her coffee, trying to warm herself during this chilling conversation. "Then Ethan's behind bars?"

"Yes." Nick had gone to the Walker Ranch with Judd and one of his deputies to arrest Ethan this morning, after presenting his evidence to the sheriff. Based on the dynamite numbers, Ethan was charged with Nick's attempted murder. He was also charged with Charlie's murder, based on eyewitnesses who'd overheard Ethan and Charlie quarreling the evening before he'd disappeared. The sheriff had seemed eager to put someone in jail so he'd be rid of Nick and his questioning of the residents.

"How'd he act when Judd went for him?"

"He didn't resist." But his hands had balled into fists and his eyes had blazed at Nick. "The only thing he said was, 'You've got the wrong man.'"

Melissa set down her cup and shifted her gaze out the window. "Do you think we do?"

Nick shrugged. "It's hard to tell. Most people arrested claim they're innocent. This is as good a circumstantial case as I've ever worked on. After twenty-odd years, what more could you hope for? There's no smoking gun that the killer buried in his backyard, no witness who saw the murder. We have to let the trial bring out all that and see if the facts prove him innocent or guilty."

"Are they going to search his place for the weapon? I mean, it has to be somewhere."

Nick nodded. "Judd's sent a crew to dig around some more in the area where the remains were discovered, though I frankly doubt they'll come up with much. Ground's frozen most everywhere. Ethan could have disassembled that weapon and buried it in any of a hundred places. Or tossed it in a lake somewhere. He'd be awfully stupid to have hidden it on his own ranch."

"I just wish I felt better about this. More relieved instead of concerned."

"I know how you feel. I'm not utterly convinced myself. Still, some of the facts are irrefutable." He reached across the table and patted her hand. "Don't worry. If Ethan's not guilty, the truth will come out."

Melissa sighed. "I certainly hope so." She finished her coffee. "So, what are your plans? Are you leaving now that your work here is finished? Or—or do you have reason to stay?"

Apparently Melissa, like several others, had heard rumors about Nick being seen in the company of Sara Lewis for several weeks now. Perhaps she'd even heard he'd been living with her. The owner of a café overhears more than most people. "I'm working on something local that I need to clear up before I return home." The stakeout at the museum was set for this Friday night, Jason Eagle had informed Nick only this morning. "After that, I'll be leaving." Hopefully not alone. "But I'll be back from time to time."

He'd already decided he wanted to finish insulating the homes on Laughing Horse, the work he'd begun. It wasn't his way to promise to do something, then quit. And he'd determined that the only way he could convince Sara to become his wife would be if he'd agree to spend equal amounts of time on the res as they did in Butte. Nick had no problem with that. If only she'd be willing to compromise.

Melissa reached into her pocket and handed him a folded check. "I believe this is the amount we agreed upon."

Nick looked at the check. "Wait a minute. This is way too much."

"No." Her voice was firm. "That's for expenses as well. And I want to know, is your insurance company compensating you for the Blazer?"

"Yes. There's still paperwork to fill out and send to the main office. These things take time, you know. But they're being very fair."

"Good. Then I don't feel so guilty about that loss. But please, you've certainly earned the rest of it—and probably more." Melissa turned as one of her waitresses beckoned her to the phone. "I have to go," she said, rising. She held out her hand. "Thanks, Nick. You've done a fine job."

He gripped her small hand in his. "I'll be in touch." He drained his coffee cup and stood, leaving money on the table for the waitress. He felt as he usually did after a case was closed—a mixture of sadness and elation. He'd probably be returning to testify at the trial.

Would Sara be his wife by then? he wondered.

Sara sat in the dim, chilly storeroom on a heavy packing box and squinted through a small crack in the door.

She could see no one in the anteroom where the delicate tapestry that Jason had on loan from an out-of-state museum was displayed. They'd decided to use it as a lure to flush out the smuggler, being careful not to make the trap too obvious. Two lights perfectly angled shone on the ancient piece, and Sara prayed fervently that they'd be able to prevent the valuable artifact from being stolen.

Jason had orchestrated the publicity himself, inviting the press and even a nearby radio station to preview the new hanging, which would then be on view to the general public starting Monday. But on this Friday night, the three of them waited to see if their bait would work.

Sara had insisted on accompanying Nick when he'd gone to meet Jason, saying that this was her department and she deserved to be in on anything that happened. Neither man had known how to talk her out of her stand, so here she was. Already it was three hours after Friday-night closing, and so far they hadn't heard even a mouse stirring.

Nick had warned them that they must not talk or move around, that they'd have to situate themselves as comfortably as possible, then sit tight. He'd been on many such stakeouts when he'd been with the police, so they'd deferred to his greater experience. That didn't mean they had to like it.

Sara glanced over at Jason, who was sitting on a folding chair, his expression that of a man listening hard. He also looked impatient and uncomfortable. The only one who seemed as if he could remain still as a statue for hours was Nick, who stood by the door as if ready to spring. She'd been watching him and he hadn't so much as moved a muscle in hours. How he managed that, Sara couldn't imagine, since she'd been rubbing her hands, rolling her shoulders and generally squirming without respite.

In the near darkness Nick, with his light hair and fair skin, stood out much more than she and Jason did. Or was it that he fascinated her, so she used any excuse to gaze at him? Incredible that it had taken her thirty years of living to be so much in love with a man. Perhaps the old adage should read "The *older* they are, the harder they fall."

Suddenly, the sound of a voice and footsteps coming closer caught them all by surprise. Jason sat up straighter as Nick held out a silencing hand. He kept his eyes riveted to the crack in the door. The speaker was male, Sara could tell, but she didn't recognize his voice, though he made no effort to keep it low. Whoever it was must feel awfully confident. She leaned closer to the tiny crack in the door.

The anteroom was shadowy, with only faint nightlights on, plus the ones shining on the glass case. Now she heard two voices and her heart began to pound. Nick had a gun, she knew, but he was one against two, since she doubted if Jason would be of much assistance if it came to a struggle. Would the thieves have weapons, or were they so confident that they believed they could get away with two valuable smugglings in as many weeks? Undoubtedly they'd be people she worked with daily. Heart in her throat, she waited.

A man she didn't recognize stepped into the anteroom, walking directly to the case. "You got the key?" he asked over his shoulder.

The second man stepped into view and Sara's heart sank.

"Right here," John Thundercloud said. He slid the key into the lock of the case just before Nick slammed open the door of the storeroom with his gun drawn.

"Hold it right there," he ordered.

"This is going to be one of the hardest things I've ever had to do," Sara told Nick as they drove back to the res.

"Alice's parents are both dead and she's never gotten along with John's folks. They're very old-fashioned and critical."

Nick turned his rental car onto the road that cut through the thick pine trees. "And she's got that baby to worry about."

"Yes." Sara was angry—at John, at the fates. "I know he shouldn't have stolen, but in a way, I understand John's frustration. Working constantly, never enough money. That broken-down house, and he's been trying to save for the medical bills he knows he'll have with the baby's arrival."

"Do you think the fellow with him, Dave Carter, is more to blame than John?"

"I can't say, since I don't know him. All John told me was that he and Dave worked together on the Gillis Ranch. Still, John had to be the one who'd taken Jason's key and had a duplicate made. He also had to have thought up the plan, since I can't see this Dave hanging around museums, knowledgeable enough to know what was valuable enough to risk stealing."

Nick sighed as he swung around the tribal center and headed for Sara's house. "A damn shame."

"Yes, especially since the things they took wouldn't be easy to sell just anywhere. They're too easily recognized. They'd have to find some shady operator in another state or take them out of the country. They haven't the money nor the connections." She shook her head angrily. "Stupid amateurs."

"Desperate men do desperate things." He pulled in front of her house and stopped the car. "Would you like me to go with you? I'd be glad to."

She touched his arm gratefully. "Thanks, but I think I should go alone. Alice won't want to lose face in front of you. This will be hard enough on her." She leaned to kiss him lightly. "You were so wonderful. Jason couldn't thank you enough."

"I was just glad the whole idea worked."

Sara took a deep, calming breath. "I'd better get this over with. I'll take my car and be back as soon as I can."

He got out with her and saw her to her Volkswagen. "It's late. Be careful. I'll be waiting for you."

She smiled wearily at him, then started her car.

Sara lay staring at the ceiling of her bedroom, tired but not sleepy even though it was three in the morning. Beside her, Nick stirred slightly as he shifted in his sleep. It had been a rough evening, one she wouldn't want to go through again.

Alice had been heartbroken to learn her husband had been caught red-handed robbing the museum. She'd cried for what seemed forever, then had tried to phone him at the jail. But they wouldn't allow her to talk with him until tomorrow.

Sara had assured Alice that she'd personally go see Jackson Hawk in the morning and see about legal representation for John. Under the circumstances of his arrest, she doubted there was much a lawyer could do. But perhaps if his motives were explained, there might be some leniency. The man wasn't stealing so he could live a wild life with wine, women and song, but rather to put food on his table. Food that he had to work twelve and fourteen hours a day to earn as it was.

That sort of pressure had broken the back of many a man and the foundation of many a happy marriage.

"Penny for your thoughts," Nick said as he rolled over. He'd sensed her wakefulness and had awakened in turn, wondering if anything specific was bothering her.

"You'd get change," she told him quietly.

"We'll talk to Jackson tomorrow. He'll think of something. And I'll get started on fixing up Alice's house as soon as I finish your mother's place." Summer Lewis had reluctantly agree to his repairs and was paying him by cooking and baking so much food that they hadn't had to fix a meal since he'd begun there.

Her head on the pillow turned toward him. "Your murder is solved and now the smugglers have been apprehended. I thought you'd be anxious to be on your way back home."

He moved closer, gathering her to him. "You're wrong. I don't want to leave. I want to marry you."

Only the steady ticking of the clock could be heard in the quiet of the bedroom, unless you counted a heartbeat thundering out of control. Sara couldn't answer, couldn't say a word. She'd been both hoping for this moment and dreading it.

"Did you hear me, Sara?"

"Yes."

"Are you not saying anything because you don't want to marry me?"

She closed her eyes, drawing in a deep breath. "I want to marry you with all my heart."

Nick felt a smile forming. "You had me worried there for a minute. I thought I'd been reading you wrong and—"

"But it would never work between us."

His own stunned silence followed. Easing to a sitting position, Nick frowned down at her. "Haven't we been over this ground so often as to be tiresome? I can't believe you're still hung up on this Indian-white thing."

"Not between you and me. I know you see no differences and you've managed to convince me. But others do.

People we must live among. My people, your people. And when that sort of pressure begins, love flies out the window. I know. I've seen it happen often enough."

Nick swallowed his frustration and tried to be reasonable. "I want you to keep an open mind, to go with me to visit my family and judge for yourself. They will love you as I do, I promise you."

She looked at him with eyes already suspiciously moist. "You want us to live with them?"

"Of course not. I have a place in Butte and my work is there. I'd like to build a house for us, let you help me design it. One big enough for children and—"

Abruptly, Sara sat up. He was moving awfully fast for her. "I've told you, I don't want to leave Laughing Horse. My place is here, where I can do so much more good."

"I have no problem with dividing our time between the res and Butte. I like it here. And besides, the work I've started here is far from finished. I enjoy fixing up the homes."

He just refused to see. "For how long, Nick? You won't be happy here repairing shabby housing, away from all your people, from everything familiar. You'll get frustrated and want to leave. But by then the whites won't accept you back, and when you run out of money, what'll you do on the res? Soon, you'll begin to resent me." Unspoken was the rest—that he'd turn to drink to drown life's disappointments. And children. She wouldn't want to raise children as she'd had to live, listening to arguments and afraid of her father's drinking bouts. "How long do you think our love will last in that kind of atmosphere?"

Angry now, Nick stood. "Life's a gamble, Sara. You have to take chances. And you have to believe. In yourself, in me and in our love. I'm willing to risk it all to be with you. I'm willing to compromise to make you happy, and it's not a sacrifice. I told you, I like it here. And if you'd give yourself a chance, you'd find you'd like it in Butte or wherever else we might wind up living part of the year."

He didn't understand, would *never* understand. "I can't live like that," she said, her voice heavy with pain.

"*Won't,* don't you mean? Won't compromise." His voice was filled with barely concealed anger.

"Either way amounts to the same thing. It would never work."

Furious, Nick grabbed his jeans and pulled them on. "No, it never will. Not as long as you believe it won't." Gathering the rest of his clothes, he looked at her one last time. "I feel sorry for you, Sara. You're afraid to live." Turning, he stormed out of her room and closed the door behind him.

Slowly, Sara laid her cheek on her bent knees and let the tears fall.

In the morning, when she left her room, he was gone.

Twelve

A cold December wind tossed light snow against the third-floor windows of Nick's office as he leaned back in his chair and watched. Down a few stories on the slick streets of Butte, the Christmas shopping frenzy had already begun and shopkeepers were open longer hours to accommodate the crowds. Carols could be heard being piped into stores and out onto the streets as bundled-up shoppers rushed about carrying gaily wrapped packages and lugging heavy shopping bags without complaint. It was the time of year when people set aside their differences, were warmer to one another and smiled more frequently.

Nick's frown deepened.

He didn't feel like smiling or shopping, nor was he thinking about goodwill toward men. He was mad at the world, at himself, at the capricious fates and everyone else.

The door to the office opened and Nate Upton came in, snowflakes dotting his dark hair. "Hey, buddy," he said in greeting as he shrugged out of his sheepskin jacket. "You still sitting there contemplating your navel the same way you were when I left?" Nate settled his lanky frame into his swivel chair at the desk across from Nick's and wrinkled his brow at his partner, whose eyes were riveted on the window. "You sure you're all right?"

Nick straightened and half-heartedly picked up a file. "Yeah, I'm terrific. What'd you find out?"

Nate spent the next few minutes updating Nick on a worker's-compensation fraud case he'd finally cracked.

Nick listened halfheartedly, the same way he did most everything these days. "Nice work." He yawned expansively. "I've been going through our pending file. Not much to be done on any of these until after the holidays." It was traditionally a slow time of year for private investigators, with most people too caught up in holiday plans to worry about other problems. January usually meant a rash of calls. "I think I'll take some time off." He glanced at his partner to catch his reaction.

Nate was digging through his file drawer. "I think that's a good idea. You haven't been yourself since you got back, if you want to know the truth."

Scowling, Nick straightened the few folders on his desk. "Are you saying I'm not holding up my end of things?"

Nate released a heavy sigh. "Don't get testy. I didn't mean about work. I meant personally." The two of them went back a long way and their friendship was solid. Which was why Nate felt comfortable in telling Nick the truth. "Something more happened in Whitehorn than the murder case you solved over there. I realize that having your Blazer blown up while you were in it and having the hitchhiker die must have been traumatic. But there's more. I can see you're not happy. No, it's more than that. You're *un*happy."

When Nick didn't reply but instead began clearing his desk, Nate knew his partner wasn't ready to talk about whatever was bothering him. "Look, we've never pried into each other's personal lives, and I'm not going to start now. I just want you to know I'm here if you need to talk." Bending to his files, he busied himself.

How would Nate ever understand what he was going through, the frustration? Nick asked himself. Nate had been happily married with two sons for years now. Then again, his friend had been very supportive when Nick had had it rough after his divorce from Beth. Maybe he should run a few things by him.

Finished straightening his desktop, Nick swiveled to face his partner. "Nate, how do you feel about Indians?"

Nate's dark, shaggy brows rose. "Indians? I know several. They're good people. I've also known a few who were losers. Why?"

"Let's just say I brought a woman here who was a Native American and told you I loved her and planned to marry her. And that we'd be living here in Butte. What would you say?"

Nate broke out in a grin. "I'd say it's about damn time you found someone. Who is she?"

He'd gotten the reaction he'd hoped for. But there was more. "Would you accept her easily? Would you and Karen have us over for dinner? Would you want our kids playing with your kids?"

"Hell, yes, to all three questions." Nate ran a hand over his beard, looking confused. "I don't know what you're getting at. You know I'm not prejudiced. There're good Indians and bad Indians, just like there are good whites and bad whites. Is that what's got you in knots—that you think your friends won't accept this woman?"

Nick shook his head. "No. I always believed you'd react just as you did. And most everyone else I know would, too. *She's* got this hangup that mixed marriages don't work. Her father was white and her mother's Northern Cheyenne. Things didn't work out for them, or for some others she knows. Sara is hung up on our differences."

Nate leaned back thoughtfully. "Do you love her?"

"Yes. More than I ever thought I could."

"And how does she feel?"

"She never said the words, though I know she cares. But she's afraid. She had a bad experience with a white man back in college. She can't get past that."

"Can't or won't let herself?"

"Yeah, that's what I think, too." He pushed back his chair and stood. "I think I'll go visit my folks for a while, work with my Dad." It bothered Nick that he'd left so much work unfinished back at Laughing Horse. It was the only time he'd ever walked out on a commitment. But staying had become impossible. Maybe he could work something out with his father and send some men to finish what he'd started on the res. If Jackson and the others would allow that.

"Okay, buddy." Nate rolled a clean sheet of paper into the typewriter. "Keep in touch."

"I will." Nick grabbed his jacket and left the office.

The applause in the main room of the day-care center was loud and enthusiastic. The kindergarteners had just put on their first ten-minute play, entitled "Billy Goats Gruff," and were giggling and bowing to the delight of their audience, which consisted of parents, grandparents, aunts, uncles, cousins and siblings. The construction-paper hats complete with little goat horns were all askew, but no one cared.

Then, as the piano music ended, the children rushed to surround their teacher, pushing and shoving to get close. Sara Lewis held out her arms and hugged as many as she could reach, smiling her pleasure at the upturned little faces that were so pleased with their accomplishments.

Finally, the excited participants, along with their admiring public, filed into the outer room for cookies and punch before the evening ended. Bending to gather up some of the makeshift props, Sara stifled a yawn. Frankly, she was ready for the evening to end right now.

"They wear you out?" Jackson Hawk asked, pushing away from the doorway where he'd been watching and strolling over to join her.

Sara glanced up at him and nodded. "If only we could bottle their energy. I'd be first in line to buy some."

Jackson smiled, but his dark eyes were concerned. "You look a little peaked, Sara. Just working too hard?" He had a feeling it was much more than that, but he wanted to hear what she'd say.

"Probably." Sara went about lining up the small chairs and putting away odds and ends.

"Can you leave that for later and come have a cup of coffee with me?"

She could use a little caffeine jolt, at that. She wasn't concerned that drinking coffee in the evening might keep her awake. With or without caffeine, she hardly slept these nights. Turning, she walked with him to the small pot she kept on the burner in the back room. "Where's Maggie?"

"At a meeting over at the tribal office, coordinating some sort of social program for Christmas." He took the mug from her and sat down at the small table along the back wall. "Speaking of the holidays, can you believe it's only two weeks away? Have you got your shopping done yet?" His dark eyes watched as she sat down opposite him.

Sara set down her cup without tasting the coffee. "I can't seem to get into the Christmas spirit this year."

She seemed paler than usual to him. Perhaps it was fatigue or the beginning of the flu. Or maybe there was something missing in her life that had stolen the color from her world.

It had been exactly three weeks since Nick Dean had suddenly left the res early one morning, Jackson knew.

The only explanation Sara had given anyone was that he'd finished his work in Whitehorn and had to get back to his life in Butte. Jackson didn't buy that story for a minute.

"Do you want to tell me what happened, Sara?"

She frowned, staring down at her untasted coffee. "What do you mean?"

"Don't insult my intelligence or our friendship. You know perfectly well what I mean."

Sara let out a ragged breath. "I told you, Jackson. Nick solved Charlie Avery's murder and even managed to apprehend John Thundercloud smuggling goods from the museum. His work here is finished, so he left. End of story."

Not by a long shot. He gazed out the window toward the streets were Nick had started to repair homes. "What about the work he'd begun out there? Everyone's asking. It had all been his idea and he'd seemed eager to help. Nick Dean doesn't strike me as the type who'd walk away from a commitment."

She shrugged, feigning nonchalance. "Guess you don't know him as well as you thought."

Jackson's dark eyes narrowed as he studied his friend. Her hand trembled as she finally picked up her mug and took a disinterested sip. Her eyes were suspiciously moist and she couldn't seem to raise them to meet his. She was wearing wool slacks and a bulky sweater, but he could swear she'd lost weight beneath all those clothes. "I'm a pretty good judge of character and I've found that I'm seldom wrong."

"Good for you. I wish I could say the same."

Jackson leaned forward. "You misjudged Nick? Did he do something to hurt you?"

Slowly, she shook her head. "No. *I* did something to hurt me. I knew things would never work out between us and I still let it go on. I should have walked away that first day, but I didn't. At least the first time I was young and stupid. This time I was just plain stupid."

"Do you think it's stupid to fall in love?"

Now her eyes did raise to his. "Twice with the wrong man? Yes, I'd call that pretty stupid."

"Who *is* the right man for you, Sara?"

She set down the mug heavily and crossed her arms over her chest defensively. "Maybe such a person doesn't exist. Perhaps I'm destined to live alone."

"Oh, bull!" Melodrama, yet! This wasn't like Sara.

"It's true, Jackson." Her voice was tremulous so she cleared her throat. "Why can't there be some good Native American man of strong character right here on the res, someone I could work alongside happily? Someone like you."

"Hey, you had your chance with me, lady." But he saw even his small attempt at humor didn't make her smile. "Are you afraid of being hurt again, or are you just plain afraid of being loved?"

Sara frowned at him. "Why would anyone be afraid of being loved?"

"Lots of reasons." He crossed one long leg over the other and prepared to enumerate them. "Commitments are scary. The thought of forever is frightening. Living alone, you more or less do as you please. When someone shares that home, you have to learn to compromise on everything from what to have for dinner to how many children to have. Or where to live. Or who will our friends be." He could tell that his words were hitting the mark.

"As I see it, those compromises are difficult enough without having to struggle against racial differences as well."

"I've said this before, but it bears repeating. Not every white man's like that guy who hurt you years ago. I got a very strong feeling that Nick's good and honorable. The folks who live on Laughing Horse, they don't take to strangers easily or often. Nick managed to win quite a few over without half trying. Your own grandmother, a lady whose judgment I trust, told me she wished he'd come back, that she missed talking with him, that he'd be good for you."

"So I should marry him because my grandmother likes him?"

"No. But maybe you shouldn't let him go quite so easily, either."

Eyes full of anguish looked at him. "Easy? You think letting him go has been easy?" She turned away, willing herself not to cry. "You of all people should understand that mixed marriages have little or no chance to survive. I don't like those odds."

Jackson wrinkled his brow. "Wait a minute, Sara. My first marriage didn't end because she was white and I'm an Indian. That's not what caused our divorce. It was because we had a different set of values, which have nothing to do with being white or red. Maggie and I have the same values, and it just so happens we're both Indian. Think about it. Do you and Nick share the same values, such as a love of family, a desire to make a home and have children, a sense of responsibility to others less fortunate, a caring nature, a basic honesty? Do any of those things ring a bell? You have them. Does Nick?"

Sara had to admit that he did—every one and several more Jackson hadn't listed. "I suppose so. But Jackson, what about his family? All right, so Nick's accepted here. How will it be when he takes me to his home?"

"Did you talk about it? What did he tell you of his family?"

She gazed off into space, remembering. "That they were close and loving, that they'd accept me. His father helps his mother with the dishes every night." She smiled. "Can you believe that, after years of marriage?"

"Well, then. What are you afraid of?"

She thought a moment, then answered him honestly. "Of history repeating itself, I guess."

"It needn't. You have the power to change that."

Sara felt a tiny bubble of hope forming inside where before there had been none. She looked at him, praying he was right. "Do you really think we could make it work?"

Jackson rose, took her hands and pulled her to her feet. "Listen to your heart, Sara. In the dark of night, when you can't sleep, whose face fills your thoughts? Who do you wish was alongside you when you see a beautiful sunset? Whose arms do you wish were holding you when you feel lonely?" He saw the answer in her face. "Then go find him. I think he's the real thing, Sara. Don't let him get away, not if you love him. Tell him you're willing to risk it all if he is. Because life's a gamble. None of us knows how the book will end."

"That's more or less what Nick said." She hugged Jackson's solid strength, blinking back tears. "Thank you."

"It doesn't look like we're going to have a white Christmas," Doris Dean commented as she rolled out dough for pies. She glanced toward her kitchen table, where her son was letting a cup of coffee grow cold as he stared out the window that faced the small barn and corral out back. When he didn't say anything, she frowned as she picked up a circle of dough and placed it in a pie plate with expert hands.

This had gone on long enough, she decided as she fluted the edges. Nick had been home a week, silent and brooding, working with the construction crew for long hours at a time, then sitting around the house and staring at nothing. Yesterday his father had coaxed him out to look at cars and trucks, since the insurance check had arrived from his Blazer accident. But Bill Dean hadn't gotten much further with him than she had, and they'd returned without a purchase. Nick couldn't seem to make a decision, her husband had informed her with a worried look.

Finished with the shell, Doris scooped some of the pumpkin mixture she'd prepared earlier into it and put the pie into the oven to bake. Dusting off her hands, she took her coffee cup over to join him.

He didn't glance up, just kept his eyes on the scene outside, where clouds inched their way through a winter sky. His lean jaw wore a stubble that he hadn't bothered to shave off this morning and his blond hair—so like his father's—was tousled from frustrated fingers pushing through it at frequent intervals.

Something was surely wrong and Doris meant to get it out of him.

"This isn't like you, Nick," she began.

Taking in an aggrieved breath, Nick shifted in his chair. He'd been grateful that, so far, his folks hadn't questioned him since his return. They'd let him talk when he wanted to and be silent when he didn't. But he'd been aware of the quiet, worried looks that passed between them. He should have known that their patience wouldn't last forever. He supposed he owed them some sort of explanation.

"I guess not," he answered, his finger tracing the rim of his cup. "Just kind of a low point in my life, that's all. I'll be fine in a couple of days." Or a couple of years.

"Would you tell me what brought you to this low point?" Doris thought she already knew. The only other time she'd seen Nick—who was usually fun-loving, confident and upbeat—like this had been when his baby hadn't lived and his marriage had broken up. She had a feeling this recent depression also involved a woman. Nothing else ever took the sparkle from a man's eyes quite the way woman problems could.

"Not much to tell, Mom."

She leaned forward, intent on prying it out of him if she had to. "Nick, you know I don't ask about your personal life. But I hate seeing you like this. Please tell me what happened."

So he did, giving her the bare-bones version and ending with what he felt was an honest assessment. "It seems I fell in love with a woman who doesn't love me enough in return." He gave a small, bitter laugh. "Twice now I've done that. Seems like I never learn my lesson."

Doris had listened quietly without interruption. She also tried to read between the lines, since she felt there was much he wasn't saying. "Sara doesn't sound like a woman who doesn't love you, from what you've told me. I'd say she sounds like someone afraid of being hurt again."

"I know that. But I tried to tell her that it would be different between us, that you and Dad and all my friends would have no problem accepting her." He ran a weary hand over his face. "She insists it wouldn't work."

"But you do love her?"

It hurt to admit how much. "Yes."

"Then you need to go to her and talk some more. If you feel that you two have a good chance, then convince her. You can be very persuasive, Son."

He shoved the coffee cup aside and stretched out his long legs. "Experience has taught me that, when in doubt, it's best to do nothing. Remember how I went after Beth, tried to tell her how sorry I was about not being there when she went into labor? She all but threw me out of her parents' home. Sometimes, Mom, it's best to let sleeping dogs lie and get on with your life."

She reached over and touched his hand. "But Nick, you're not getting on with your life. You're sitting here in pain." Doris decided to try another tactic. "Do you feel there's a similarity between Beth and your Sara?"

Nick shook his head. "They're not at all alike. Beth was young, needed constant attention I didn't give her and was selfish enough to want things her way most of the time. Sara's generous and giving and wants to help everyone and anyone."

Doris had always felt that Beth had been unfair in judging her son, but she'd kept those feelings to herself. "Are you still wrapped in guilt over not being there when Beth went into labor?"

He'd spent a lot of hours going over the subject, so he could answer her from his recent reexamination. "No. I realize that I did everything humanly possible. I had no way of knowing she couldn't contact me or that she'd go into labor so early. She probably should have called sooner to have someone else drive her to the hospital when I couldn't be reached. But I don't blame Beth, either. She was young and frightened. Funny thing is that it was Sara who made me see that I had to let go of my guilt." He swallowed hard, wondering how he'd go on from day to day without Sara.

"Sara sounds like a good woman, Nick. Isn't there some way you two can work things out?" Doris wasn't one to give up easily and hadn't thought her son was, either.

"I don't know. Maybe in time. It's up to Sara, I feel. I asked her to marry me, but she wouldn't. If she changes her mind, she knows where to find me." Nick stood and stretched. He needed exercise, something to do that didn't involve thinking. "I think I'll take a ride on Flame before it snows again. We could both use a workout. See you later, Mom." He walked toward the back door, grabbed his jacket and went outside to saddle his mother's mare.

Doris sat for several minutes staring after her son. She was not the interfering sort. Never had been. But there were times when a person had to act out of character.

Keeping an eye out the window on her son as he led Flame out of the barn, Doris Dean picked up the phone.

The wind was cold as it slapped at his face, but it felt good. Nick urged Flame on with a gentle nudge of his knees and the mare responded quickly. She was getting used to their daily rides and looked forward to them as much as he did.

Since he'd talked with his mother three days ago, Nick had taken Flame out every afternoon as part of his routine. He'd go to work mornings with his father to the site west of town where Dean Construction was putting up a new subdivision, doing mostly indoor-finish carpentry work. Then he'd leave about two and go for his ride on Flame across the frozen fields. As long as the snow held off, they'd be able to go daily. There was comfort in routine, in hard work and in exercise. And it tired the body so a man could sleep nights.

A few more days and it would be Christmas. He'd finally forced himself to do a little shopping. Several items for his parents to put under the tree. Some gifts for Nate, Karen and the boys, which he had sent to them. And then, on the spur of the moment, he'd bought a soft handknit sweater for Summer in blue and a crocheted shawl for Manya, wrapping and mailing the packages himself. He'd enclosed just his card, with no note. He hoped they would wear them and remember him.

He'd wanted badly to send something to Sara, but at the last minute he'd walked out of the jewelry store. She didn't want his gift, didn't want him. The sooner he realized that, the sooner he'd be able to forget.

Liar, he thought. He'd never forget her.

Flame spotted the small barn up ahead and put on a burst of speed. Bareback, Nick crouched low and held on. He had to stop sitting around feeling sorry for himself and worrying his parents, he thought. As soon as Christmas was over, he'd already decided, he'd go back to Butte and throw himself into his work. Keeping busy was the answer. The days would pass, one after another, and he'd get through them somehow.

How? was the question.

He was perhaps three hundred yards from the corral fence when he realized someone was standing there watching him. A woman with coal black hair blowing every which way in a strong breeze. As he slowed Flame, he saw that one booted foot was propped on the lower rung of the fence as she leaned on the top one. She had on jeans and an open sheepskin jacket.

Nick blinked several times to assure himself he wasn't hallucinating. No, it was her, all right. Sara.

Slowing to a walk, he let Flame take him to the railing, then slid from her, allowing the mare to find her own way into the barn. Heart pounding, he stood looking at Sara across the fence.

Sara swallowed around a dry throat, wondering if she'd done the right thing, after all. Nick's mother had been so sure, so convinced that he'd welcome her with open arms. But the blue eyes she loved were hesitant, wary. "Hi," she managed to say, her voice husky with emotion.

"Hi." He stuck both hands into the back pockets of his jeans and took two steps closer. "A little far from home, aren't you?"

She squinted up at him, silhouetted as he was against a hazy afternoon sky. "Am I?"

"Yeah. I thought you never strayed more than a couple of miles from Laughing Horse. Or you'd turn into a pumpkin if you did."

She stepped back, holding her arms out at her sides. "Then I guess I'm a pumpkin." She hadn't rehearsed what she'd say, only knew that she'd had to come, had to be with him. Jackson had convinced her to try and Doris Dean's phone call had finalized her plans. She hadn't been sure her Bug would make the trip, but it had. Now here she was, face-to-face with the one man she needed more than the air she breathed, and she was scared to death.

Nick didn't smile, didn't move a muscle.

"I've missed you," Sara began, knowing it would be up to her. She'd sent him away and she'd have to win him back.

Don't punish her, he warned himself. If she'd come this far—which couldn't have been easy for her—and probably had already been through a question-and-answer session with his mother, the least he could do would be to meet her halfway. "I've missed you, too."

Encouraged, she met his eyes. "I was wrong, Nick. I don't care anymore about what people think. *We* are the only ones that matter. I want to be with you—if you still want me." Why didn't he move, why didn't he say something? Oh, God, was she too late?

Slowly, Nick pulled his hands from his pockets and moved closer to the fence. "Are you sure?"

Sara nodded. "Very sure."

With one quick leap, he was over the fence and standing very near. "Why do you want to be with me?" he asked, knowing his future hung on that one question.

"Because I love you."

The right answer. Yet there was more. "But you love the res...."

"Yes, I do, with all my heart. But I love you *more*." She dared to take a step closer, slipping her arms around him, looking up into those wonderful blue eyes. "Do you still care a little for me?"

Nick let out a rush of air as he pulled her into his arms. "Only more than life itself." And he bent his head to kiss her.

Her remembered fragrance wrapped around him and he felt at last as if he'd come home. His hands thrust into her magnificent hair and her pliant mouth moved under his. The kiss went on and on, neither able to get enough. By the time it was over, they were laughing and crying all at the same time.

"I was so afraid you wouldn't want me anymore."

"Never. That would never happen." She was back in his arms. He would never let her go again.

"I've been such a fool. I still don't think it'll be smooth sailing all the way, but I don't care. Our love is worth fighting for." She snuggled against him, knowing she held the world in her arms. "You never doubted that and I'm so sorry I did."

"I had concerns, too, you know."

She leaned back to look up at him. "About me?"

"No, about me. I wondered if that old urge would return, that when things got uncomfortable, I'd run."

"Do you want to run now?"

"Yeah." He smiled down at her. "I want to run—to you. Right to you. You *are* my home, Sara. On the res, off, wherever. All I want is to be with you. All I need is to know you love me."

"I do. With all my heart."

"Then you'll marry me?"

"Any day you name."

"Great. And it's going to make that lady who's watching us from her kitchen window awfully happy, too."

They both turned to wave to Doris Dean, then Nick bent his head and kissed his bride-to-be once more. It was a kiss filled with promise for the future they'd share together.

* * * * *

MONTANA MAVERICKS

continues with

WAY OF THE WOLF

Rebecca Daniels

Available in February

Here's an exciting preview....

One

"You going to hang him, Wolf Boy?"

Detective Sergeant Rafe Rawlings stopped when he heard the familiar nickname.

"That's up to the jury, Mrs. Wheeler," he said politely. He moved away before Lily Mae could finish her analysis of Ethan Walker's character. He slipped through the crowd of spectators that lined the courthouse corridor. He wished avoiding Raeanne Martin would be as easy. But it wouldn't. They'd be on opposite sides of the courtroom, but it wouldn't be enough.

He wasn't sure if it was some perverse act of providence, or just plain bad luck that had Raeanne appointed defense counsel on this particular case. All he wanted to do was stay out of her way, but as chief investigator of Charlie Avery's death, it would be necessary for him to be in court throughout the entire trial, and that would make avoiding her a little tough.

When she'd first moved back to town, he'd managed to keep their encounters to a minimum, brief and impersonal. It would have been impossible to avoid her completely. Whitehorn was a small town and they were, after all, old friends. When they were younger she'd been one of the few who'd stuck up for the "wolf boy" and his oddness. She'd tried to draw him out of his shell. And she had once been his best friend's wife.

Still, after seven years of her being away Rafe had managed to convince himself he was over her, but that hadn't made her return any easier.

Rafe made his way into the courtroom, taking his seat behind the prosecutor. Raeanne came in behind him and spoke a few words to Harlan, nodding to Rafe, before setting out her things.

He watched her as she worked, as she addressed the jury, talked with her client, leafed through her notes. She was capable, confident and thoroughly at home in the courtroom, and this served to infuriate Rafe even more. She looked wonderful, too. Slim and professional in her suit, with her dark hair framing her delicate features.

After Andy's death she'd leaned on him, depended on him—had *needed* him, and for a while he'd thought he might have a chance. But he'd been a fool. She didn't need him, she didn't need anyone. To her he would forever be one of her strays, one of her underdogs, one of her charity cases.

Rafe closed his eyes. Why couldn't she have stayed away? Why did she have to bring all the old memories to the surface again? She was part of his past, part of a fantasy he'd held on to for too long. He no longer had room in his life for fantasy.

He opened his eyes just then to find her looking at him from across the courtroom. A sudden surge of emotion swelled in his heart. She was the woman he knew he could never have, so why was it so hard for him to let go?

Raeanne dropped her head, feeling the dull throbbing at her temples spread to her nape. The first day of any trial was never easy, but this one had been exceptionally difficult.

The judge hadn't done her any favors today. His rulings had been swift, harsh and usually in favor of the prosecution. She had to be on guard constantly. Add to that the fact that there hadn't been a moment today when she'd not been aware of Rafe sitting across the courtroom, watching her with that cold, dark gaze of his, and it was a miracle she'd been able to concentrate at all.

At least she could be grateful he'd gotten up and left immediately after court was adjourned. She wasn't up to another awkward meeting with him.

And her client was turning out to be just as stubborn. Sure, the evidence to Charlie Avery's murder was mostly circumstantial, and it had been a long time ago. But Ethan Walker's pig-headedness during the pre-trial stages hadn't won any sympathy from the jury. And there was enough information to suggest that Ethan could have killed Charlie Avery and left his bones on the Laughing Horse Reservation.

Raeanne gave a sigh as she stuffed the last of her files into the already crammed satchels she'd brought. She wished she could pack away her thoughts about the trial as easily. She started for the elevators, eager to get home.

"Oh, no," Raeanne groaned, feeling the load in her arms beginning to list dangerously. One of the satchels started to fall.

"Got it."

Raeanne turned as Rafe reached from behind to catch the heavy packet before it hit the floor.

"Let me help you with those," he said, tucking the satchel under his arm and reaching for the others.

"Thanks." Raeanne watched in a kind of trance as he relieved her of her burden, too tired to protest. The very last thing she needed was to be alone with Rafe.

"It's been a long day," he commented quietly, trying to pretend he didn't see the exhausted look in her eyes. She seemed so small standing there, so vulnerable, like she might need someone to lean on, someone to help her.

The silence was awkward as they waited for the elevator and their few conversation attempts quickly died away. Finally Rafe made a remark about a mutual friend and they began to relax and talk about various acquaintances. They barely noticed crowding into the elevator or going to Raeanne's office.

But when the subject got around to the case, the camaraderie established abruptly disappeared.

"What I'm talking about, Detective Rawlings," Raeanne said, picking up a pencil and jabbing it in his direction to emphasize her point, "is that it's been *alleged* that my client killed Charlie Avery, and despite what you and the rest of the Whitehorn Police Department seem to think, a person is still innocent until proven guilty—*even* in Blue Lake County."

The emotion in her voice sent an icy finger traveling down Rafe's spine. Raeanne was never better, never more passionate, never more articulate than when she was defending one of her strays. The same passion she'd once used to defend him from the kids at school, she now used to defend creeps like Walker.

But it had been so different with Andy. She'd never pitied him, never gone running to shield and protect him. She hadn't needed to. She'd looked up to Andy, admired him.

Rafe recognized the familiar gnawing in the pit of his stomach. How many times had he wanted Raeanne to look up to him, wanted to earn her admiration, to be her hero?

He thought of her skill in the courtroom, how strong and competent she'd appeared, and the anger swelled in his chest. For some thoroughly irrational and absurd reason, her strength made him furious. He didn't want to be lumped together with all the rest of her charity cases. He wanted to be someone special in her life, and it made him angry and frustrated to know that would never happen.

"Ethan Walker murdered Charlie Avery," he said in a cold, unemotional voice. "The prosecution's case is flawless and there are no rabbits you can pull from your hat to change that. So give the jury the best argument you can, but it's not going to do any good. Like it or not, lady, Walker is guilty."

Raeanne leaned forward until they were practically nose to nose. She knew all too well the reputation Wolf Boy had for being intimidating, but she wasn't about to be pushed around. "Stick around, Detective Rawlings. We'll just see about that."